W9-BLO-687

Praise for *Elmina's Fire*

"A sparkling, spiritual gem of a tale that splendidly illuminates the searing soul-searching of Cathars and Catholics in medieval Languedoc. Carleton's achievement makes historical fiction a retelling of history and a discovery of self."

—STEPHEN O'SHEA, author of *The Perfect Heresy* and *The Friar of Carcassonne*

"With *Elmina's Fire*, Linda Carleton has succeeded in recreating the challenges of an important if little-known period of the High Middle Ages. In telling her compelling story of desire and the human condition, she captures the world of the medieval Catharism as well as the portentous events that were destined to shape the modern world."

—JAMES MCDONALD, Cathar Historian, St-Ferriol, France

"In Elmina, Linda Carleton has given us a most unusual heroine: a humble young woman of the Crusades whose epic struggles with her past actions, her faith, her convictions, and the mysterious demons that plague her follow her into a cloistered life. Elmina's narrative is addressed directly to God. We are merely eavesdroppers on the most intimate of confessions, in which the stakes are life or death. In serene prose undergirded by deep historical knowledge and the passion of one who knows her subject intimately, Carleton weaves her tale like the weavers in her 'Good Christian' ostal, a tapestry both terrifying and beautiful."

—KATHY LEONARD CZEPIEL, author of *A Violet Season*

"This meticulously researched novel describes the quotidian world of a religious order. It is rich with details of a medieval life that was shattered by the Albigensian Crusades. Carleton shows us the urgent and all-encompassing reach of the Catholic Church, and the physical, material, and familial hardships with which it crushed the faithful. She bravely explores the fragile lines between physical and spiritual seduction, art vision and madness, faith and betrayal. *Elmina's Fire* is a vivid and nuanced portrayal of both the anguish and the ecstasy that is one brave woman's search for truth and the love of God."

—Diane Bonavist, author
of *Purged by Fire: Heresy of the Cathars*

"*Elmina's Fire* grabbed me from the start and held on. More than once while reading I felt myself holding my breath. Linda Carleton has written Elmina's story so close to the bone it has the feel of memoir—more remembered than imagined."

—Joan Hunter, Fifth House Lodge, Bridgton, Maine

"*Elmina's Fire* is a passionate story of a young woman's spiritual struggle in the Languedoc region of 13th-century France, a place renowned for its troubadours and poets—and its violent crusades. Elmina, a young woman caught in the crosshairs between warring religions, tells her story to God. Her life is riven by dualisms that she cannot mend. Doctrinal beliefs, whether Catholic or Cathar, have set mother against father, sister against sister, body against soul, spirit against matter, good against evil. Historical yet timely, *Elmina's Fire* is a deep exploration of religious beliefs and their consequences."

—Patricia Reis, author of *The Dreaming Way* and *Motherlines*

"On the eve of the Albigensian Crusade, Elmina, a sensitive young Catholic nun, is confronted with the horrors perpetrated by the Church and her unintended complicity in its evil. Despite the 'trials of the soul' that it reveals, *Elmina's Fire* leaves the reader with the hope that there is always forgiveness and redemption possible, whether in this lifetime or another."

—Leah Chyten, author of *Light, Radiance, Splendor*

"Based on true events, *Elmina's Fire* transports readers to southwestern France in the 13th century such that they feel the agonizing decisions the main character makes as she searches for her own spiritual truth. This is a beautifully written, historically accurate debut novel."

—Marianne Bohr, author of *Gap Year Girl: A Baby Boomer Adventure Across 21 Countries*

ELMINA'S FIRE

To Penthea
in appreciation for
your grounded presence
and poetic soul.
Linda

ELMINA'S FIRE

A NOVEL

LINDA CARLETON

She Writes Press, a BookSparks imprint
A Division of SparkPointStudio, LLC.

Copyright © 2017 by Linda Carleton

All rights reserved. No part of this publication may be reproduced, distributed, or transmitted in any form or by any means, including photocopying, recording, digital scanning, or other electronic or mechanical methods, without the prior written permission of the publisher, except in the case of brief quotations embodied in critical reviews and certain other noncommercial uses permitted by copyright law. For permission requests, please address She Writes Press.

Published 2017

Printed in the United States of America

Print ISBN: 978-1-63152-190-4
E-ISBN: 978-1-63152-191-1
Library of Congress Control Number: 2017930589

For information, address:
She Writes Press
1563 Solano Ave #546
Berkeley, CA 94707

Cover design © Julie Metz, Ltd./metzdesign.com
Cover photo © TK
Formatting by Katherine Lloyd/thedeskonline.com

She Writes Press is a division of SparkPoint Studio, LLC.

This is a work of fiction. Names, characters, places, and incidents either are the product of the author's imagination or are used fictitiously. Any resemblance to actual persons, living or dead, is entirely coincidental.

Dedication

*For all who have needed to walk away
from the spiritual abuse of church
and for those who have chosen to stay
in the hope of helping it to change*

CONTENTS

PROLOGUE

The Aude region of the Languedoc in the south of France still holds the sorrow of its tragic past. The Pyrenees and the Black Mountains loom in the distance, casting a protective shadow and offering the illusion that the land is safe from evil marauders. The sun still sheds a mystical sheen over the vineyards, olive trees, and ochre grains, grown up like a phoenix from the ashes of its past. Winding roads connect the towns that still perch high atop jagged promontories, their fortifications now only imagined. Signs dot the landscape announcing that the Aude is Cathar Country, but there are no Cathars living there today. Stone steeples rise from the highest point of every village proclaiming the victory of the Roman Catholic Church and the Cathars' destruction in the wake of the Albigensian Crusade.

Because the Aude extended south from the city of Albi, its people were once known as the Albigensians. They were in many ways an autonomous group, existing outside the medieval feudal structure. Until the thirteenth century, the region remained beyond the reach of the king of France. It had no central governance and did not abide by the laws of primogeniture. As a result, there was a growing pool of increasingly impoverished nobles who vied for control of its territory and its great cities: Toulouse, Beziers, Narbonne, and Carcassonne. Knights and *routiers* razed the countryside, and farmers and villagers attempted to escape their ravages by fleeing to fortified cities or towns.

Throughout most of medieval Europe, the Church in Rome exercised a stabilizing influence in unsettled times, but not so in the Languedoc. The ties binding the Church to the people had never been strong in the south of France, and by the thirteenth century they had become severely frayed. Many village churches stood empty for lack of a parish priest. Some clerics had left to seek their fortunes in the Crusades and never returned. Those who remained were largely uneducated and notoriously corrupt, living in an opulent decadence funded by the sale of indulgences and extraction of heavy tithes on both the land and all that was produced. Even Pope Innocent III decried their dishonesty and ineffectiveness.

It's not surprising that much of the Languedoc held the Roman Church in disdain and began to look favorably upon rival religious movements. Today we call the largest of these groups the Cathars. Eight hundred years ago, the medieval Church referred to them as the Albigensians, but the group spoke of themselves simply as "Good Christians."

In many ways the Good Christians were not unlike the Catholic Church. They both used Trinitarian language to speak of God and shared the New Testament of the Bible (although the Good Christians used the Waldensians' Occitan translation). They both organized themselves into parishes and diaconates, appointed bishops, and claimed to be the true heirs of apostolic succession. Both the Catholic Church and the Good Christians were divided into a kind of clergy and laity. The Good Christian leaders were the *perfecti*, those *bons hommes* and *bonnes femmes* who had received the sacrament of the *consolamentum*. The followers were referred to as *credentes*, or believers.

One reason the Good Christians were admired was that they strove to uphold the moral teachings of Jesus. The *perfecti* maintained an ascetic existence supported only by voluntary contributions. They dressed in simple black robes and ate only enough to stay alive. They refrained from sexual contact and refused to consume meat, milk, or eggs—anything that was the product of fornication. The *perfecti* traveled from village to village to preach their truth. They set up hostels, they made medicines and healed the sick through the laying on of hands, and many *bonnes femmes* opened homes or *ostals* to educate the daughters of the impoverished nobility who could not afford a dowry.

Despite their similarities, the Good Christians ran afoul of the Church in Rome. In part it was their belief system. The Good Christians adhered to a Gnosticism that the Church had proclaimed to be heresy in the fourth century. But an equally important part of the Church's opposition was political and economic. The Good Christians rejected the need for the sacraments and the role of priests as intermediaries between God and humanity. They ridiculed the system of feudal tithes and the practice of selling indulgences. The Good Christians considered the Roman Catholic Church to be an arm of the Devil, and they were outspoken in their opposition to it.

When Pope Innocent III commenced his reign in 1198, he noted the decline in revenues coming from the south of France and attributed it to the growing influence of the Albigensians. His first strategy was to send papal legates into the Languedoc to preach against the heresy. These first legates were joined by two Castilian priests: Diego de Acebo, the bishop of Osma, and his canon, Dominic de Guzman, the man who would become the founder of the Dominican Order. Legend has it that Dominic worked miracles and rescued nine women from an Albigensian *ostal* to form his first monastery outside the town of Fanjeaux in the abandoned village of Prouilhe. History has recorded little about these women but their names. One of these names was Guilhemina de Beaupuys. I've chosen to call her Elmina.

Chapter 1

FANJEAUX

*L*ord God in Heaven, if that is where You be, it is Elmina here begging to speak with You for one last time. You know, of course, that I have reached the end, and I no longer even know to whom I pray. If You are the God of the Holy Catholic Church, the One whom I have loved and tried to serve here at Prouilhe, I will soon be damned to the fires of Hell—not for what I've done to Amelha and to my people, but for the sin I will commit tonight. For the priests say that the razing of the Languedoc and burning of the heretics were done for Your great glory, but that to take my own life is a mortal sin that cannot ever be forgiven.

But, Santa Deu, what if the priests are wrong? What if the heretics knew the truth all along? If so, the life I thought was serving You has been offered instead to Satan. But death will bring about release from all its torments and the promise of a new life in a different time and place. If those Good Christians had it right, I may yet get another chance to love and serve You better.

I beg that You will hear me out. Perhaps in offering to You my story, I will release some of the turmoil that does burn within and rest in peace tonight.

✳

The fire within that has reduced my soul to ashes has been with me since I was but a small child growing up in the hilltop *castrum of* Fanjeaux. My mother wanted me to be a good little girl, cheerful and obedient, but I was not. It was as if a demon made its home within my soul and tormented me with a fiery rage.

Poor Mama was quick to remind me of the trial I had been. She had been scarcely more than a girl herself when she was given in marriage to my papa. I wonder sometimes if she, too, had been reluctant to marry and become a mother. Of course, she and Papa had hoped their firstborn would be a son, someone to carry on the noble name of de Beaupuys and maybe even find a way to restore its fortunes. But that was not Your will. Instead, in the year of our Lord 1191, You gave them me, a cursed girl child who would one day require both an education and a dowry.

And I did not make it easy for my mother to love me.

"You began screaming before the midwife had finished pulling you from my womb," Mama often complained. "You cried both day and night. There was no point in trying to comfort you. If I picked you up, you just screamed the more loudly."

It was as if my soul already knew that it was born into a hostile world. Flames of orange and crimson singed my earliest memories. They swirled within my dreams and haunted many of my waking hours.

"Stop screaming like some God-forsaken soul dangling above the fires of Hell," Mama would complain as she picked me up from my leather cradle. She'd walk me back and forth across the rough-hewn boards of our *fogana*, that stone-walled "house within a house" that is designed to ward off both evil spirits and the cold. But I did not feel safe in the *fogana*. The smoke from the stone-lined fire pit filled my nostrils with bitter ash and its flames shot up into the room. Mama said I would stiffen every time the servant girl Jeanette laid faggots on the fire and cry until my face turned red.

My fears did not abate as I grew older. Whenever the coals burst into flames, I would crawl into the farthest corner of the room and hide my head under a moth-worn woolen blanket. Neither my mama's pleading nor her threats could coax me out until the fire had settled into blackened embers. Only then would I creep back to her and whimper to be picked up.

"Oh shush, Elmina," she would say. "Quit your foolishness. There is nothing here that can harm you."

I wanted to believe her. The walls of the *fogana* embraced me with warmth from the coals. The room filled up with the rich smell of beans and chicken as Jeanette stirred her *cassoulet*. Often my aunties were there, chattering around the wooden table and beckoning me into their circle. I'd curl up at my mama's feet or even venture to climb into a *tanta's* lap, and for a short while I might feel safe.

But always the flames leapt up again. I'd grow dizzy, and my stomach would clench as if some mean man had reached down inside and twisted it. I'd set again to screaming and cling tightly to my mama's linen hem. She'd pry my fist from her skirts and once more pick me up with poorly feigned patience. Again she'd hold and rock me. Again when I refused her comfort she would put me down, and I would crawl into my corner to cover my head and suck my thumb and try to disappear into a safe dark place where the world's inferno could not get me.

Santa Deu, I used to wonder why You would curse a little girl with such a fiery demon in her soul. Why would You make one who was so frightened to live in the world You created? It wasn't just the fire. I startled at loud noises—the squeal of the piglets from the yard behind our *fogana* and the clacking of the wooden carts upon the cobbled streets beyond our steps. I flinched each time I heard a knock upon our oaken door or when the neighbors flung open their shutters to empty their chamber pots. I was scared of things floating in the air, feathers and pollen and the ash from cooking fires. It was as if each sound and sight reminded me of some not quite forgotten terror.

My only comfort came when Papa picked me up.

"Hush, little Elmina," he'd coo as he lifted me into his brawny arms and I nestled into the softness of his beard. "There is no need for you to cry. God will not forsake you. He has ordered the world to keep you from harm. Our Savior is with you and the Blessed Virgin watches over you." Then he would hum a soft melodic Ave in his tender baritone and hold me so close that I could believe that it was Your own embrace.

Mama would hiss, "Don't fill Elmina's head with your Church nonsense," but Papa paid her little heed. Despite Mama's objection, he insisted that she be present when I was baptized in the big stone church. I do not know why Mama acquiesced. Perhaps Papa grew angry. Or maybe she held a secret hope that I might be cleansed of my accursed nature. But that is not what happened. Instead, shortly after my first birthday, the demon envy joined the fearsome legions in my soul.

I can almost recall the scorching August day on which Amelha burst into my world. I sometimes wondered if Mama had made another baby just so she might get a better one than me. And she most surely did! Right from the start, Amelha was Mama's favorite child. She filled the house with her enormous energy and cheerful spirit. She'd gurgle and wiggle her legs in such a way to make the whole household want to pick her up and squeeze her tight.

"You are now a big sister," Mama instructed me. "It is your job to teach Amelha, and protect and love her all the days that she should live."

And, God, I tried. I stroked baby Amelha and held her in my little lap. I sang her lullabies just like Mama taught me. I even rocked her cradle and hummed Papa's Aves to her.

"Baby Amelha, Baby Amelha," I would coo, and she'd look up at me with those sparkling blue eyes of hers and smile. She was so full of joy! Amelha danced her life to a tune I could never hear. And everyone adored her for it; everyone, that is, but me.

I am so sorry. How many hours I have spent in prayer, wishing it might have been otherwise. I wanted to smile back at little Amelha, to laugh with her and love her like a big sister ought to, but I could not. The demon envy had thrust its sword right through me. Each time Papa lifted Amelha into the air, she squealed with delight and my heart withered. *Why wasn't Papa spinning me that way?* I'd wonder while my gut twisted into wretched knots. The very presence of Amelha's happy nature and adventuresome spirit made me feel putrid in comparison. I could not be like her, and I could not control the jealousy that festered like a smoldering cinder in my heart.

It seemed to grow hotter each time Amelha smiled. When my eyes looked at hers, they'd go as hard as iron, and I could feel my chest on fire. I'd start to rock her cradle harder and faster. Sometimes I pinched her just to make her cry. Then Mama would rush in and shove me to the side. She'd scoop up Amelha and sing to her. She'd shoo me back into my corner, where I'd seethe beneath my blanket. Slowly the smoldering cinder turned into a glowing coal.

Santa Deu, so many times You've listened to my confessions. And You've received my penance for the way I treated poor Amelha. We were always together, and after the birth of our twin brothers, it was easy to escape from Mama's watchful eye. I found ever-new ways to torment Amelha. I told her she was ugly; that her face was crooked and I was the pretty one. I tore the left arm off the flaxen doll Papa had given her. I shoved her and took food from off her plate. I stole Mama's cheese and blamed it on her. Sometimes we would play horse and rider. When she rode me, I bucked and reared 'til she went crashing to the ground. And still Amelha wanted to be with me.

Sometimes in the evenings, when he came home from overseeing his farmlands, Papa would take us out to walk along the narrow cobbled roads of Fanjeaux. I think he did it just to give Mama relief from our incessant fighting. He held our hands and steadied us as we climbed down the steep stone steps that led from our front door onto the *Carrièra des Esquirols*.

I always tugged on Papa's hand hoping he would go left so we could climb up the rocky path that led toward Your stone church. It was as if its massive walls and bell tower pulled at my soul. They lured me toward another world where there were no sudden noises or floating ash or fire.

And sometimes Papa obliged.

"Take care where you put your feet," he'd caution us as the road narrowed, pointing to the brown sludge running down its center gully. But we had no need of his warning. Who would step into such putrid waste if she could help it? We always watched our feet as we wove our way up the hill, past Goodwives coming from market and shepherds returning home with their sheep. We'd turn left and walk along the *Rota des Tesseyers* where the weavers worked until we reached the *Lac de Jupiter*.

I caught my breath each time I saw the church tower's reflection in the rippling water of the *lac*. How could it be that there was a spring-fed pond at the very top of our *castrum*, our city on a hill? In olden times it had been part of a Roman temple, but now women used it to do their washing while children splashed and frolicked about. Amelha shouted out greetings while I clung tightly to Papa's strong hand and we made our way past the noisy throng to the front steps of the church.

Ah, God, I was then but a little girl, but I recall those moments as if they were yesterday. There was a round stone cross set upon a base of granite. Carved into its center was a marking that looked almost like a man's hand.

"Whose hand is that?" I asked Papa.

"It is the hand of God, the work of an ancient carver," he responded with no intimation that the carver might have been anything other than a good Catholic.

I touched my hand to its hard fingers and felt a warm tingle. I quickly jerked away.

"Do you want to go inside?" Papa asked.

"Oh, yes!" I answered, but Amelha shook her head.

"Do not worry, we won't be long," he reassured and gave her hand a tug. Then he took us up the steep stone stairs. Over the entrance was a carved tympanum. It stood as wide as half a house and taller than a priest and it was painted in bright colors. On its right side there were winged angels; on the left there were bones and men being consumed by fire.

"What's that?" Amelha asked.

"It is the Last Judgment. If you say your prayers and attend Mass whenever the priest comes to Fanjeaux, you will abide in Heaven like them," he told her pointing to those carved figures resting at God's right hand.

"What about those others?" Amelha asked him.

"Those are the sinners who have turned their back on God and on the Church," was all that he replied.

"I do not want to be one of them," I responded and Papa gave my hand a tight squeeze.

"Do not worry," he said. "If you are a good girl, the Devil will not come for you. Our Lord Jesus suffered and died on the cross so that your sins will not be counted against you."

I shuddered. *How could it be that he thinks me to be a good girl? Does he not know about my demons?* I wondered, but Papa took no notice. Instead he said,

"Come, let us go inside."

The heavy iron hinges creaked as Papa pulled open the great oak doors. I stood transfixed. The nave was dark as deepest night, and my eyes struggled to take it in. I reached out my hand and felt dampness seeping through the stones of the church's ancient walls. Ah, God, back then its moldy odor was for me a sweet bouquet! The room was like a giant cave. It had vaulted ceilings held up by six stone columns with angels hovering on top. The floor had been worn smooth by the shuffling feet of penitents. Our footsteps echoed as we slowly made our way toward the east wall. Over the apse was a round window made of stone. It looked like three glowing rose petals joined in the center. Papa noticed me staring at it.

"See how they are fitted together at the center there? Those petals are the three parts of God. The Church calls them the Holy Trinity: the Father, Son, and Holy Ghost," he explained. "God the Father created you and me and everything that is. His Son, Jesus, lived in the Holy Land a long, long time ago. He taught us how to live and died to free us from our sins. Then God sent his Holy Ghost to be with us and look after us."

I was not sure I understood at all; but, God, as I let Papa's voice flow over me, it felt like the words came right from Your own mouth. My eyes shifted to the fading daylight seeping from the window across the apse. It spread its gentle glow over the carved altar where a wooden statue of a young woman kept her watch.

She was so beautiful! Soft brown ringlets fell from her veil and spread across her shoulder. She was clad in robes the color of the summer sky. She held a precious little boy close to her breast and seemed to beckon me into her care.

"Who is that?" I whispered to Papa as if my voice might break her magic spell.

"That is our Blessed Mother, the Virgin pure who gave birth to Our Lord Jesus. Do you see how gently she holds him?"

My head slowly nodded.

"My dear Elmina," he continued. "She holds you just the way she holds Our Savior." And for a minute I imagined I was held in the arms of a mother who loved me.

Papa showed us how to kneel before the altar and make a cross upon our chest.

"You can pray to Mother Mary for anything your heart desires," he said, "and she will carry all your prayers straight to her Son in Heaven."

Of course I did believe him. The Blessed Lady was so very calm.

Just looking at her stilled my anxious heart. And I imagined that her Dear Son must be just the same—gentle and filled with deep compassion. *Santa Deu*, I was only a little girl, but in the dark quiet of that church, I sensed Your tranquil presence all around me. It seemed as if I breathed Your very spirit in its musty air. With Papa by my side, I knelt before Our Lady and prayed out loud.

"Please Mother Mary, I desire to be a good girl and to sit at God's right hand on the Judgment Day. Please make Mama love me and help me to be a better big sister."

Immediately, a beam of light from the round window filled the darkened apse with a Heavenly glow. I felt a warmth that made me tingle from my hair down to my toenails. My head grew light as if a choir of angels were caressing it, and, for a moment, I felt as if nothing could ever harm me.

But much too soon Amelha grew restless. She started to whine and squirm, and Papa signaled it was time to go. And, God, I beg that You can forgive me, for at that moment I forgot my prayer and hated her again. I wished that she would go away so I might kneel inside Your church forever.

Chapter 2

LE JEU D'ADAM

But of course Amelha did not go away, not then. And so we went back into the daylight, through the oak doors, down the stone steps, and past the wall of houses that formed an inner sanctum around the church plaza. Like ours, they were the last remaining pride of other noble families of Fanjeaux. They stood two or three floors above the street, with thick stone walls and windows that were shuttered to keep out the rain and cold. Each house had two wood doors, one for people and a larger one for carts and animals. A few of them were well kept, plastered with a fresh paste of lime and water, but others were, like ours, in sore repair. The plaster was crumbling, and the paint on their once-colorful shutters had mostly peeled off. The stone and plaster showed which families had met hard times.

When we got home, Mama always asked us where we had been. I knew enough to stay silent, but Amelha had no such instincts.

"Papa took us into that musty old church," she told Mama. "And Elmina was praying to a wooden statue!"

Mama turned to Papa with a cold fury.

"I've told you that I do not want my children fouled by the filth the Roman Church spews on our land," she hissed.

"I will not deprive my girls of salvation," Papa answered quietly. Mama glared, and my heart sank. I could tell that our next outing would not be to the church.

Sure enough, the following day Papa turned right onto the *Cariérra des Esquirols* and we walked to the *Rota des Faures* where all the blacksmiths worked. I hated the din of the hammers pounding on anvils, the peddlers screeching for us to buy their wares, the screams of children chasing one another, and the crowds of townsfolk shouting their *bienvenuts*. The noise made me afraid, and I longed all the more for the quiet of Your church.

That day we saw a man who had no legs riding in a wheelbarrow. I held tight to Papa, but Amelha walked right up to him and inquired, "Where are your legs?"

He smiled at her and shook his head. "I lost them in the Holy Land," he replied.

"I hope you find them soon," Amelha answered, and he chuckled.

I stared wide-eyed as he passed by and then asked Papa, "What really happened to his legs?"

"He lost them in battle. I fought with him in Constantinople," Papa responded. "He gave his legs to save the Holy Land from infidels."

I was incredulous.

"You fought in the Crusades?" I asked. "Were you a knight? Did you have a black horse and your own sword? Did you kill any infidels?"

Before Papa could answer Amelha piped up, "What are infidels? Are there any here?"

Papa took a deep breath. "Infidels are enemies of the Holy Church. Here in Fanjeaux . . ." He hesitated and let out a long sigh. "Here in Fanjeaux, we do not let infidels trouble us," is all he said.

※

Sometimes Papa took us down the hill all the way to the first wall that circled Fanjeaux. We would look past the fortifications and watch as shepherds traipsed home with their sheep after a day of grazing in the fields. And, God, what fields they were! Furrows of grain and olive trees undulated across a rolling valley all the way to Montréal. Their greens and ochres shimmered with the light of Your creation.

"This land is in your blood," dear Papa reminded us. "Look west toward Belpech and you can see lands once controlled by your grandparents; look east toward Montréal and all you see was owned by your mother's family."

"Do we still own it?" I asked him.

"Only a little garden plot. The rest we share with your cousins and their in-laws. The tithes upon our lands are no longer enough to provide us with much of an income."

"What happened to our lands?" I pushed.

"It is hard to keep land within a *domus* anymore. We aren't like the Franks, and we don't give our lands to just our first-born sons. That means all the children inherit land and with each generation their holdings get smaller. The taxes aren't enough to support everyone, so lords from the Languedoc are forever fighting one another."

We must have looked alarmed, for he stepped in to reassure us.

"You don't have to worry. Three walls and a deep ditch surround Fanjeaux," Papa said, pointing to the watchtowers beside the city gate. "See these turrets? There are fourteen of them where guards keep watch both day and night. We will always be safe within the walls of this *castrum*," he promised us. "Why, not even the pope's army could get through them."

And, God, back then I trusted he was right.

By the time I was eight years old, three brothers had come along and the house filled with babies crying and little boys running about. Mama was so busy that sometimes I could sneak away. I'd climb the path up to the church all by myself. With all my weight, I'd pull open its oaken doors and step into its darkened stillness. How I treasured those times. Most often there was no one there, and I would kneel before the Blessed Virgin and pray. Sometimes I was certain she spoke to me as well. I heard her gentle voice echo in the space between my ears. She told me of the Father's love and reassured me that her Son, Jesus, forgave me for being a bad big sister.

One afternoon, when I was kneeling in prayer, I heard the doors creak behind me. I startled and turned in the darkness to see two shadowy presences walking toward the altar. They were young women dressed in white woolen robes, and their heads were covered with white veils. The oldest one was tall and stood erect as if she were a fine lady; the younger was shorter and rounder. They walked up to me and extended the hand of friendship.

"*Bona tarda,*" the older girl offered. "My name is Guillelmette and this is my sister Raymundine. It is good to find a girl like you praying in this church."

"I love God, and I love the Church," I answered quietly.

"There are not many in Fanjeaux who do," she replied. We stood in silence for a moment before she added, "Have you ever considered that you might be called to religious vocation?"

"I don't know what that is," I admitted.

"It is becoming a nun," she replied to my blank look. "We are Cistercian novices preparing to become brides of Our Lord Jesus Christ. We live in a convent in Toulouse."

"Why are you here in Fanjeaux?" I inquired.

"We grew up here and now we've come for a last visit with our mother, Na Gracia. Soon we will give our lives to the Blessed Savior by taking solemn vows of poverty, chastity, and obedience. Then we will spend all of our days in prayer and sacred work for the glory of God."

My eyes widened in wonder.

"Can anyone become a nun?" I asked.

"Anyone who has been baptized and whose father can pay the order's dowry," she replied.

I've been baptized, I thought and my heart leapt. *I wonder if Papa would pay a dowry so that I could be a nun.*

I wanted to stay there and talk with these two novices, but the setting sunlight that crept up the church's walls told me it was time to go. I quickly curtsied and replied,

"I need take my leave to help Mama and Jeannette prepare our dinner. I am most pleased to have made your acquaintance." Then I ran home. Papa was not yet there and Mama had not even noticed I'd been gone.

It wasn't long before Amelha too had grown big enough to explore Fanjeaux. We were almost always together, and we tussled every time we left the house. I longed to head up the steep path to the church, but Amelha wanted nothing to do with it. She froze whenever she saw the bell tower. She'd pull away from me, as if its very walls might crush her, and then run down the hill as fast as her little legs would take her. I had no choice but to follow after.

And so, we usually explored the other parts of town. We wandered down the *Rota des Tisseyers* and watched the weavers at their work. We headed down the Forgers' Road where blacksmiths, bakers, and tanners all had their shops. We even visited *ostals* run by the Good Christians, where we knew we'd be welcome and could always get a cool drink and maybe a piece of horsebread. Amelha loved to bid *bonjourna* to these *bonnes femmes* who let girls live with them and taught them how to read and write.

Back then, I did not know that the Good Christians were shameful heretics. I hadn't learned it was a sin to read the Bible in Occitan or for their perfecti to heal the sick through laying on of hands. Even Catholics like my papa admired the perfecti and their simple ways. Most of us had aunts and cousins who had chosen to follow the Good Christian path, if not as perfecti then as believing *credentes*. There was even a rumor that the Catholic priest who led Mass once a month and on feast days was a secret supporter.

Each Thursday, Amelha and I would go with Mama to the market square. Everyone in Fanjeaux was there! Not just artisans from town but vendors from as far away as Mirepoix and Carcassonne would come to sell their wares: warm bread and quince preserves, needles and linen for embroidery, belts, dice and iron nails—anything you could want.

Sometimes the sounds and bustle of the market scared me. One day a hunch-backed man took hold of Mama's skirts. "Lovely lady, lovely lady," he implored, "any man would need help to feed the appetite of one so fine as you." Then he thrust under her nose a basket filled with odd-looking dried meat. "Take these home to your husband and I promise you will be grateful," he added with a wink. Mama pulled herself loose and quickly ushered us away.

"What were those things?" Amelha asked.

"They were parts of a bull that you don't need to know about," was her reply.

There was an old black-robed woman who sold herbs and medicines that promised to cast out demons and cure any ailment. The most mysterious was a hairy brown root that she called the *main de gloire*. It looked to me, then, like a magic dancing elf, but the herbalist would not allow me to touch it. Her gleaming eyes stared into mine and seemed to look into my very soul. I even wondered if she could predict the future.

"Only the wisest of practitioners can touch the mandrake root," she warned me. "It shrieks and moans when pulled out of the earth, and it can kill you if you don't know how to handle it. Lovers who smell its fruit will be driven to ecstasy. From its roots comes mandragora, a tincture that can heal the deepest pain. But," the wise woman added, "it can drive you mad and make you sleep forever."

It did make me shudder. I wondered if You had created that

dangerous magic plant, or was it made by the Devil himself? I quickly turned away to look at other things. There were both men and boys on stilts and *jongleurs* dancing in the streets, singing the songs of the troubadours. It seemed to me that they might have smelled the fruit of the mandrake themselves, the way they carried on and crooned about the passion of chaste courtly love.

I must have been near ten years old the time we met the *troubairitza* who came all the way from Dia. Her name was Beatriz, and I felt certain she had tasted the root of the *main de gloire*. I saw her first the day she came to Fanjeaux for the Feast of Mary Magdalene. Dear God, she set my blood to boiling in ways I cannot tell You about. She sang in a low voice that could have been the Magdalene's herself: "*Quant ce vient en juin . . .*

> When the month of June comes
> I breathe a floral odor in the air
> My sisters dance
> And dream of sacred love.
> They strut and prance
> With such great joy
> A fire begins to burn
> Below my waist.
> Once more I beg to know,
> Papa, why did you give me
> to become a nun?"

I was not yet a woman, God, but I was sure good Catholic girls don't think of things like this. They sing gentle songs to the Blessed Virgin, the One who watches over us and keeps our chastity. The rich, low voice of Beatriz ignited a burning terribly new to me. I stood as in a trance while she crooned her lament and longed to run up to the church and hide.

Amelha, on the other hand, did not seem to be troubled by the song at all. She dragged me over and asked Beatriz, "How can a girl become a troubadour?"

Of course I shrank away, embarrassed by her forwardness, but I could hear what Beatriz replied.

"There is but one way to become a *troubairitza*, and that is to sing about what rests within your heart."

From that day on it became impossible to shut Amelha up. She sang herself to sleep with lullabies Mama had taught us; she hummed along as villagers danced to the *estampidas*; she crooned romantic *cansos* and the *albas* sung by lovers to welcome the dawn. She tried to get me to join with her. Sometimes I'd hum along, but my heart did not want to sing as the troubadours did. Dear God, even back then its sole desire was to chant hymns and raise my voice to You.

On market days, the troubadours were not the only ones who vied for our attention. Gaunt perfecti from all around the Languedoc stood at the corner of the market spreading their message. They dressed in long black robes and claimed to live just as the early Christians had, traveling in pairs and holding everything in common. They fasted and they ate no meat or eggs or cheese—no products of vile fornication. They called Your Holy Church "the Whore of Babylon" and claimed that it spoke with the voice of Satan.

I know that it was wrong to listen to their blasphemy; but we were still young girls, and it was hard not to. We never saw Your priests except at Mass. None of them ever came out into the market square to defend the Church. I don't know where they were; the heretics claimed they were too busy collecting tithes or enjoying their wine and concubines. There was even a rumor that our own itinerant priest would soon abandon the parish to seek his fortune in the North. It almost seemed as if Your Church ignored us, while these heretic perfecti looked into our eyes and talked as if the fate of our souls really mattered.

⁂

Each time they did, Amelha always looked right back. She'd sit down at their feet and ask whatever questions came to into her mind.

"Where does God live?" she wanted to know. "Has he really gone off and left this world to the Devil? If so, why does it matter whether we are good or bad?"

"God lives in Heaven and in our souls," the perfect answered. "God has not abandoned the world; God gives everyone the spiritual power to overcome its tethers."

Amelha even dared to ask about the Church. "Why does Papa have to give his best lambs to the priest?" she once demanded.

"The priests are controlled by demons," he replied solemnly. "They take what is not theirs from your papa and all the people."

Amelha stomped her foot. "I do not like the priests," she said. "I hope that they and their demons stay far away from me."

The things those perfecti said, God, they scared me. They talked as if the whole world were one giant battleground between forces of good and evil. They said the Good God created our souls as divine sparks in his own image. But then a Bad God came along and stole them. This Evil God enwrapped all souls in flesh and then created earth so he could hide them. Everything we see—the rivers and the rolling fields, the cattle and the sheep, and the birds of the sky—the Devil made it all that we might be enslaved to matter. The perfecti claimed that if we would hope to free our souls, we must renounce the pleasures of the world and be like them.

Dear God, back then I could not make sense of their words. How could it be that the world is not Your creation? As I sat in the warm sun next to Amelha, I averted my eyes and shivered.

I liked the feast days better than the market days. There were no perfecti on the street corners and Papa would always take us to church. Saint Nicholas Day began a whole month of celebrating the birth of Your Dear Son. On Michaelmas, we gave thanks for the harvest, and after church we'd frolic with horn dancers in the square. In August the whole town ceased from their labors and gathered for the Feast of the Assumption of the Blessed Lady. Jugs overflowed with the best wine of the new harvest; choristers poured out from church singing hymns to the Virgin Mary. Peasants and nobles danced together in the street to celebrate the union of her undefiled body with her soul in Heaven. Even back then, I dared to hope that I might grow up to be chaste and pure just like she was.

Still, Easter was my favorite feast day. We always woke up with the rising sun to gather in the market square and wait for the priest. He arrived with his deacons clothed in full regalia, with a gilt-edged chasuble draped over his snow-white linen alb. We all began chanting together. Then the priest lifted high his golden cross and led us up the hill and through the church's open doors. Dear God, I still remember how beautiful it was! The altar was draped all in white and even the Blessed Virgin wore a crown of white lilies. Most of the town was there, even many of the Good Christian *credentes*.

I stood transfixed throughout the Easter service. On this one day the priest let all the people share in the Holy Eucharist. He washed his hands and chanted his blessing in Latin. Then he lifted the perfect circle of the Host high in the air and broke it, just as Jesus was broken on the cross. I felt my own heart break and held my breath until that magic moment he reunited the halves in sacred wholeness and then lowered them to the table. Then one by one we walked to the altar to receive the precious gift of His body.

Each year, we spent six weeks preparing for just this moment. Throughout the forty days of Lent, we all became as somber and ascetic as the perfecti. We'd eat no meat or even eggs. (When the hens kept on laying, we'd hard-boil the eggs to save for Easter). On some days of fasting we did not eat any food at all. On Maundy Thursday there would be a play, the passion or one that told the story of sin and redemption. And then, on Good Friday, all the

Fanjeaux Catholics would mourn together. Even the *bons hommes* carpenters refrained from using nails or iron tools out of respect. Amelha and I spent most of the day in church with Papa while Mama stayed home with the little brothers. It was dark there and somber. No candles were lit, and all the bronze ornaments were put away. Even the crucifix was covered with a black cloth. One by one we all crept up to the cross upon our knees, lamenting not just our own sins, but those of the whole fallen world. After confession, we stood silently contemplating all our wicked ways.

It may seem strange that every year I looked forward to Good Friday. As I think back on it, I realize that with the whole village fasting and lamenting, I felt less alone. For I could see that others also knew the affliction of sin upon their souls.

And, God, that Lent of the year 1203, I felt the stain of sin as I grew toward womanhood. I was only two months short of my twelfth birthday, and I knew that one day soon, Papa would come home with the news that he'd arranged my marriage to a man. How I dreaded that day! When Amelha and I strolled through the streets of Fanjeaux, I'd begun to notice how young men would turn their heads. I cringed when they whistled and made sucking noises as we walked by. But Amelha seemed to enjoy it! She was only ten years old, but she seemed fully ready to burst into the life of a woman. She sang with troubadours and danced with the *jongleurs*, and she flirted openly with all the boys who looked her way.

Not me. I knew not how to enter womanhood. I marveled at Amelha's winning ways and felt a hopeless failure beside her. Something inside me shriveled when I thought of marriage. Sometimes I would return a man's gaze with a tepid smile, but it felt false. And often on those walks I recalled Guillelmette and Raymundine and dreamed of entering a convent. I wished that I might run away into the sacred darkness of the church.

※

Of course I knew that envy was a mortal sin, even before that Maundy Thursday when Amelha and I saw *Le Jeu d'Adam*. It was a market day, and we could see immediately that something was different. Because of Holy Week the crowd was muted, but still the market bustled with activity. The usual tradesmen were all there and the peasants who came from surrounding villages. But there were new vendors as well, with fancy goods from Toulouse in the west. I even heard some people speaking French as we wandered from stall to stall. There were wealthy nobles dressed all in silk and priests I didn't recognize with flowing robes and jeweled crosses around their necks.

Amelha tried to start up conversation with each person there. I stood on the outskirts listening in, until I heard the echo of a familiar voice. Amelha heard it too. And this time when she grabbed my hand she pulled me toward the church!

Sure enough, just at the corner of the *Rota de l'Eglise*, we saw her, lute in hand, amid an entranced throng. Beatriz! Her silken gown was grey in recognition of the holy season, and she was singing a different kind of song. *"O Mary, no ploris,"* she crooned.

"Dear Mary, do not weep
For all that lives within the Heavens
Knows your sorrow
And the depth of your compassion.
Seek not your Lord
Amidst these mortal ruins
But know that
He abides within your heart
This day
And evermore."

As I pressed my way to the front of the crowd, I thought for a moment that Beatriz was looking right into my eyes. Even Amelha, who usually had no use for Church music, stood there transfixed. Together we followed Beatriz up the hill to the cobbled plaza stretching before the west wall of the church. Over the oaken doors was the familiar tympanum.

Today, though, the west wall had been transformed. Carpenters had built a stage with stairs ascending all the way to a wood platform above the tympanum. On it stood a chorus of white-robed angels, surrounded by a bounty of fruits and flowers. It could have been the floor of paradise or the garden of Eden. And there, leaning out of the tower window was a tall *figura*. He wore a pointed hat and held a bishop's miter, but his eyes seemed as angry as the Devil's. I heard the loud voice of a herald and the crowd suddenly grew silent. *Le Jeu d'Adam* was about to begin.

A dazed character came leaping onto the platform and a voice issued down from the *figura* in the window above.

"Adam," it boomed, "I am your God and you must call me Sire! A *ma imagene t'ai feit de terre.* I have formed you in my image from the loam of the earth."

"That is a lie," I heard someone yell from the crowd. "Do you not know that a Good God would not create mortal flesh?"

But the *figura* appeared not to hear, and Adam reached a bony hand longingly toward the Heavenly apparition. Again, God's voice echoed over the crowd, "You must promise one thing. *Ne moi devez jamais mover guere.* Never make war against me."

Who would make war with God? I thought incredulously.

And as Adam fell to the ground in humble obedience, my knees began to quake. Didn't my own mama at times malign the Church? Did she and her friends not rail against its tithes and defame priests who sold indulgences as corrupt dogs? I began to wonder whether the *figura* was talking to Adam or to somebody else. And suddenly I grew afraid.

I watched in horror as Adam and Eve took a bite from the apple and were cast down the scaffold stairs onto the stage below. It was there that the next scene unfolded. The two were bent over in toil, and they had borne two sons. Abel wore white robes, for he was the good son—the cheerful, obedient one who sang while laboring in the fields. Cain was the evil son, dressed in blood red and fiercely jealous of his brother. They tilled the earth together, and Abel remarked:

> "In serving God, let us not be churlish
> Let us be at all times obedient to the Creator;
> Let us so serve that we will win back his love,
> Which our parents lost by their folly . . .
> Let us pay his tithes and all that is justly his due."

And so God, each presented his own sacrifice. Cain had only a pile of grain, but Abel—he had the gifts that You adore. As he bent on his knees to offer incense and a lamb, I could feel Cain's fury. "Let us go into the field," he said menacingly. As he began to lead his brother away, Cain looked briefly toward the church and the paradise he might have known. But then he turned away to complete his murderous task. As Abel lay lifeless upon the stage, the choir asked of Cain, *"Ubi est Abel, frater tuus?"* and God repeated in Occitan, *"Cain, u est ton frère Abel?"* Cain's response still swirls within my spinning head: "Am I my brother's keeper?"

We watched as three devils dragged Cain away to the deepest fires of Hell and the angels gently carried Abel toward its nether regions to await the coming of Our Savior. And when both of us walked down the hillside to our home, I shivered.

The next day was Good Friday and I spent the day in church with Papa and Amelha. As I confessed my sinful heart, I prayed for its release. My soul, like Cain's, had been branded with the sin of envy, and I begged God to show me a different path. That Easter, I once more stood transfixed before the sacred host and gratefully took Christ's body into my own. How I wanted to believe that my soul had been wiped clean; but, Dearest God, the flames of envy and desire still burned within me, and I knew it wasn't so.

That summer, as the days lengthened and the white olive flowers turned to fruit, I entered my twelfth year. Finally the day arrived for Papa to talk with me of my future. He came home early from the fields, and Mama sat with him at the table. They bid both Amelha and me sit down. Papa released a sigh as he began to speak.

"Guilhemina, you have come of age," he said, "and Amelha too will soon become a woman. The time has come for us to talk with you about what lies ahead."

My stomach lurched.

"There are many things that you don't know," he said to us. "You both were born to noble blood, and you deserve to be given in marriage to a man of your station."

My gut twisted in knots.

"But Elmina and Amelha," he continued, "our *domus* is poor. We barely get enough in taxes to feed and clothe you and all of your brothers. We have no money to provide a dowry for either of you, and we cannot support you here at home forever." He cleared his throat as if his words were caught there.

And then Mama began to speak. "There is a Good Christian woman in town whose name is Signora Bonata. She is a gentle soul who can provide you with not only food and shelter but an education too. You will learn your letters and be taught a useful skill. Perhaps you will marry a *credente* from the village, or you might choose to live as—"

Papa regained his voice and cut off Mama's words. "We can do no better for you. You must go now and pack your belongings. Tomorrow I will take you to the *ostal* of Na Bonata. And you can live there secure in knowing that you are no longer a burden on the *domus* of your family."

"But Papa," I pleaded, "I love the Church. I don't wish to live with the perfecti or marry a village tradesman. Couldn't I just become a nun instead?"

I heard Mama whisper beneath her breath, "My own daughter will not become a servant to the Whore of—"

"What Mama means," Papa quickly interjected, "is that there are no convents here in the Languedoc. And we have not the dowry to send you to one in Toulouse. You will do as we have said."

Dear God, how my heart ached. When I asked, "Will Na Bonata take us to church on feast days?" Papa simply shook his head.

It was Mama who answered, "The Good Christians will teach you a better way to know God."

But I did not want a better way. I wanted to be in the warm bosom of our Blessed Lady. And I feared that You would think I was turning away from You, and that I too was declaring war against Your Holy Church.

"Papa, please don't make me go away," I whimpered, but Papa had already turned his back. Amelha and I both knew that our fates now rested in the hands of Na Bonata and the Good Christians.

Chapter 3

THE OSTAL

anta Deu, when Papa turned away, I stopped breathing. The room began to spin around me, and I thought that I might faint. I wanted to grow tiny, so small that Papa would not find me. I loved Papa, and Mama too, and even the brothers. I loved living so close to the church and its quiet darkness where I could be alone with You. *Why would Papa send me away?* I wanted to know. How could it be Your will that I go to live with the Good Christians? After I climbed into the sleeping loft, I prayed all night that You might change my papa's mind. But You did not answer my prayers.

And so the next day, just as he had said, Papa took Amelha and me to the *ostal*. He held tight to our hands as he brought us down the winding path through the market square. We walked along the *Carrièra des Faures*. The cobblers and tinsmiths were already hawking their wares, but I heard nothing other than the screaming inside my head.

Amelha seemed to take this change as yet another great adventure, waving *bon jorn* to each shopkeeper as we walked along.

"Will there be other girls at Na Bonata's *ostal*?" she asked Papa. "What will they teach us there?"

Papa probably answered her, but I was too dizzy to hear what he replied. I dragged my feet, aware that every step was taking me farther away from home. When we reached the towering stone walls of the Durforth palace, we turned right. For a moment I wondered if our new home might be found there, but no. We walked right by and climbed down a steep dirt path to a row of houses built against the city wall. Their plaster was crumbling, and there were dogs picking through the debris in their front gutters. *Please, God,* I prayed silently. *Don't let this be where I'm going to live. And please don't hold it against me that I must learn the ways of the Good Christians.*

Papa had become quiet as a monk, and I wondered if he was asking Your forgiveness. He said nothing until we stopped before a small stone house with cheery yellow shutters and golden mimosas growing in its window boxes. Its front steps and gutters were swept clean and its door stood open as to welcome us. I could see a workshop where girls sat weaving at their looms under the watchful eye of a small woman clad in a black robe. Papa stepped inside, and Amelha and I both trailed behind.

"Good morning, Na Bonata," he said in a formal voice that I hardly recognized. "I wish to present my daughters, Guilhemine and Amelha."

Amelha offered a curtsy, while I looked down and clung to Papa's tunic. He gave me a little shove and I slowly looked up at Na Bonata. She was short and thin, with long grey braids that wrapped around her head. And Dear God, You cannot deny that it was so: her amber eyes were beautiful, as fluid as honey, and gentle, kind, and welcoming. I took in a deep breath, and in that moment I almost forgot that those eyes belonged to an enemy of Your Church. I did not want to like her, but I most surely did. When Signora Bonata looked at me, I knew she saw the sadness in my soul and still she held out her hand.

"I bid thee welcome, Guilhemine."

"If it please you, I am called Elmina," I dared to answer.

"Elmina it is," she said in agreement, and I reached for her out-stretched hand.

The signora introduced us to a young dark-haired woman sitting at the looms. "Magdalena, I'd like you to meet two new students," she said. As Magdalena rose, I could tell she was older than me; she was tall and had the kind of figure that men liked to woo. When she put down her weaving, I could not help but notice a strange carving on her loom. It was a flower with six petals, surrounded by a circle. More petals grew outside it in a pattern that looked like it could go one forever. I could not take my eyes off it. Magdalena took no notice of my fascination, but Amelha did.

"What is that picture?" she inquired.

"It is the *Flor de la Vida,* the Flower of Life, and it contains great power." Her dark eyes flashed as she spoke, and I felt a twinge of fear.

I looked away and nodded without speaking, but Amelha returned the flashing gaze. She smiled broadly. "I can tell that it is filled with magic," she replied. "My name's Amelha, and I hope you can teach me how to draw it."

Magdalena's eyes responded with a twinkle. "Na Bonata can teach you that and many other mysteries. I bid thee welcome." She gestured toward a thickset girl whose frizzy red hair was escaping from the braid down her back.

"Please meet my friend Jordana," Magdalena said. Jordana seemed reluctant to put down her weaving and offered but a nod.

"And this is her sister Alaide," Magdalena went on. Alaide was feeding yarn to Jordana. She added a coquettish smile to her nod of welcome. Alaide was so very pretty! Her eyes were wide set and of deepest blue. Her nose was long and graceful. She had woven bright yarns into the braids of her wheat-colored hair. Alaide held her head high as if her beauty raised her a notch above the rest of us, and I accepted it was so.

Then Magdalena pointed across the room to two younger girls who held distaffs and spin.

"These are Curtslana and Paperin, younger sisters to Jordana and Alaide." Curtslana seemed shy and did not look up right away. I wondered briefly if perhaps she were as frightened of the world as me. Paperin was only seven or eight years old. She jumped up and bounded over to say hello. Paperin's smile was so genuine, I almost returned her greeting, but Na Bonata interrupted us.

"I must talk privately with Signor de Beaupuys." She turned to Magdalena and asked, "Would you please show Elmina and Amelha the *ostal*?"

Magdalena grinned her concurrence. She led us through the workshop into a dark stone room. It was smaller than our own *fogana* but not so very different, a dark hall with a fire pit at one end and a long table with more girls sitting on benches at the other. The smell of turnips roasting in the fire was a sharp reminder that this is where I would now take my meals. A spark leapt up, and I drew back. I turned my back on the fire to face the girls sitting at the table, talking and giggling as they kneaded bread and chopped onions. The sharp odor reminded me of Mama's warning.

"Only peasants eat onions!" she once told us. "They ruin the complexion."

But none of these girls seemed to be sorely afflicted.

"Blanca, Riccarda, Gentiana," Magadalena announced, "Please greet two new students, Elmina and Amelha."

Blanca was cutting onions, taking great care to be sure that each piece was exactly the same size. Riccarda looked to be the same age as Magdalena and seemed to be overseeing the kitchen. Her bulging breasts sagged onto her round belly as she bent over Blanca's work nodding encouragement. Gentiana was kneading bread with a touch so gentle that it seemed like a caress. All three returned my wary gaze with welcoming smiles. I took in the loving care with which they were preparing their meal, and, God forgive me, at that moment I forgot they were heretics and hoped I might become their friend.

⁂

Then Magdalena led us to a steep ladder ascending to a timber loft. "That is where we all sleep," she said. "Do you want to take a look?" Amelha was already bolting up the ladder, and I climbed up behind. The floor was covered with straw-stuffed mattresses and a rough linen curtain hung behind them from the rafters. "The beds of the perfecti are back there," explained Magdalena.

"What are perfecti?" Amelha inquired.

"Na Bonata and Sister Bruna are perfecti," she responded. "They have received spiritual gifts through the *consolamentum*. They will teach us all they know so that we may one day follow in their path."

"What's a *consolamentum*?" Amelha asked again.

"You must be patient," Magdalena replied. "It's the Good Christians' sacred rite. In due time you'll learn all about it."

She then pointed to a plump mattress tucked into the corner underneath the rafters. "That bed is for the two of you," she said. I startled. For the first time, I realized that I was grateful for Amelha and glad I that I would not be sleeping with a stranger. I glanced at my sister with a smile of relief. She returned it with a big grin. Together we crawled back down the ladder after Magdalena.

"I'll show you the classroom," our guide offered and led us through a door in the back of the *fogana*. Three more girls sat at a round table, intently copying letters onto wax tablets with wooden styluses. Another black-robed woman stood attentively above them. She was tall and thin, and her graying brown hair was pulled in a tight knot behind her head.

"This is Sister Bruna," she said by way of introduction. "She is instructing some of our day students, and she will teach you to read and write your letters."

"Papa has already taught us to write," Amelha piped up proudly, but the sister barely acknowledged us before going back to work. Already Bruna scared me, but Magdalena took no note.

"Come over here," she urged. "I want to show you something

wonderful." She pointed toward the eastern corner of the room where a leather-bound book sat open on a carved wooden stand. We gathered round, and I saw a bright illustration of Jesus hovering over an empty cross. His head was surrounded by a halo of purest gold; its rays shone all about him. The book reminded me of the illuminated Bible that the priests read from in church, and I felt a familiar tingle. But something was different.

"What is this book?" I dared to ask Magdalena.

"Why, it's our Bible," she responded. "It was copied by Na Bonata's brother in Minerve."

I stared at the sacred book. "It's not so big as the Bible in our church," I observed. "And it's not written in Latin."

"Of course not," Magdalena replied. "It is just the New Testament. And it's in Occitan so that we can all read it. Only the Demon Church uses a Latin Bible."

I flinched as my eyes widened, but I dared not answer back. Amelha reached to turn the pages of the Occitan Bible, but Magdalena quickly intervened. "There are only two books like this in all of Fanjeaux," she warned. "Only the perfecti are allowed to touch it.

"Come, let's go to the gardens," Magdalena continued as she ushered us out of the classroom and led us through the back door. We stepped into a lush garden of raised beds enclosed by a wooden wall. On my left were leafy greens—spinach and lettuces and kale. There were spiky onion shoots and small artichokes and green beans forming on the vine. Magdalena called to a woman who looked to be overseeing the garden, "Aude, come meet Elmina and Amelha."

Aude was about the same age as Mama. She was kneeling among the turnips and basking in an aura of light. At Magdalena's words, she stood up with a regal bearing and walked over to greet us.

"Benvengut!" she exclaimed. "I am most pleased to make your acquaintance." Turning to the beds on my right, she offered, "You've seen our kitchen garden. What we have here are medicinal herbs. Through them, God helps us to heal all kinds of ailments."

I looked upon more varied leaves and flowers than I'd ever seen in my short life. Some grew in the earth; others were planted on raised platforms or were hanging from clay pots. Aude began reciting their names: aloe and angelica, coltsfoot and cardamom, wormwood and feverfew, horehound, henbane and St. John's wort. My eyes grew wide as she pointed to the red flowers of the poppies growing along the back wall and to the thick green leaves and lavender flowers of the mandrake.

Two girls were kneeling in the dirt and watching us. "Berengaria and Clarette, I bid you meet Elmina and Amelha." The older one was Berengaria. She stood there as if she too were planted in that garden. She waved a handful of weeds at us and gave a welcoming smile. The younger girl raised her head shyly to look at me. Her bright blue eyes shone with a clear intelligence, and as soon as they met my own, I knew that soon we would become fast friends. My heart leapt with the hope that I might be allowed to tend the gardens alongside Clarette. And, God forgive me, among these *bonnes femmes* I was already starting to feel at home.

When Amelha and I returned to the *fogana,* Papa was gone. My heart wept, and Na Bonata seemed to know its sorrow. She put a hand on my shoulder, and its warmth flooded through me. Then she explained that our days would soon be occupied with completing chores, studying our letters, and learning the Good Christian way. We would also be taught a skill that could one day become for us an occupation. We might learn how to spin and weave, we might become skilled cooks or bakers, or we might learn how to tend the garden and combine herbs into medicines.

For once in my life, I spoke up before Amelha. "Would it please you to have me work in the garden?" I asked with bated breath, and the signora nodded!

"And Amelha, what work do you wish to do while you're here?" Na Bonata inquired.

I could hardly believe it. This time it was Amelha holding back, as if she were afraid to admit the desire of her heart. But I could tell that there was something she wanted to ask, and so could Na Bonata.

"What is it that you wish to say?" she inquired.

Amelha raised her eyes and spoke so softly, I could scarcely hear. "I want to make music," she whispered. "I want to play the lute and be a *troubairitza* like the great Beatriz."

The signora smiled and I could see the sparkle in her amber eyes. "Dear Amelha," she replied. "It requires wealth and patronage to live as a *troubairitza*. But we would be most pleased to have you sing for us. Magdalena both sings and plays the lute. Perhaps you would agree to work with her in the weaving shop. I am sure she would be happy to teach you what she knows."

And so Amelha and I began our lives at the signora's *ostal*. In the morning we were occupied with our studies. Since we already knew our letters, it wasn't long before we were able to decipher words from the Occitan Bible. I still remember the first time Sister Bruna read to us from the Gospel According to John, and we carefully copied her words onto our tablets.

"If ye love me, keep my commandments," she read to us that morning. "And I will pray the Father and He shall give you another Comforter; even the Spirit of Truth, whom the world cannot receive, because it seeth Him not, nor knoweth Him."

They were beautiful words. As the soft cadences of Bruna's voice lilted over us, I could almost feel the comfort of the Spirit, descending like a dove. But then Bruna began to speak the phrases more harshly, "The world cannot receive him, because it seeth Him not," she repeated. "The world remains under the grip of the Evil One, blinded and held captive by the poisonous teachings of the Roman Church."

My chest tightened as I caught my breath. I crossed myself to ward off her blasphemy. I thought of the gentleness and beauty of the Blessed Virgin and the dark womb of her Church, and I felt a tear form.

"I don't like it when you talk like that," I said quietly. "I love the Holy Church." Every eye in the room turned upon me.

"Elmina," Sister Bruna replied, with a tinge of warning in her voice. "You speak from ignorance. You do not yet know of the Church's wickedness."

"How can the Church be wicked?" I replied. "It was formed by God."

"It's not always been thus," said Sister Bruna. "There was a time when all the followers of Jesus loved our Heavenly Father. They lived simply, owning no property and sharing all they had. Those who received the Gnosis of the Spirit, men and women alike, served God as deacons and as priests. And they went about preaching and sharing the Gospel with all they met.

"But then the Devil took hold of them, and the Roman Church was born. Its bishops and the pope in Rome created God in their own image. They distorted the teachings of Jesus. They burned the Gnostic writings. And they persecuted the holy men and women who followed them. The Harlot Church—your Church—began to teach that Jesus was a physical man born of a woman's flesh. They claimed his body died and was resurrected. But that could not have been. The Good God would never have subjected Himself to the filth of human flesh, nor could resurrection in material form ever offer our souls the hope of spiritual salvation."

As she spoke my tears flowed freely. I didn't understand all of her words, but I heard her say that Jesus could not have been born of the Blessed Virgin.

"But Our Savior was not corrupted when he was born to woman," I stammered in reply. "The Virgin Mother was both chaste and pure."

"My dear Elmina," Sister Bruna responded. "You still have much to learn. In time you will understand more, but for right now the gardens await your care." She picked up the Occitan Bible and placed it back upon its stand.

Santa Deu, I was so confused. I asked myself, *Why did these women call themselves Good Christians when they despised Your Holy Church?* Sister Bruna had said that Jesus was not born of Mary. Did she not know that the Blessed Virgin watches over us and takes our prayers to God? Bruna had said that Jesus never died. Who was it then hanging from the crucifix over the altar? How could he have been resurrected on Easter if he had not died? If Jesus did not give his life upon the cross, who would forgive my sins and conquer my demons? I felt dizzy and a cold chill shot up along my spine.

But I did just as Sister Bruna bid. I went outside and tended to the garden. Aude, Clarette, and Berengaria were already hard at work. They showed me how to sow seeds through the holes of a dibber and pull out tender shoots to give each plant the room to grow. They taught me the names for every herb and whether each one wanted sunlight or shade, dry soil, or damp. Soon, Aude said, we'd learn the sacred art of turning plants into healing balms and medicines.

Dear God, how close to You I felt in that garden. In the rich dampness of the soil, I knew Your grace. My heart swelled in adoration as I considered the many living things You created to nourish us and heal our ailments. I thought to myself, *How could Aude have such tender regard for every plant and still believe that they were created by the Devil?* I was only twelve years old, but I knew something was wrong with what Sister Bruna was teaching us.

I could not help but wonder if Clarette and Berengaria felt the same way. That afternoon, as we plucked weeds from the soil and gathered the first ripe fava beans into our baskets, I dared to ask, "Do you believe what Sister Bruna taught us today about the Blessed Virgin?"

Berengaria looked down and said nothing, but Clarette checked to see that Aude was out of earshot then answered. "Bruna is a good woman who loves the Word of God," she said, "and she has much to teach us. But I try to close my ears when she speaks against the Blessed Virgin and the Holy Mother Church."

I sighed with such relief. Here in this garden was a friend who also loved both Mary and the Church. But God, I was sorely confused. The perfecti were so kind and good. I wondered *God, do You hate them for their blasphemy? Or is Your love so strong that You embrace them despite their hatred for Your Church?* And, God, after all that has happened, I wonder still and dare to hope You do.

That summer, the three of us worked together under Aude's tutelage, and slowly we began to learn the craft of making potions, teas, and tinctures from the bounty of our garden. It seemed a miracle that You had created all this from a handful of seeds! Aude showed me a Latin book with colorful drawings of more plants than I'd ever seen.

"What is this book?" I asked, slowly turning its pages. "And why is it in Latin?"

"It is called *The Book of Simple Medicine*," Aude replied. "It was written fifty years ago by a German nun named Hildegard."

A nun? I thought and wanted to know why she had a book made by a Catholic. But I asked instead, "Where did you get it? Do you know how to read Latin?"

"It was a gift from my brother. I read a little Latin, but he made translations for me," Aude answered pointing to neatly penned Occitan inscriptions in the margins.

I did not even think to ask about Aude's brother or to wonder then how he knew Latin. I was too interested in all she had to teach me. Folk from the town would come to us for relief from their pains and illnesses. We dried coltsfoot so those who suffered from the croup and coughs could burn it and breathe the smoke. We ground up wormwood leaves and mixed them with mint to treat stomach pains. We made a balm of hemlock to rub on aching joints.

I even learned to make a love potion from mallow and a sleep tonic by mixing mandrake root with poppy seeds, henbane, and vinegar.

When I began my bleeding, it was Aude who taught me to make a tea of comfrey, nettle, and blackberry to reduce my monthly flow and to carry nutmeg to conceal its smell. The sisters all tried to reassure me; they said the bleeding was a natural part of living in an evil world and nothing to be concerned about. But I was not so sure. The whole womanly realm confused and frightened me. I was ashamed of my ripening body, and my blood reminded me of the stain of sin upon my soul.

Aude told me the bleeding meant I soon would have to make a choice. I could enter the world, live with a *credente* and bear his children. Then I would be responsible for entrapping those new souls in the flesh of my womb. I might one day choose to do as Aude had done and return to the Good Christians after raising a family. But if I did not wish to be a wife and mother, I could prepare now to receive the *consolamentum,* that solemn laying on of hands that would initiate me as a Good Christian perfect. I could forego the sensual pleasures of youth and live my whole life in service to the Holy Spirit's light.

Dear God, I did not feel prepared to handle such a choice. I did not wish to be a wife or be confined to a lifetime of raising children. But even though I loved the *bonnes femmes* at the *ostal,* I did not want to become a perfect and declare war upon Your Church. Most of the time, I could ignore the choice that lay ahead, but each month when I bled, I knew the day of reckoning was growing near. Then I would lie awake at night praying that somehow You might make for me another way.

Amelha, on the other hand, seemed to have no such worries. She spent her days in the workshop, learning the arts of spinning and weaving. How fully she gave her heart over to those Good Christians! In the classroom she was quick to learn and filled with curiosity about their ways. In the evenings, she and Magdalena made music together. Magdalena played the lute, and their voices blended in perfect harmony as they crooned the songs of the troubadours. But, *Santa Deu*, how their words vexed me!

They sang the *cansos* of courtly love that were on the lips of all the *jongleurs* of Fanjeaux. They swooned with longing, as if making their love calls to a far-off suitor or to some distant God. One night they sang the song we'd heard from Beatriz during Holy Week.

Dear Mary
Do not weep
For all that lives within the Heavens
Knows your sorrow
And the depth of your
Sweet compassion.

"Why do you sing of Mary," I asked Magdalena, "when you don't believe her to be the Mother of Our Lord?"

"Ah, Elmina," she answered. "Mother Mary is not the one of whom we speak. We sing to Mary Magdalene, the first apostle. It was she who knew great, unrequited passion for Jesus and then transformed it into spiritual love upon his passing. It is to her, the bride of Christ, that knights offer their fealty and troubadours address their hymns of love."

"The Magdalene?" I gasped. Surely she was mistaken. Was not the *domina* of the troubadours the Blessed Virgin?

But Magdalena kept on talking. "This fabled lover was at Jesus's side throughout his life and at the foot of the cross when he died. She loved Jesus in all the ways a woman loves a man save one; and then, when Jesus left the physical plane, the Magdalene became his apostle. She devoted the rest of her life to preaching the gospel of the Kingdom."

Dear God, as I listened to Magdalena speak, I felt dizzy with confusion. My soul adored the Blessed Virgin; it did not wish to sing of Mary Magdalene. And yet, I harbored a secret desire. I wished that I too might love from afar as the troubadours and Mary Magdalene had loved. During the day I imagined the Son of God appearing on our doorstep and at night I dreamt of the exquisite pain of unrequited love. *And God have mercy on me, for I started to imagine that if Mary Magdalene could love both man and God as one, perhaps one day someone might come along who'd let me do the same.*

Chapter 4

CONSOLAMENTUM

I had been with the heretics for just over a year that summer of 1204. *Santa Deu*, I am ashamed to admit it, but during that time, I never once climbed up the *Rota des Faures* to pray in the dark comfort of Your Church. It was as if the Good Christians were severing the hold it had once had upon my girlhood soul.

Instead, as the olives ripened and the lavender blossoms gave off their pungent scent, I studied with Bruna and lost myself to reveries of love. How I longed for the pure love of the troubadour, an ardor that would be both passionate and chaste. But my body was tormenting me with a different kind of longing. By day I stole secret glances at young men in the market and at night I dreamt of the godly savior who would become my champion. I might have given myself completely to fantasies of romance had not word of the Troubles come to our door.

We first learned of them from the Good Christian bishop, Guilhabert de Castre. He was often a visitor to our *ostal*, instructing Aude and the other women who were preparing for their *consolamentum*.

Sometimes he would remain after dinner for music or conversation. On that June evening, he and his companion, Brother Martin, had just returned from Toulouse. They sat at a small table set aside for men. We ate in silence, and afterward Guilhabert revealed some disturbing news.

"Pope Innocent III has issued an edict giving the Catholic Church the right to confiscate the property of Albigensian heretics and anyone supporting them."

"What is an Albigensian heretic?" I wanted to know.

"My dear Elmina," Guilhabert replied. "That is how the Roman Church refers to the Good Christians. They call us Albigensians and claim that our faith is heresy against the Pope's religion."

"And most of the good people of Fanjeaux are friends to the Albigensians," added his companion. "Count Raymond VI of Toulouse and Raymond Trencavel of Carcassonne could lose all of their holdings if they continue to allow us to remain within their territories."

"But our liege Raymund Roger, the Count of Foix, is a vassal of Raymond VI," Blanca exclaimed. "He has made his support for the Good Christians clear. His sister Esclarmonde will soon receive the *consolamentum* with Aude. Surely he would not turn his back on all of us."

"I cannot know what any of the lords will do under the Church's sway," Guilhabert responded.

"The Roman Church seeks nothing but its own power and wealth," Amelha piped up in disgust.

I gave her an ugly look, but she continued and took no note of me. "Yesterday the troubadours at the market sang a *sirvente* about the Church. Would you like us to sing it for you?"

The bishop nodded and Magdalena brought out her lute. Dear God, they made me squirm as, in perfect harmony, the two blasphemed Your Church:

A land once ruled
by gallant noblemen

now falls under the sway
of filthy swine
disguised as churchmen,
bishops, monks, and priests.

They leach our blood.
They steal our last few sous
for their indulgences.
They take the grain from our fields
and cast their lust upon our women.

Pray tell if ever you have seen
a treachery more vile
or an hypocrisy so great
as that of clergymen.

When they finished, Guilhabert could not help releasing a chuckle, but then his face grew grim.

"You must take great care where you play your music," he warned. "The pope and his legates would not look kindly on such words."

I cringed. I was still naïve enough to ask of Guilhabert, "Why would the Holy Father look upon anyone with unkindness?"

"Elmina," he replied with both gravity and compassion, "you must know this. The world is held in the grip of an Evil God, and the Roman Church is his handmaiden. The pope says that because we accept neither the vicious Jehovah of the Old Testament nor the authority of the bishops and the priests, we are the enemies of God. Those churchmen seek to destroy us and claim our lands for themselves. In Paris they have already burned our people at the stake, and now Innocent III has asked nobles throughout the Languedoc to call a crusade against us. Thus far they have refused, but I'm not sure how long the pope will take no for an answer."

Burned people at the stake? I wanted to inquire. I closed my eyes but could not shut out the vision of flames that danced behind them.

Guilhabert took no notice of my distress and continued. "For now, the Church has simply challenged us to respond to their charges of heresy in public debates on all matters of Christian belief and practice. Papal legates have already been dispatched throughout the territory. We all will be called, each in our own fashion, to defend our way of life against the Serpent Church. And you, Elmina, cannot remain sitting on the fence. You will have to make a decision as to which path you will follow."

My stomach clenched at hearing Guilhabert's words. I closed my eyes and felt the room begin to spin. How could I choose a path? I did not wish to turn my back on the Church I had loved since I was small. I thought of the *Jeu d'Adam* and the *tympanum* over the church's door. Papa had said that those who turned their back upon the Church would burn in hell.

But if I did not join the Good Christians, how would I survive? Perhaps I could beg Mama and Papa to take me back. Papa would have mercy on me and wish to help me if he could, but not Mama. She had no patience for either the Church or me, and I knew well that they could not afford to keep me.

And God, I must confess that I had come to love the Good Christian women as a family. Na Bonata was kinder than my own mama had been. Aude and even Bruna were now my *tantas* and I had not just Amelha but eleven more sisters. I thought perhaps I should just agree to take a *credente* for a husband. But I did not wish to leave these dear women to become a wife. How could I have turned my back and walked away without a family or dowry to support me? I'm sorry, God. I was but thirteen years old that summer, and I had then neither the strength nor the courage to choose Your Church.

And so I opened my eyes and continued to listen to Guilhabert. He announced that the first of the debates would be held in but two weeks time, and all of us who were of age would travel

to Carcassonne to stand as witnesses. The *ostal* buzzed with anticipation as we worked together to prepare enough food for the week.
Clarette and I picked cucumbers and cabbages and helped Alaide
pickle them in vinegar, honey, and mustard seed; we kneaded dough
for bread and packed dried apples and a barrel of wine.

The night before we left, I hardly slept. We arose before dawn,
then rolled up our blankets and tied them on our backs. Amelha,
Alaide, Blanca, Curtslana, and Paperin waved their subdued fare-
wells. I must admit I felt a touch of selfish pride that I was going and
Amelha had to stay at home.

At daybreak we walked the short distance to the southern gate.
The rusty hinges creaked as two watchmen pushed open its heavy
doors. Then we set off by foot across the rolling hills toward the
fabled city of Carcassonne. How I was filled with excitement! I had
traveled north before to visit Papa's family, but this was different.
We were going into a different world, a city that has long stood as
a towering symbol of our freedom from the Franks. And Guilhabert
had made us feel as if we were all a part of something important.
This was a sacred mission, and I was honored to be joining it.

No clouds troubled the sky on that September day. Good
Christians from all the *ostals* of Fanjeaux filed out of town behind
Guilhabert. We walked all morning, stopping only to refresh ourselves with watered wine. I worried what would happen if we went
too slow, but there was no reason for concern. When we passed the
castrum of Montréal looming to the north, I knew that we'd surely
reach Carcassonne before nightfall. By mid-afternoon we began
to see its massive walls and turrets emerging on the horizon. They
sparkled white and grey in the sunlight as if beckoning us toward a
magic kingdom.

And there were so many people on the road, black-robed perfecti and blue-robed apprentices like us, churchmen and priests
dressed up in silken vestments, and lots of curious townspeople from
as far away as Castres and Toulouse.

We were walking with a group of *bons hommes* from Béziers, exchanging news and rumors, when we saw a cloud of dust approaching on the road from Narbonne. Soon a whole retinue came into view. Knights on horseback led the way. They carried red shields emblazoned with a black-and-yellow-checkered eagle. Following the knights were footmen and wagons laden with beer barrels and supplies. Finally three horsemen appeared, dressed in silken finery and accompanied by heralds who bore the white and yellow banners of Pope Innocent III. So those were the famous papal legates! I'd never even imagined such a display of wealth and power, and I couldn't help but wonder if the Church had come to debate the Good Christians or to conquer them. We all reached the outer wall of Carcassonne together. There was a loud creaking when the guards lowered the bridge. All of us stood back and let the legates pass first through the wide iron gate.

Then it was our turn. I could hardly believe my eyes. We crossed the drawbridge and entered through two huge walls of stone, each one as thick as any legate's steed. The debates were to be held at the Trencavel castle, so we all walked the whole length of the city. Its narrow streets were so crowded with hawkers and animals that I almost lost sight of Guilhabert and Na Bonata. I hastened my steps and slowly we ascended the steep road. To the left I could see the towers of the Basilique Saint Nazaire soaring above the red-tiled rooftops, but I knew better than to beg to go see it. We headed directly toward the Trencavel castle. At its gates stood armored guards bearing the crimson and black herald of Count Roger Trencavel. Guilhabert presented himself, and we were ushered into the great courtyard.

Santa Deu, what a sight it was! The castle was taller than five houses, with leaded windows on the lower levels and narrow slits above just wide enough for a bowman to shoot an arrow. I spun slowly around and counted twenty-six round turrets. Its strength and grandeur made me fret. These walls were so much stronger than those of Fanjeaux; I worried that our own castrum was not as safe as Papa once had told us.

I quickly brought my attention back to the courtyard.

There were more people there than I had ever seen, both Catholics and Good Christians together. They were all calling to their friends and vying for a place to set up camp. Some had, like us, arrived on foot; others had their horses in tow. We found an empty corner near the southern wall and laid out our blankets and supplies while Guilhabert unpacked his manuscripts.

The next day, the weeklong disputation began. We filed up the stone stairs that led to the upper chamber. There were more people than could fit inside, but we were with Guilhabert and so were given leave to enter. We stood shoulder-to-shoulder as less fortunate bystanders gathered outside underneath the windows. I looked around the room at the high walls covered with a golden ocher plaster. At one end of the room was a real fireplace. I was grateful that it was summer and there were no flames bursting around its massive andirons. At the other end was a tapestry of knights on horseback. I wondered if they were fighting in the Crusades, and for a moment I imagined that one was my dear papa. Above us the ceiling was painted an inky blue, dark as the sky at night, and spangled with a thousand stars. In every corner of the room stood iron candelabras. I had never imagined such opulence.

We all shifted on our feet as the debate got under way. And what a spectacle it was! Guilhabert and three companions stood on the right side of the fireplace. To the left were the papal legates. I had heard that these legates were Cistercian monks, but they looked more like fancy noblemen to me. They were clearly well fed, jowly and round in the belly. They were dressed in bright silk and bore gold rings on their fingers and jeweled crosses hanging from their necks. What a contrast to Guilhabert and his brothers who were clothed in their long black robes tied with a rope of hemp. Seated before them were the judges, thirteen Albigensian *credentes* and thirteen Catholics who had been chosen to decide which side best presented Your divine truth.

Dear God, even back then I knew that those Cistercian Legates had to be an embarrassment to You. They claimed the Church to be the upholder of virtue, but did not Jesus tell a rich young man that he must sell all he had if he wished to enter the kingdom of Heaven? When the legates began to speak they sounded more like kings than Your disciples. The famous Peter Castelnau derided the Good Christians as "Cathars." He said that they raped one another and buggered cats! I thought of Aude and Bonata, and I could barely stifle my laughter. *How could those churchmen dress in such finery and still claim to be defenders of the people?* I knew that their jeweled crosses and gold rings had been bought with money they'd extracted from the poor. I did not see, God, how Your legates could end up on the winning side of this debate.

Guilhabert wasted no time in pointing out their decadence. He contrasted the life of Good Christian perfecti with that of the Church's priests. "It is the Good Christians," he said, "who are the legitimate descendants of the first apostles. They live chastely in community and share all their belongings. They provide hospice for the sick and hospitality to the traveler. They wander the countryside preaching Jesus's message of peace and liberation from worldly pride.

"The priests, on the other hand, live in notorious sin. They pay no heed to their vows of chastity. They are boorish and uneducated; they do not serve the needy or even preach the Gospel. If they cannot extract enough money from the poor with their tithes and their indulgences, they abandon their parishes and move on. Saint Martins at Prouilhe has been vacant for years and now even the church at Fanjeaux stands without a priest."

The church now has no priest? I thought. *How could I not have known?* I felt a twinge of sorrow. But as I listened to Guilhabert, I knew he spoke the truth. And, God, You knew it too. Even the pope himself has now condemned the corrupt clergy of the Languedoc as, "dumb dogs who can no longer bark."

The papal legate Peter Castelnau pointed his bejeweled finger at Guilhabert and said that the Cathars are damned because they don't accept the sacraments, but Guilhabert ridiculed him.

"The God who created our souls in love has no need for priests to reconcile us to himself. And it is not possible for a corrupt priesthood to perform a holy sacrament," he retorted.

The pompous Castelnau responded by citing Augustine's claim of *ex opere operato*. "It is the holiness of God that makes a sacrament valid and not the priest who performs it," he said, but no one was listening. The room had begun to fill with chuckles, and we could hear jeers wafting up from the courtyard below.

Guilhabert took advantage of the crowd as he objected to the papal legate's claims.

"The churchmen," he argued, "have just accused the Good Christians of all the vices and excesses that they themselves inflict upon our people. It is they who are hypocrites and fornicators. It is they who steal from the poor. The Church is not the bride of Christ, but the harlot of the apocalypse." The bystanders roared their approval.

By the end of the week, you could hardly hear those poor papal legates at all over the crowd's taunts and mocking. And yes, God, I joined with them and stopped listening to the churchmen's words. I saw the hypocrisy of Your dear Church and it made me cringe with embarrassment and anger. *How could something so beautiful have become so corrupt?* I wondered. I could not find the answer. And so, *Santa Deu*, I took the side of Guilhabert. I cheered for the perfecti and taunted those pompous legates. For the first time, I too committed blasphemy against Your Church.

※

The next morning, we rolled up our blankets and set off for Fanjeaux. We were all tired, but our load was now light and we were filled with the pride of victory. As we walked, Aude and I fell into conversation.

"How could anyone believe the words of the pompous legates?" I said. "Do you remember when they said that the Good Christians bugger cats?"

We both began to giggle.

"Why is it that the Church appears to be so frightened of us?" Aude mused and answered her own question. "It's about riches. They know we speak the truth and think we will convince people to withhold tithes and taxes."

"I used to love the Church, and now I'm not so sure," I responded. "If I had any money I do not think that I would want to give it to them!" And then I ventured to inquire, "What about you? Have you always been a *credente*? Were your family all Good Christians?"

"Not all of them," Aude responded wistfully. "But I became a *credente* when I attended an *ostal* many years ago."

"How is it that you have chosen to receive the *consolamentum* and become a perfect?" I asked her.

"It has long been my hope to abide with the Holy Spirit," she replied. "When I was young, I chose to marry and raise a family, but I always dreamed of returning to the Good Christian way. It is now a great joy to study with Guilhabert. My only desire is to live simply and in accordance with God's commandments. I do not wish to be encumbered by property or the temptations of the world. I long only to serve the God of love, the One who lies beyond the chaos of this earthly realm. I sense his healing presence all around me, and I too hope to become a healer. Guilhabert tells me I have the gift. Already I have learned the use of herbs and medicines, but once I become a perfect I'll learn the laying on of hands and receive the power to heal across great distances."

"Is it only the perfecti who can learn to heal like that?" I inquired.

"Yes," Aude replied. "Only those who are freed from the confines of their bodies can use God's power for healing. When we
receive the *consolamentum* we are cleansed of all our sin. From that
day on we do not allow it to pollute our souls. We remain chaste and
travel always in the company of another. We fast and eat no more
than is necessary to keep us alive. We do not consume the flesh of
any beast created through the sin of fornication."

"But I've seen Guilhabert eat fish," I countered.

Aude chuckled. "Don't you know that fish are chaste?" she
replied. "They're generated by God's grace from the waters. Just as
Christ abided in the abyss of this mortal world, they live without sin
in the depth of the seas."

I nodded. There was a glow around Aude, the same one I'd
noticed the first day we arrived at the *ostal*, and I accepted what she
told me. Dear God, You have to know: I even contemplated what
it might be like to follow in Aude's footsteps. I wondered whether
the *consolamentum* could heal even my envious heart and let me too
abide within Your Spirit.

As the days grew shorter and the last of the tomatoes ripened on the
vine, we busied ourselves with preparations for the *consolamentum*.
Aude had been fasting for forty days, arising before sunrise to eat a
little bread and drink the water she would need to sustain herself for
the day.

"I seek to replace my hunger for food with a hunger for God,"
she told me earnestly one morning in the garden. She said that she
had learned the art of making the *Flor de la Vida*. She'd had ecstatic
visions, intimate encounters with the light that were far too won-
drous to put into words, and she had learned to draw their essence
into a sacred circle.

The night before the ceremony, Guilhabert arrived and led
Aude away for the night of trials. That evening I struggled to sleep,

imagining her ordeal and what it would be like to endure the trials myself.

The next morning friends and family from as far away as Foix assembled at the Durfort palace. And there was Aude, standing with Rays de Durfort, Fays of Saint-Germaine, and Raymond Roger's beautiful sister Esclarmonde. They were surrounded by a host of black-robed perfecti. It seemed to me as if a white light glowed around all four of them. You know, God, they really did believe that this *consolamentum* was a sacred sacrament, that it would set their souls free not just from sin but from the whole cycle of birth, death, and rebirth. Back then, I had not learned that this sacrament was the devil's rite, and I believed it too.

And so it was that I observed the *consolamentum*. We milled about in the Durforth courtyard until the black-robed Guilhabert appeared. Then the crowd grew suddenly silent.

"Before we begin," Guilhabert announced, "I wish to commend our sisters Aude, Rays, Faye, and Esclarmonde. They have been accepted to receive this holy sacrament because of their pure hearts and virtuous devotion to Our Lord."

I blanched. Guilhabert had said, "*They have been accepted.*" In all my agonizing over whether to follow the Good Christian path, it had not occurred to me that the perfecti might not find me acceptable. *Surely a girl who loves the Church and whose heart is consumed with black envy would not be chosen to receive the* consolamentum, I realized and hung my head. Guilhabert began the rite.

"In the beginning was the Word," the pale, black-robed bishop intoned, "And the Word was God and the Word was with God. He was in the beginning with God. All spiritual things were made through Him, and without Him was not anything made that was made."

The slight change from the beginning of the Gospel of John barely registered, all *spiritual* things were made through Him . . . Bishop Guilhabert continued to read from Scripture:

"'If ye love me, keep my commandments. And I will pray the Father and he shall give you another Comforter, that He may abide with you forever . . . '"

Then he walked over to Aude and spoke directly to her.

"'Wherefore be it understood that your presence confirms the faith and teaching of the Church of God as the Holy Scriptures tell us. For in former times the people of God separated themselves from the Lord their God. And they abandoned the will and guidance of their Heavenly Father through the deceptions of the wicked spirits and by submission to their will.'"

Dear God, You know that I did not hesitate that day over the blasphemy these Good Christians were speaking. I thought they told the truth when they claimed themselves to be the true followers of Jesus's teachings. I knew that they were claiming aloud for all to hear that Your Holy Catholic Church had been deceived by Satan and had abandoned the will of the Heavenly Father. And in that moment I believed that they were right. *Dear God in Heaven, perhaps I will burn in Hell for saying this, but it is possible that I still do.*

The *consolamentum* continued.

"We deliver you this holy prayer that you may receive it," intoned Bishop Guilhabert, and Aude solemnly replied, "I receive it of you and of the Church of God."

It was time for Aude to speak the Paternoster. Line by line she repeated the sacred words for the first time:
"Our Father, which art in Heaven," she intoned.
"Hallowed be thy name . . .
Give us this day our supernumary bread,
And remit our debts as we forgive our debtors. . . ."

✳

Santa Deu, how my heart quivered in longing as I listened to Aude recite Your prayer. I understood that they were praying for spiritual bread, but it didn't matter. I wondered if I would ever be allowed to say the Paternoster again.

What followed was a recitation of scripture, all read in the Occitan language and pointing to the Paraclete, the Holy Spirit in our midst. Finally the bishop arrived at the *melioramentum* preceding Aude's vows.

"Do you give yourself to God and the Gospel?" asked Guilhabert.

"Yes," she replied, bowing and taking a step forward.

"God bless you and keep you," responded Guilhabert. They repeated this solemn dance three times before the bishop added, "God bless you and make you a Good Christian and bring you to a good end."

Then the vows commenced.

"Do you promise that henceforth you will eat neither meat nor eggs nor cheese nor fat?" asked the bishop, "and that you will live only from water and wood, that is fish and vegetables, that you will not lie, that you will not swear, that you will not kill, that you will not abandon your body to any form of luxury, that you will never go alone when it is possible to have a companion, that you will never sleep without clothing and that you will never abandon your faith for fear of water, fire, or any other manner of death?"

"Yes," Aude replied solemnly.

Bishop Guilhabert continued, "If you wish to receive this power, you must keep all the commandments of Christ and the New Testament, according to your ability . . . also you must hate this world and its works and the things of this world."

I released a gasp and quickly stifled it. Aude loved the gardens and all the beauty and abundance of the world. How could Guilhabert be asking her to hate it? Then I recalled how he had taught that the Devil had made all beauty to seduce us. I felt a dizziness descend upon me. I feared that I might faint, but I grabbed hold

of a stone pillar and the lightness passed. I heard Guilhabert as he
recited from the Epistle of John,

"'If any man loves the world, the love of the Father is not in
him. For all that is in the world, the lust of the flesh and the pride of
life, is not of the Father but is of the world. And the world passeth
away and the lust thereof, but he that doeth the will of God abideth
for ever.'"

When the vows were completed, it was time for Aude to receive
the laying on of hands that would seal her fate as a Good Christian
perfect. She bowed her head and Signora Bonata stepped forward
and stretched out her hands. Even I felt something shift around me.
Aude was surrounded by radiance so white I was certain that it was
Your Holy Spirit. As Na Bonata cupped her palms around Aude's
temples, I felt my own hands tingle. Slowly, she hovered her fingers
over her eyes, her mouth, her throat, until every inch of her body
seemed to be consumed by holy fire.

Santa Deu, I still do not know what transpired there. The Church
would say it was the Devil's doing and Aude had just consigned her
soul to Hell. But You must know that I am not so sure. I felt Your
presence in that room, and I think that could I feel such power just
one more time, I even now might find relief from my torment.

That evening, as we returned to the *ostal*, Amelha walked beside
me. "That was so wonderful! I can't wait until I come of age," she
gushed. "I too wish to receive the *consolamentum* and live as a
perfect. What about you, Elmina?"

I could not put words to the confusion that was swirling in
my head. I was stunned by Amelha's certainty that she would be
accepted to receive the *consolamentum* and the old familiar jealousy
reared its ugly head. "I do not know," I hissed at her, "and you are far
too young and foolish to be sure of what you speak." Amelha stifled
a cry and ran off. I walked the rest of the way in silence.

Chapter 5

THE PATH TO PERFECTION

D ear God, how I prayed to You that autumn, as the nights lengthened and the frost descended on the gardens. Do You remember? I begged to understand what had happened at Aude's *consolamentum*. What was that feeling in the room? Why did my hands tingle when Bonata touched her temples? Was it the Holy Spirit or a more sinister power? I didn't know if I was living among saints or demons.

One chilly afternoon when we had finished carrying onions and turnips and the last of the kale to market, Aude and Berengaria said they would mind the stall. Aude gave Clarette and me leave to return to the warmth of the *ostal*. But as we left, I felt an old, familiar pull.

"Do you remember the church on the hill?" I asked Clarette.

"I've not been in it," she replied. "But I remember how I loved to go inside the church in Pamiers before Mama sent me to the *ostal*."

"Come with me!" I said and took her hand. "I'll show you our church."

We headed down the *Rota des Farques* as if going toward the *ostal*. But then we sneaked off to the left and wound our way to the top of the hill. Together we stood staring at the church's reflection in the *Lac de Jupiter,* and my eyes filled up with tears. I glanced at Clarette and realized that her eyes too were moist with longing. "What are we going to do?" I asked her quietly.

"Let's go inside and pray," is all she said. Together we walked around to its western wall and pulled open the big oak door. The hinges creaked, and we slid into the musty darkened nave. Strings of cobwebs served as a reminder that its priest was there no longer. Silently, we crept up to the altar where the Blessed Mother still kept watch and knelt before her. *"Ave Maria, gracia plen,"* we began, as the gentle countenance gazed down upon us, "Hail Mary, full of grace, the Lord is with thee. Blessed art thou among women, and blessed is the fruit of thy womb, Jesus."

"Holy Mother," I added, "If it please you, I beg that you might guide us in the way Our Father wishes us to go. Guilhabert tells us that you are not the mother of Our Lord. He says that we do not need any assistance from you to loose our gaze from this world and fix our eyes upon the one beyond. But, Dearest Lady, I have not been able to do that on my own. My heart still longs for the peace and comfort of my Mother Church. Could you please help us find our way back home to her?"

We knelt together in silence until Clarette adjoined, "And Blessed Mother, if it be your will, I ask that you allow Elmina and me to remain together." We both added our Amen.

But God, that winter we did not hear Your answer to our prayers. We'd put the gardens to bed, the snows had arrived, and yet only one thing had changed. Clarette too had begun her bleeding. It was another reminder that soon we would have to leave the *ostal* unless we started to prepare for the *consolamentum.* Gentiana and Riccarda had started their studies in the fall; we were the next in line. It was in the first month of the year of our Lord 1205 that Na Bonata came to us and asked that we join her at the table. "There is something we must discuss," is all she said.

We entered the dark hall, and the first thing I saw was the fire pit. I sensed that there were demons dancing in its flames, and my heart set to trembling just as it had when I was a little girl. Then I looked at the table. On one side sat Sister Bruna and Aude with Riccarda and Gentiana; on the other were perched Berengaria, Magdalena, and Amelha. Na Bonata had taken her place at the head of the table, and she motioned us to sit beside them.

"Elmina and Clarette," the signora began, and I drew a deep breath. "You both have come into your womanhood, and it is time for you to make a decision. Your fathers have entrusted you into our care and now we must choose a path for each of you. If you wish to have a family, we will arrange your marriage to a Good Christian *credente*. Or, if you think that you have been called into a life of service to the Lord of Light, you may join with Berengaria, Magdalena, and Amelha, and begin studying with Bishop Guilhabert."

I gasped and glared at my sister and my friend. Berengaria returned my gaze and offered a resigned shrug. Amelha would not even look at me. The two of us had not spoken of our futures since the night of Aude's *consolamentum*. Had I really believed my caustic words had made her reconsider her path? And now, Dear God, she was consigning her life to these Good Christians. I offered a quick prayer, but I could hear no answer. I looked around the room for help and was drawn into the liquid amber of the signora's eyes. In that moment, O God, I made a hasty decision. I thought about the Church's debacle in Carcassonne and the beauty of Aude's *consolamentum*. I had come to love these women and girls who had become my family. And if I am honest, I must confess, I did not want to have Amelha choose the holy path while I was relegated to a life of servitude as wife to some *credente*. And so I turned my back upon Your Church. I decided to remain at the *ostal* and give my life to the Good Christians. I'm sorry, God, but I could see no other path.

Taking a deep breath, I met Na Bonata's gaze and answered, "If he will have me, I will learn from Guilhabert." Clarette paused just a moment before doing the same.

And so it was that we began our evening studies with Bishop Guilhabert. For the next year, he taught us every week, and women from other *ostals* in Fanjeaux came to join us. First he spoke about the Good Christian Church.

"We are descendants of the first Church," he said, "older by far than the Church of Rome and the true heirs of the original apostles. Our bishops have been ordained by the laying on of hands since the first days of the early Church. Our ancestors were Gnostics who knew that the divine presence lay in their hearts. Since the Council at Saint-Félix-Lauragais in 1167, we Good Christians have had four bishoprics here in the Languedoc. Our bishops teach and offer the *consolamentum* to those who have been chosen to follow our path."

"Pray tell us more about the *consolamentum*," Clarette inquired. "Is it like holy baptism?"

"Most of you have been present to witness our most sacred rite. It is offered to any candidate who seeks a blameless life and is deemed worthy to receive it. Like baptism, it cleanses us of sin. It is through the *consolamentum* that we receive the power of the Holy Spirit and become spiritual emissaries of Our Lord, Jesus Christ."

"Is that what was in the room the day Aude had her *consolamentum*?" asked Amelha.

"So you experienced it?" Guilhabert smiled.

I felt my heart constrict with jealousy. "Me, too," I quickly interjected. "I felt my hands tingling and the whole room filled with light." I dared to hope Bishop Guilhabert would praise me, but he simply nodded.

"That is what we all feel in the presence of the Holy Spirit," he replied. "In the *consolamentum* we receive the gift of healing through the laying on of hands. Then we can use it to help others and learn to pass it."

I remembered that Guilhabert had told Aude that she had the gift of healing. I looked down at my own pudgy fingers. I sensed no divine energy flowing through them and doubted they might become instruments of the Holy Spirit. I ventured to ask Guilhabert, "How can you tell if someone's hands are good for healing?"

"All hands are good for healing," the bishop replied. "The gift does not rest in your hands but in your heart. When your heart is pure and resting in God, healing flows through you."

Once more I felt the hopelessness of ever having a pure heart and hung my head.

As the weeks went by, Guilhabert taught us more of the Good Christian way of understanding God and the world, and I started to see how the different beliefs all fit together.

"The world is overrun with evil," Guilhabert told us. "Most men look no further than the selfish cravings of their own bodies, and there is no end to their cruelty."

I cringed thinking of my own jealousy and how I'd treated Amelha.

"Look at the violence that pervades the Languedoc, the horrid diseases that ravish our towns, and the wickedness of the Roman Church. A loving God would never have created a world so given to lust and devastation," Guilhabert continued. "Nor would He allow so much misery to still surround us."

Guilhabert went on to explain that there must be two Gods, a Good One and a Bad One. The Good One is the God of the New Testament, a God of Light and Love who shimmers as a backdrop underneath the world of matter. It is the Good God who created our souls and to whom our souls will finally return. This God abides in Heaven. He sees the misery of our lives and sends the Holy Spirit to accompany and strengthen us, but He cannot enter into the morass.

The other God is a Bad God, a kind of demiurge whom some people call Satan or the Devil. This God was the Jehovah of the Old Testament, the God who created our world as his own playground. He is a jealous God, one who requires unwavering loyalty and obedience to his laws. When his people disobey, Jehovah extracts cruel retribution and punishes them with pestilence, death, and worse.

"What other kind of God," Guilhabert asked, "could slaughter Babylonian babies, incinerate the priests of Baal, or demand that Abraham sacrifice his own beloved son?"

I have to admit that I had no answer.

"Our problem," Guilhabert went on, "is that this Jehovah has entrapped our souls in a prison of flesh. He has created all manner of temptations. He's made the warmth of spring, the petals of the rose, even the tender beauty of a maiden to keep us tethered to this world. It is the illusion of pleasure and beauty that keep us mired in his own sinful playground. When we look for the hand of God in the physical world, we fall prey to Satan's clever scheme."

Could that also be true? I dared to think. *Could all the bounty and the beauty of this world be nothing more than evil trickery meant to keep us from knowing the Good God?* My breath grew shallow with confusion, and I gave my arm a pinch to keep from growing faint.

Guilhabert explained to us why his people have declared war upon the Church.

"The Catholic Church worships the God who created a world of dust and entered it in human form. Can you not see? The Church has fallen into the clutches of Jehovah. It holds that our salvation rests in the battered body of Jesus Christ, proffered to poor credulous souls by avaricious priests.

"Such thinking is absurd," Guilhabert contended. "Salvation cannot be found in tortured flesh, and mortal priests cannot procure it for us. This lie just keeps our people enslaved to their greed. We call the Roman Church the Whore of Babylon because the evil of its seduction is very great."

My head swam with the impact of this blasphemy. I tried to ward it off, but even so a thought took hold: *Perhaps Guilhabert is right; perhaps the Devil is not just our enemy, but the very God who created us. If that be so, two Gods of equal power vie for dominion over us. And wherein lies my help?*

My mind could not absorb the confusion. So many times I'd felt as if two Gods were battling within me. One kept me safe and wrapped me in a warm blanket of love. The other offered bitter condemnation and threatened to consume me in its fire. *But no, I thought, something is wrong. It is my dear papa who has wrapped me within his arms and the Blessed Virgin who has kept me safe from the fire. And yet the Good Christians would say they are evil.*

"Fortunately," Guilhabert concluded, "the Good God has provided us a way out of our bondage. He sent Our Lord the Christ as a pure spirit to show us the way to freedom. In him we find the path to perfection that each of you is now preparing to follow."

I swallowed hard. The Good Christian path seemed to lead more toward puzzlement than perfection.

"What if we can not become perfect?" I dared to ask him.

"All people reach the freedom of perfection," Bishop Guilhabert replied. "If you do not do so in this lifetime, you will keep returning to earth until you do."

Another life? I could not take in all that Guilhabert had to say. Sometimes after class I would need to go outside and walk among the gardens so I might feel my feet firmly grounded in the earth. I'd kneel down, and as the rich loam sifted through my fingers, I would inhale the sweet lavender and let its fragrance cleanse the sore confusion from my mind.

I liked it much better when Na Bonata taught our classes. She introduced the art of healing and told us how the perfecti become channels for God's healing energy. She explained that they could send this energy over long distances.

"There are no physical limitations in the spiritual realm of the Good God," she said. "You can send power to cleanse the soul of evil thoughts and ease the pain of every ailment. You can use herbs to balance the humors and even prevent illness."

"Can you send healing to anyone?" inquired Amelha. "What about the churchmen and the pope? Could you clean even them of evil thoughts?"

The signora chuckled. "You can send healing energy to anyone, but when their hearts have been sealed shut by the Devil, they are not likely to receive it."

One evening, Aude talked to our class about medicine. She took everyone out into the garden and Berengaria and I recited the names of each plant. She held up the book that her brother had given her and showed them recipes for the tonics and tinctures we had made together. She took us to the shed where herbs were drying and asked me to tell the group how to prepare mandrake root to make a sleeping tonic. How proud I felt at all that I had learned! I even dared imagine that for once Amelha envied me.

Another evening Aude and Na Bonata came together to talk about the art of drawing within the sacred circle.

"Can you teach us to draw a *Flor de la Vida* like the one carved on Magdalena's loom?" asked Amelha.

"Of course I can. It's very easy," the signora replied. She picked up a piece of charcoal and tied a length of twine to it. She instructed Amelha, "Just put your finger on the twine and hold it fast. Now move the charcoal around it."

Amelha drew a perfect circle on the table, and my heart tightened in envy.

"Next place the end of your twine on any part of the circle. Hold it fast and then draw another circle."

Amelha did as she was told.

"Do you see where the circles intersect? Place the twine at one of those intersections and draw another circle, and then another until you have made a flower," continued Na Bonata.

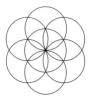

"This is the seed in which all things find their being," she said.

I wondered what she meant, but she went on. "God's kingdom is like an everlasting circle. Right here in its center is the divine heart. Each circle is the love of God, sent out in all directions. Look at the petals formed when the circles meet. They make a rose of the purest perfection, the rose each one of you can be.

"Now watch," Bonata said. She took the charcoal from Amelha and added more circles to the drawing.

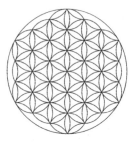

As I looked down upon the *Flor*, I thought that I could feel its energy moving within me.

"The roses could go on forever," I commented.

"Indeed they do," replied the signora. "They are your souls, all roses and all held within the fullness of God's love. Do not forget this *Flor*. Thinking upon it can give you great healing in the most trying of times."

"Can I make one too?" I asked the Signora.

"Not now," was her reply. "There is more that I want to show you." She brought out three drawings and tacked them to the wall. One was a *Flor de la Vida* colored in hues of ochre and crimson. Another was a golden sun against a deep blue starry sky. The third was of a young woman kneeling in prayer, her head surrounded by a glowing orb.

"They are beautiful," I gasped.

"Indeed they are," responded Na Bonata. "Aude painted them all, on paper that her brother brought from Constantinople. They are all spirit drawings, bestowed on those who are ready to receive the *consolamentum*."

At that moment I felt glad that I had chosen to remain on the Good Christian path. *Perhaps one day the Spirit will bestow such gifts on me*, I mused and looked forward to that day I might learn to draw within the sacred circle. I scratched out the *Flor de la Vida* in the dirt path of the garden and I dreamt of a time when I too might be given paints and paper. I even dared to hope that I might be chosen to receive the *consolamentum* and the spiritual gifts.

But even then Na Bonata's soothing words rang hollow. I knew that this could never be. I was not cut out to become a rose of the purest perfection. My soul was haunted by demons of fire, and my heart was tainted with the sin of envy. I wore the robes of a Good Christian novitiate, but they provided scant coverage for my many doubts and the jealousy that still burned within me. Amelha's presence in the classroom reminded me each day of this poisonous envy. She hung on Guilhabert's every word. Her cheerful spirit filled the air, and everyone adored her.

Amelha still said good morning with a lilt in her voice; she walked through her day with a cadence in her step; she hummed as she wove. She sang her troubadour songs in the market square and filled the house with them at night. I could not compete with Amelha's cleverness or her indomitable spirit. I took in the Good Christian teachings, but my soul would not allow me to digest them. I realize today that Bonata and Guilhabert must have known this all along.

Chapter 6

DOMINIC

Of course, God, You knew of my sinful heart, You who have searched me and are acquainted with all of my ways. And the priest Dominic knew it too. The very first day that we met, he took one look at me and saw it all.

It was a market day in the spring of 1206. The sun had returned to the southern sky and its warming glow had finally seeped into the stone walls surrounding Fanjeaux. All ten of us had walked up from the *ostal* to enjoy the festive day. The streets were filled with townsfolk and peddlers. The troubadours and *jongleurs* had returned after their winter hibernation. And a black-robed perfect was again preaching at the corner of the market in the *Place des Halles*. Amelha and Magdalena, of course, joined with the troubadours and had begun singing. Berengaria, Clarette and I had set up the produce stand and were standing among our sisters on the sidelines.

"Listen to how lovely Amelha sounds," said Riccarda. "You must be so proud of her."

"Indeed!" I lied and looked away. "She sings like an angel of God." Even in the festive warmth of the spring sun, I could feel my heart chill and my brow tighten. *Why does everyone always admire Amelha?* I asked myself. *Don't they know that I can sing too?*

Then I looked up and noticed an odd-looking preacher watching me. He and his companion stood not ten paces from the market stalls. They were barefoot and simply clad like the perfect, but their robes were white. They wore no decoration, save a black and white cross stitched on the black cloaks draped over their shoulders. *What mode of men are these?* I wondered.

I took scant notice of the older man, but not so the younger! Dear God, You know that he was fine to look at. He must have been about the age of my dear papa. He was tall and lean, and he stood full upright as a man who is certain that he knows the truth. His red-blond hair curled around his bald tonsure and fell softly upon his ears. And his eyes, they were the color of a winter sky, shifting from grey to blue with every shaft of Heavenly light that fell upon him. They flashed with fervor as he spoke and bore into my soul.

"You cannot hide from God," he proclaimed in a Castilian accent. "I saw the green-eyed look you gave to the young *troubairitza*. Have you not heard the words of God that 'a sound heart is the life of the flesh; but envy is the rottenness of the bone'? The God who created you knows your every thought."

I shrank back, but he took a step forward.

"God knows the evil lurking in your soul," the preacher continued, "but He does not despise you for it. He longs for your redemption and to welcome you back home."

How can I return home to God? I wondered, but the Castilian continued on before a question could rise to my lips.

"You who wear the heretics' robes would claim that you are trapped within an evil world. But just look around you! Nothing is further from the truth. See the pure white flower growing from this crumbling wall?" he said pointing to a vine of Silver Lace. "Look at the strength with which it clings to life; look at its perfect symmetry. There is no flaw within it. This flower speaks in all its intricacy to the Glory of God. How much more might your own heart do the same if you allowed Our Savior to cleanse it of its sinfulness."

The preacher's deep voice drew in a curious crowd. I too wanted to hear him better, for he spoke of the Creator God whom I knew in the gardens. I took a step toward him and Clarette followed.

"You who call yourselves Good Christians have been told that this fallen world is the Devil's handiwork, but that is a lie. Its sin and suffering are not the product of some Evil God; they are of *your* own making. It is *you* who disobeyed God. It is *you* who have succumbed to temptation; *you* who ate of the Tree of Knowledge and now pretend to know more than God's Holy Catholic Church."

I thought of how Guilhabert had ridiculed the Roman Church, but something told me that this preacher spoke the truth. My head started to spin. *What if evil and suffering truly are of our own making?* I thought. *Then my fiery torment must be because my sin is very, very great.* I hung my head and tried to avoid his gaze.

A black-robed perfect shouted out from the crowd, "And who was it that tempted Eve in the Garden?"

"You know full well it was the Devil himself, disguised as a serpent," Dominic spun around to reply.

"And where did this Devil come from?" demanded the heckler. "Did your Good God decide one day to create Satan and let loose a force for evil on the earth? What kind of sadistic deity do you worship?"

God, You know that I will never forget the way Dominic's piercing eyes glared at the speaker. "Only a heretic and enemy of the Church could speak in such a way. God created only good. But good cannot sustain itself without the constant choice for good, so God gave his angels freedom. Satan was not content to be a servant of God's good; he wanted to become as God himself. And so he chose against the good. He descended from Heaven to tempt the weaker sex, knowing that all men soon would follow."

"And what transpired next?" pursued the interrogator knowingly.

"Adam and Eve did sin, and so were banished from the garden," Dominic replied.

"And where did they then go, if not to live in Satan's playground?" the heretic countered with triumphant glee. "Or did the God you worship then create a fallen world to house them?"

My heart pounded and I did hold my breath. *Please, answer well*, I found myself pleading in silence. *Please defend God against this heresy.*

But the red-haired preacher did not answer the perfect directly. He simply repeated, "God saw what he created and proclaimed it good." Then he turned his attention back to us. His eyes flashed blue with his impassioned words.

"My dear young ladies," he addressed us. "You know that evil hath descended from the weakness of a woman, and that your flesh carries the filth of that first sin. I beg of you, do not follow Eve into temptation. The error of your heresy is the work of the Devil. It is abhorrent to the One True God. My own heart is tormented by the great agony your souls will suffer if you do not renounce your sacrilege and return to the Church."

Dominic's breath quickened and he began to beat upon his pulsing chest as if taking our agony onto himself. For just a moment our eyes locked again. A bolt of lightning shot down my spine and spread throughout my body.

Dear God, I was not sure what had happened, but I still bear the shame of it. My fingers started tingling and my knees almost gave way. I felt the fire beneath my waist of which Beatriz had sung and flushed full red. My mind raced with terror. *Are not such sensations good proof of a most sinful heart?* I thought. I forced myself to look away and grabbed Clarette's hand.

"We must now take our leave," I croaked. The two of us made a hasty retreat back to the darkened recess of our booth. I busied myself with rearranging the piles of beans and onions, but I could feel the preacher's eyes still boring into me.

That evening we talked with Guilhabert about what had occurred. "Who was that man?" I asked, "and why did he blame all women for the sin of Eve?"

"I do not know his name or where he comes from," Guilhabert responded curtly. "But he would not have spoken that way unless he served the pope and the Devil's Church. This preacher would have you bow down to the evil Jehovah and believe in such a God as would curse all of mankind for the disobedience of one woman."

"He told us that the very flesh of woman is cursed," I answered him.

"Dear Elmina, listen to me. A woman's body is cursed no more than a man's," responded Guilhabert. "All flesh is the creation of Jehovah; it is no more or less evil than other forms of matter. But our desires serve the Devil's purpose by binding our souls to the earth. There is nothing wrong with the *credentes* who live in the flesh and enjoy its pleasures. But one day, their souls will long for liberation. Many of our perfecti have lived a carnal life—look at Bruna and Aude. But they have chosen to leave it behind. They have received the *consolamentum* and released the curse. And, Elmina," he added, "you too could do the same."

But God, You know my heart. I did not pass that week releasing the curse of my flesh. Each time I thought of the red-haired preacher, the tingling in my spine returned and I had to pinch my arm until it bled to quiet the shameful sensations that warmed my womb. I prayed that none of the sisters could read my thoughts. I tried to seem attentive to my studies and my work in the garden, but Clarette noticed when I yanked out sprigs of fresh young parsley and left weeds to grow in their place.

"Elmina, you have been distracted all week long. I'm sure it couldn't be that red-haired preacher who caught your eye in the market," she teased.

I could feel my fair skin blush.

"I speak the truth," Clarette added. "You are as red as you were in the marketplace!"

"But you cannot say a word to the signora," I warned. Clarette put her hand to her lips in a solemn pact of silence.

"I do not know what to make of the preacher," I whispered. "He frightens me, but I cannot stop thinking of him. He is not like the other priests, and his words cut through the sore confusion in my head."

"That is most surely so," Clarette responded. "He dresses in simple robes like the perfecti and wears neither jewelry nor shoes."

"And his form is not soft like that of the priests who visit Fanjeaux," I added and could feel my cheeks redden again. "I had not noticed that," Clarette chuckled. "But I could tell that he speaks with great fervor, as if he were intent on sharing his own soul."

"I know," I replied, "and yet the God he speaks of scares me. He would consign us all to everlasting Hell for following the Good Christian path. Would a Good God really do that?"

Clarette stared down at an onion peeking through the dirt. "I do not know," she replied. "Guilhabert tells us the only Hell is here on earth, but what if he is wrong? I long to be with God in Heaven when I die. I too am fearful He will damn the souls of heretics unto the everlasting fire."

She paused as she skillfully plucked weeds from among the young stalks.

"Shush," Clarette whispered, "Aude approaches. We will go to the market again next week."

The following Thursday, I tried to disguise my impatience as I slipped on my robe and packed up tender herbs and greens to take to market. As I walked along the cobbled path, I could feel my heart racing. My eyes searched the usual throng of peddlers and black-robed perfecti to no avail. When we approached the corner where the red-haired priest had spoken, my heart sank. He was not there, and in his place stood the older Castilian. He too ranted against the Good Christians, but I turned a deaf ear. I lowered my head, moved on to our stall, and listlessly set out our produce. This Thursday it was our turn to oversee the table, so Clarette and I remained as the others wandered off.

"What will you do all afternoon without the red-haired preacher to entertain you?" Clarette teased. "The churchman who preaches on the corner today surely lacks his, uh, fervor. Perhaps his friend has—" she began to offer, when we heard a familiar voice resonate behind us. I swung around and there he was, striding up the *Rota des Faures*.

"Your mother, the Holy Catholic Church, calls you home to the One True God," the voice implored. Both of us turned as one.

"Can you not hear the Blessed Virgin weeping for the loss of your precious souls? Her tender heart yearns for you and calls each of you by name. She will intercede on your behalf and protect you from all harm if you but offer your hearts to God."

I thought of the Blessed Lady standing guard before the altar only one hundred paces from where we now stood, but my image was interrupted by a different presence. The red-haired preacher was walking right up to our table!

He bowed his head, and his red curls dropped over his flashing eyes.

"Good afternoon, my young ladies," his voice boomed. "What have you to sell this fine day?"

"L-l-lettuces," I stammered.

"And spring herbs," Clarette added. "We have here parsley and chervil and over there are dill and chives." She lifted a fistful of young shoots, but the preacher seemed not to notice.

I glanced up and our eyes met for a moment longer than I had intended.

"My name is Dominic de Guzman," he announced. "I am traveling through the Languedoc with the good Bishop of Osma. We are most pleased to have found our way to your enchanting city. I would be delighted to make your acquaintance. Might I inquire as to your names?"

Clarette gave me a warning nudge, but I hardly felt it. My heart was pounding as I responded, "I am called Elmina, and this is my dearest friend, Clarette."

"They are lovely names," Dominic replied. "I can see by your robes that you follow the Albigensian way. Might I inquire, are your parents of a similar persuasion? Did they never teach you the beauty and truth of the Church's creeds?"

Dear God, I thought of all the times I had stood with Papa during Mass and the festival days we had observed together. I remembered the Aves he would sing to me, and a wave of longing flooded my heart. "Yes," I replied softly, "I was baptized, and my father accompanied me to church. I grew up with love for the sacraments and for the Blessed Virgin." I did not tell him of Mama's disdain for churchmen.

Clarette shifted uncomfortably as I spoke. She finally broke her silence and added, "I too grew up in a Catholic family."

Dominic responded with a quizzical look. "You are both Catholic girls. Why then are you joined with the Albigensians?" he asked.

"We have joined them because our families are poor," Clarette responded. "They cannot afford to educate us or provide for us a dowry. They sent us to the perfecti so that we might learn to read and gain a useful trade. The sisters teach us the Good Christian way and will provide a dowry if we choose to leave and marry a *credente*."

"And if you do not leave?" Dominic asked.

I kept my head lowered and responded, "We will prepare to receive the *consolamentum*."

I could almost feel the revulsion that shot from the preacher's eyes.

"How could Catholic parents do such a thing?" Dominic demanded.

"Please do not look harshly upon them," I spoke in defense of

Papa and Mama. "My parents are good souls with many mouths to feed. And Signora Bonata is a kind and faithful woman. The sisters all live simple and upright lives. They instruct us in the gospel of the New Testament and the sacred arts of healing. They care for the sick and welcome any stranger who appears on our doorstep to share the meager bounty of our table."

I glanced up as Dominic took in this information. I thought he might ask more, but instead he just replied, "Your parents have betrayed their Christian duty. Your 'sisters' are Albigensian heretics, and they are preparing your souls for Hell."

He turned as if to walk away, but then he stopped. "I wonder," he mused so softly I almost missed it, "if your *sisters* are as kind as you suggest, perhaps they would share their meager bounty with two white-robed strangers."

Chapter 7

TRIAL BY FIRE

I t was only two evenings later that we heard a loud knock on the *ostal* door.

"Elmina, would you see to the visitor?" called Signora Bonata as she stirred a cauldron of pottage on the fire.

Dear God, when I opened the door and caught sight of the two Castilian priests, I dared not raise my eyes.

"You do not belong here," I whispered to Dominic.

"Well, good evening, my dear Elmina," he boomed. "I wonder if we might have a word with the kind and faithful Sister Bonata?"

I blushed at hearing my words from the market echoed back in so mocking a manner. I quickly withdrew to fetch her and hovered in the shadow of the doorway as Na Bonata approached. She looked warily at the rough wool robes and bare feet of the two churchmen standing before her.

"We are wandering priests just recently arrived in Fanjeaux," I heard the older man say. "I am Diego, the bishop of Osma, and this is my canon, Dominic de Guzman."

"You do not wear the garb or carry the accoutrement of any bishop I know," Bonata responded. "What brings you to our home?"

Dominic nodded. "It is true we are not clad in the finery of many priests. We live instead by the teachings of Our Lord, who instructs men of God to abide simply in poverty, chastity, and obedience. I understand this is also the way of the Good Christians. I have heard that you run an *ostal* for young women and that your Bishop Guilhabert will be instructing them this evening. I wonder if I might have a word with him."

"Guilhabert will arrive shortly," Bonata replied curtly. She hesitated before extending an invitation. "We are just sitting down to supper. Would you care to share our soup and bread?"

"We are fasting, as is our custom in the evening," said Dominic, "but it would be an honor to sit at your table."

When the three of us returned to the hall, Clarette and I exchanged brief glances, and twelve sets of eyes struggled to maintain their modest downward gaze.

Bonata introduced our visitors. "Berengaria, Clarette, and Elmina, perhaps you have already made acquaintance with one of these fine monks?" *How did the signora know?* I wondered. I held my breath and nodded. I'm certain that Dominic noticed the flush upon my cheeks. "Alaide, Jordana, Riccarda, Curtslana, Paperin, Gentiana, Blanca, Magdalena, Amelha. Please greet Diego, bishop of Osma, and Dominic de Guzman."

It was Amelha who broke the stunned silence as Bonata directed the priests to take a seat at the small table reserved for male visitors.

"Why have you come to our home?" she inquired with a sarcastic edge to her voice. "Do you not fear that you might become tainted by our 'heretic' ways?"

Dear God, You know how much I wanted to reach across the table and shush Amelha. But I just gave her a hard look and turned my eyes to Dominic.

"I have no fear of your kind," Dominic replied softly. "I seek only salvation for your souls. I understand that most of you are Catholics; you have been baptized into the Holy Mother Church. God longs for you to recant of your heresy and return to Him. Our Savior awaits your communion. Do you not know that if you persist in this great error, your souls will perish? And my own heart beats with anguish at the thought of so much suffering amid the flames of Hell."

"You're wrong!" Amelha exclaimed. "A Good God would never destroy the souls that He Himself had created."

"Ah, dear Amelha," Dominic responded. "Do you not understand? It is not God who would destroy your souls. God sent his only Son to die upon the cross that you might be redeemed from Satan's hellfire. By following the path of heretics, you have, by your own volition, chosen to make your bed with the Devil and lie with him for all eternity."

Dear God, I knew not what to think. I wanted to defend these *bonnes femmes* who had become my dear family. I wanted to tell Dominic that Amelha was filled with the Spirit of God and would never align herself with Satan. But I did not. My head swirled with confusion. The room seemed to spin around me, and for an instant, I feared once more that I might faint. Suddenly it seemed as if I could not distinguish the house of God from the abode of Satan. I only knew that if Dominic were right, I too was making my bed with the Devil.

It was Signora Bonata who rose to Amelha's defense. "You may not speak to my daughters thus," she quickly interjected, with fierce flames flashing behind her amber eyes. "You do not speak the truth. And I will not have you—" she began to assert, but at that moment Bishop Guilhabert and Brother Martin came through the door and strode purposefully toward our visitors.

Guilhabert took it all in, the monks' bare feet and simple robes, Dominic's fervor, and the tension in the room. He took a firm step forward.

"*Bon vespré*, my good men," he exclaimed loudly, extending his arm in a powerful handshake. "We do not often have the privilege of hosting such, er, worthy guests. Pray tell us, what has brought you here today?"

The older man took hold of Guilhabert's outstretched hand. "I am the bishop of Osma and this is my canon, Dominic de Guzman," he asserted. "We are recently arrived in the Languedoc and wish to learn of your customs. I was told at the market square that I might find you here this evening."

"And what is it that brings you to our region?" inquired Guilhabert. "Might you be engaged in the disputations of the papal legates?"

"We have made their acquaintance," admitted Diego. "It would please us greatly to dissuade your charges of their heresy and help them reconcile their souls to God."

Guilhabert responded with a frigid stare. "I would be most pleased to engage you in public debate, but you will not spread your poison in this house among my sisters and my daughters. Please take your leave."

"We were preparing to go," replied Diego. "However, we would welcome the chance to engage in another disputation.

Guilhabert drew in a long deep breath. "Shall we say two weeks hence at the home of Raymond, brother to William de Durfort? We shall each write our arguments in advance and present them to a panel of judges."

The bishop and his canon assented, and again the men shook hands. The two churchmen nodded farewell to us and departed.

The next two weeks flew by. Guilhabert had left for Carcassonne but assured us he would be back within the fortnight. Diego and Dominic, too, had traveled south. The Thursday marketplace was filled with its usual activity, but in their absence I took little note of it. I simply waited for the date of the disputation to arrive.

As it drew near, perfecti from all over the Languedoc arrived in town. Our home filled with visitors, but Guilhabert was not among them.

"What if he fails to return in time?" I asked Na Bonata.

"There is no chance of that," she replied. "He is working with the bishop there to prepare his manuscript."

True to his word, Guilhabert arrived in town the evening before the scheduled debate. That night, I hardly slept. I couldn't help but think back to our trip to Carcassonne almost two years earlier. I knew I should be loyal to the perfecti, but I did not want to see Dominic suffer the same humiliation as had those papal legates.

The first morning of the debates dawned warm and clear. Guilhabert had asked that Magdalena, Amelha, Berengaria, Clarette, and I attend to further our training. And so it was that we all walked together along the now familiar path to the palace of Raymond de Durfort. It looked as if half of Fanjeaux had gathered in its great hall to witness the event.

The debate began much as it had in Carcassonne. Once again, Guilhabert stood up and spoke of the decadence and corruption of the Roman Church. There was the same murmuring of support from the townspeople, but something had changed. The papal legates there, with Diego and Dominic, had shed their rings and jeweled crosses. This day they all wore white tunics.

"Look upon us, friends," Diego responded. "Do you behold before you a priesthood displaying ornaments of wealth and power? Are not we now living the same life of poverty and chastity that you have so proudly proclaimed?" He lowered his eyes in penitential reverence. "Yes, there are priests among us who have not honored their vows and sacred callings, and for that I am most truly sorry. But would you deny your Mother Church because some of her sons have sinned? Would you shun the beneficence of the sacraments because of their mistakes?"

Then Dominic stepped forward. "My brothers and sisters," he continued. "Our Lord entered the womb of the Blessed Virgin, unstained by mortal sin, that he might be born to live as man among you. He fulfilled the word of the prophets and became a suffering servant that you might know his truth. And he died upon the cross that your souls might gain eternal life."

"You speak in error," Guilhabert cut in. "Our Savior never did assume the bonds of flesh. His Spirit found a brief abode with Jesus of Nazareth as it does with Good Christian men and women still. But the Lord suffered no pain as he was nailed to the cross, for his soul was free of its mortal coil."

How could it be that Jesus felt no pain as the nails pierced his flesh? I wondered. I began to sweat as the heat from the summer sun penetrated the palace walls, and I wished in vain for a cool drink.

"Search your hearts," Guilhabert was saying. "Would the Good God, whose Spirit abides therein, suffer his own Son to the torture of crucifixion? Would he afflict any of his beloved children with pestilence and starvation? Would he be so jealous as to allow the slaughter of those Christians who love Him?"

Dominic raised both his arms to Heaven. "No," he proclaimed. "The One True God does not condone the slaughter of the innocent. He is slow to anger and abounding in steadfast love. He forgives the repentant and welcomes the lost sheep back into his fold. He established the Church and offers the blessed sacraments to all who would be saved. His only foe is evil itself, and those who through their stubbornness remain its ally.

"The heretic who calls himself a bishop has instructed you to search your hearts. I do the same. What do you find there? Is it the God who created this world in all its glory and a Savior who lived and died to reconcile each one of you to His creation? Or do you find there the Antichrist, disguised as a distant spiritual 'god' who knows not of your earthly struggles—a god who would have you deny the glory of this world that he has made?"

How I was filled with terror at the thought of searching my own heart, for I knew just what I would find there. I had listened to both Guilhabert and Dominic and I could not tell which man spoke the truth. How was I to discern the right path to salvation? How was I to avoid the fires of Hell?

Despite the heat, a cold dampness began to creep over my skin. I felt the great hall spinning and a shroud of darkness started to cloud my vision. A wave of nausea flooded over me, and I dropped to the floor.

But, God, despite what others say, You must know that I did not pass out completely. I could not have, for I bore witness to a miracle that is now branded on my soul.

I sensed that Dominic had seen me fall and taken compassion upon the struggle within me. His voice softened as he addressed the crowd.

"My friends," he said. "It is well and good to carry on debates, but God most surely lies beyond the bounds of human reason. If you wish to know which of us speaks the truth, we might better appeal directly to Him."

The murmuring crowd grew silent, and Dominic turned to the judges. "Both Guilhabert and I have come prepared today with carefully crafted manuscripts. We could continue to debate into the night and let our good judges determine the merit of our reason. But I propose instead that we submit our arguments to a trial by fire."

A gasp arose from the room, and all eyes shifted to the judges. The foreman spoke.

"If you submit to such a trial each side will place its manuscript upon the fire. God will judge error by allowing the flames to consume it, but the truth will not burn."

"Guilhabert," the foreman asked. "Do you concur with such a trial?"

You know, God, I imagined for a moment that I saw Guilhabert hesitate, and I wondered if he too was thinking of the tales from Montréal. But he quickly recovered and replied, "If it be the will of the judges, I so concur."

The crowd parted as servants left to fetch wood and build a fire on the hearth. And when it was aglow with flames, the two men stepped forward.

"Who would you have go first?" asked Dominic.

"Guilhabert called for this disputation and made the first remarks," the judges replied. "Let him begin."

Guilhabert stepped forward and held his precious manuscript as if it were an offering to the flames. The room fell silent as we all held our collective breath. His vellum fell upon the blaze. It seemed for a moment as if it would not burn, and the crowd gasped. But then a corner began to glow, and then another. A black smoke arose from the heretic's arguments and they burst into flames.

As Guilhabert's manuscript burned, the crowd released a deep moan, and Dominic stepped forward. He raised his arms in supplication to God, bowed his head, and laid his work upon the fire. I heard a rush of wind and thought for a moment that the calf skin had burst into flames. But that's not what happened. The writings were propelled out of the fire and landed on a wooden beam above it.

"Return it to the fire," the judges ordered, and again the vellum was expelled in a rush of wind and carried to the rafters. After the third attempt, Dominic reclaimed his precious manuscript and knelt in thanksgiving as the crowd stood dumbfounded.

Then I felt a gentle shaking, and I faintly heard a voice.

"Elmina," it urged, "you must awaken."

Slowly I opened my eyes to find Amelha, Clarette, and Berengaria all bending over me. Bonata was cradling my head in her lap.

"Where am I?" I asked as the hall came into focus. I reached for Berengaria's arm, and awkwardly made my way to my feet. Then I remembered what I had witnessed.

"Did you see what happened?" I asked them.

"You fainted from the pressing of the crowd," responded Amelha.

"But the trial by fire," I continued. "Did you see how the Holy Spirit swept Dominic's manuscript from the flames?"

A concerned look passed between Bonata and the others. "You were passed out," the signora replied. "There was no trial by fire. I fear you are delusional."

But, God, it was not so. I know full well the thing I saw. I did not imagine the trial by fire. As we walked home, I inquired of Berengaria what she had witnessed.

"Dominic was most persuasive, and God has surely favored him," was her only reply.

Guilhabert and his companions accompanied us to the *ostal*. When we returned, everyone there wanted to hear how it had gone.

"I do not know what to make of the Castilian preacher, Dominic," Amelha replied reluctantly. "He mimics the poverty and habit of a perfect, and he admits that priests have been corrupted with the sins of lust and greed. It is hard to make a case against him."

"I do not trust him," Magdalena inserted. "His words are meant to deceive. Dominic tries to win our hearts through fear of Hell, but we know that there is no Hell save that which sinful man creates on earth . . ."

Signora Bonata halted our conversation. "It is past time for you to be in bed. Bruna, Aude, and I will bid Guilhabert and the brothers *bon vespré* and join you shortly. As we clamored up the ladder and removed our robes, I could hardly wait to speak of what I had seen. I reminded them of how Dominic had demanded that we look into our hearts for God. "Do we find there Our Lord and Savior, born of the Blessed Virgin's womb and come to deliver us from the bonds of sin, or do we fin the Antichrist who would deny the glory of God's creation?" I asked.

"Dominic stopped the debate and called upon the judges for a trial by fire," I exclaimed. "Guilhabert placed his arguments upon the flames and they were consumed. But Dominic . . . the Holy Spirit swooped into the fire and lifted his manuscript up to the rafters, not just once but three times. It was a miracle!"

"Elmina knows not of what she speaks," Amelha rejoined. "She fainted and was laid out on the floor."

"'Tis true I fainted," I replied, "but only for an instant. I saw it all, and I know that God himself has favored Dominic."

"And could it be that you too favor him?" Amelha chided.

The room erupted in laughter.

Then Clarette cut in with her quiet, serious tone. "This is more than a case of mere infatuation. Dominic has shown that the Church is determined to wage war against the Albigensians. He is but the vanguard of a coming legion. It was only a few decades ago that Good Christians were put to trial by fire at the stake. Listen to me. We have all been baptized within the Catholic Church. Do we wish to turn against it and put our own lives in peril?"

The room was silent. This was the first time any of us had spoken aloud the fears that trembled in our hearts.

Curtslana finally said timidly, "I fear that if Dominic be right, we will be twice subjected to a trial by fire. Even if we escape the stake, God will subject us to the fires of Hell for our heresy."

Gentiana looked around the room at all of us before she spoke. "I do not know which path is right or true. I only want to live in harmony with all of you. I fear that these debates are tearing us apart."

"And well they should," interjected Jordana. "If there is to be warfare, we must all take our stand. Too long have we been swayed by the heretics to whom our parents have consigned us. I, for one, do not wish to be subjected to a trial by fire for a faith that never was my own."

"But we have no other choice," inserted little Paperin. "There is no place for poor Catholic girls like us to go."

"Unless we agree to marry and bear some brute *credente's* children," I added.

"My heart is sick," lamented Blanca. "When I was young, I loved the Mother Church, but now I am confused. Na Bonata and the sisters have received us with such kindness and their faith is strong. I do not know what path to follow."

"I do," replied Magdalena. I am certain of the Good Christian path that I am called to walk. I despise the Church and the evil that lurks behind the reasoned guise of Dominic. This night Guilhabert has spoken to each one of us. The time has come to search our hearts and choose."

⁂

The next day at the *ostal*, the mood was somber. Bonata, Aude, and Bruna spoke to one another in hushed voices and that evening when we finished our class with Guilhabert, we were sent to bed even before the sun had dropped behind the western wall. We awoke the following morning to find Guilhabert and his companion still there.

"Sit down, my daughters," he said to us. "We must speak with you of important matters." All twelve of us lowered our eyes and took our places at the table. "We are facing difficult times," he continued. "And soon the Roman Church will not content itself with sending fatuous clergymen to challenge the Good Christian way. You are hearing falsehood preached about our faith, and I see the way the Castilian preachers lust after your souls. It is no longer safe for you to roam the streets of Fanjeaux. Henceforth you may no longer go to town unless accompanied by a perfect, and I forbid any of you from exchanging words with those sons of Satan."

Guilhabert was looking directly at me as he spoke, but I dared not hold his gaze. I felt as if my heart had been rent in two.

"I have something else to say," he went on. "You may no longer remain on the fence. You must search your hearts, and, in one month's time, you will either receive the *consolamentum* or leave our *ostal* to make a different life."

I let out a short gasp. "This is not right," I dared exclaim. "Blanca and Paperin are not even of age."

It was the first time I had ever seen Guilhabert lose his temper. His fist slammed onto the table. "You will hold your tongue," he shouted. Then he took a deep breath, and his voice became as a mere whisper.

"It is my job to protect all of my daughters from the evil that is surely coming. There is no more that I can do for you, Elmina," he declared. "I have seen how you look with longing upon those preachers. We have taught you all we can of the Good Christian way. If your heart remains with the Demon Church, it is time you left this *ostal*."

"No, no!" I sobbed. "Please do not send me away. My heart is not given to demons; it only longs for God." I looked around the table at my Good Christian family. I could see that I was not the only one who was alarmed by the bishop's words.

That evening, Guilhabert called a meeting at his abode for all the perfecti. Na Bonata bid us again retire early before Aude, Bruna, and she took their leave. One by one we climbed the ladder and hung our robes. At first none of us spoke. It was little Paperin who broke the silence.

"What are we to do?" she whispered. And in that moment, God, I knew that You were calling me.

"We must take our leave tonight," I replied, "before they start to guard our every move. Guilhabert and Bonata would have us all declare war on God's Church. Do you wish to take arms and join in such a battle? Listen to me! You all heard Dominic last night and witnessed how the Spirit favored him. If he speaks the truth and we remain in this house, our souls will be condemned to the eternal fires of Hell. But if Guilhabert be right and we choose the Church, our only punishment will be to live again on earth. We were baptized and raised as Catholic girls. God is calling us home."

I stood and slipped on my robe. "Who will return to our Holy Mother Church with me?"

"Where will we go? And what will become of us when we arrive?" asked Alaide.

"We shall seek refuge in the old stone church. And it is the One True God who will take care of us from this day forward," I replied.

Clarette was the first to don her robe and stand beside me. She pulled Berengaria to her feet. One by one each girl arose until only two remained. "Amelha and Magdalena," I pleaded. "You, too, must join us. Do not commit yourselves to be the Church's enemy. Do not give your lives to the heretics and consign your souls to Hell."

I reached out my hand to my sister. "Please, Amelha, come with me," I pleaded. "I'm so sorry for the times I was a cruel and jealous sister. The sin within my soul is very great, but I have always loved you. And I have great fear for what will happen if you stay."

Amelha took my hand in hers and kissed it. "Elmina, my dear sister," she replied. "Since I was but a little girl I have adored you and wished to follow everywhere you go. But today I cannot. This *ostal* is where my soul belongs." She released my hand and reached instead for Magdalena's. I stood in silence as hot tears rolled down my cheeks. I knew there would be no use arguing with her.

That night we fled the *ostal* that had become our home. The moon shone its cold light as we climbed the steep path and crept past the Durforth palace. We ran along the *Rota des Faures* and through the market square until we reached the church. We didn't stop until we stood outside those oaken doors, looking up at the tympanum of the Last Judgment. One more step and there would be no turning back. I pulled open the door, and we walked through together.

And, God, as we entered Your holy church, we dared to trust that You would be there in the darkness of the nave awaiting us.

Chapter 8

FLIGHT

You know, God, that our trust in You was not mistaken. As we slipped into the dark nave of Your Church, we saw a candle flickering in the apse and heard a fervent murmuring. Of course I was afraid. I knew not if the voice was a priest or legate who would abhor our heresy and send us back to the *ostal*. I did know that if we were forced to return, we would be cast out. Guilhabert would never have allowed us to receive the *consolamentum*. The stone walls of the church still held the day's warmth, but I was shivering.

I grabbed Clarette's hand and held my breath. At first I could see nothing but the flickering candle, but as our eyes adjusted I made out a lean figure kneeling at the altar. My heart leapt, and I knew that it was Dominic! He was so deep in prayer that he did not immediately discern our presence. With fear and trembling, we crept up the aisle and threw ourselves at his feet.

Dominic responded with a start. He glared at us and quickly returned to his prayerful pose.

Berengaria spoke first as if she had rehearsed her words.

"Servant of God, come to our aid," she pleaded. "If what you preached last night be true, our souls have long been blinded with error; for those whom you style heretics, we call Good Christians. They are the guides in whom we have hitherto trusted with our whole hearts. But now we know not what to think. Have pity on us and pray to the Lord your God that He may make known to us in what faith we must live and die if we would be saved everlastingly."

Dominic did not move. I feared that he had not heard Berengaria, or else did not wish to acknowledge us. *Could it be we were mistaken?* I asked myself. *Might we have left everything behind only to be rejected by Dominic and the Church?* As the priest continued in silent meditation, we all held our breath and prayed as one that he might deign to answer us. And, Dear God, once again You heard our prayers. Dominic stood up, and his eyes quietly took in the ten of us kneeling before him. Then he placed his hands upon Berengaria's shoulders.

"Have patience and fear nothing," he finally answered. "Our Lord will send a sign and make it clear what you must do. We will ask God together."

We did as we were bid. As we knelt on that hard stone, I begged You, God, to show us the way. Then a soul-piercing screech cut through the night. I opened my eyes just in time to see a monstrous beast leaping into the rafters. It was as black as soot, and its eyes flamed just like the fires of Hell. Some will say I was mad, that no such beast exists, but, God, You know I saw it. And I was not the only one, for we all gasped as the creature leapt into the air and disappeared into the belfry.

"A black cat is a deadly omen," exclaimed Blanca. "I fear we've made a grave mistake."

"'Twas not a cat," was Dominic's reply. "It was Beelzebub himself, the master you have hitherto served. God has permitted you to behold its likeness so that you might see the horror of your ways and repent."

"God has delivered us a sign," I gasped. "Pray tell us, Dominic, what He would have us do. We fled the *ostal* so we would not be forced to take the sacred vows of heretics. Our *consolamentum* was scheduled to occur within the month. Now we cannot return. Please help us, for we have no other place to go."

Dominic bowed his head, and I feared he had no answer for us. I know now, God, that he had heard our plea and was asking You what he must do. But before he could offer his reply, Blanca began to cry.

"Dear friends," she whispered. "I am afraid, and I should never have come here. Na Bonata will be so upset when she finds us gone, and I don't want to make her angry. I love the Mother Church, but I love the signora and Guilhabert too. I cannot stay with you. Please pray to Mother Mary and ask God to have mercy upon my soul." With that, Blanca spun about and bolted through the nave.

I started to run after her. "Blanca, don't turn your back upon us now," I pleaded. She did not look around. "Blanca, if you won't save yourself, I beg of you, do not reveal where we have gone," I yelled to her back as she disappeared down the cobbled lane.

Then suddenly I felt the firmness of a hand upon my shoulder. "You must let her go," insisted Dominic. He looked from me to the eight other girls still huddled at the altar and told us his decision. "With God's help, I will do all I can to assist you," he said. "We have no time to waste. I will take you to the *domus* of Na Gracia, a fine Catholic noblewoman. Perhaps she will offer you all shelter." He bid us follow him. In silence we all stood and trailed after Dominic, down the *Rota de la Gleisa* toward the Aymeric gate. And there along the northern wall we saw a stone house bigger by half than Papa's.

Dominic stepped forward and knocked loudly on the door. A dowager dressed in fine silk appeared and Dominic bowed deeply.

"My Lady," he began, "I greet thee in the name of Our Lord and I offer His blessings to your good daughters." The lady acknowledged this greeting, and he continued. "I have come on behalf of these dear Catholic girls who have fled the clutches of the Albigensians and have no other place to go. I beg of you to shelter and protect them in your home."

Na Gracia looked upon the nine of us, and her wary brown eyes met the fear in our own. She stepped outside to speak with Dominic. I couldn't hear their words, but I could see when she nodded her consent. The two returned, and Dominic delivered the good news.

"Our friend Na Gracia has graciously offered to let you stay," he said. "Her daughters live now in a convent at Toulouse, and you may remain here and do her bidding until other arrangements can be made. I will retire in prayer to ask God to divulge His plan for you."

We all nodded together. Na Gracia led us into her home and bid a servant show us to our quarters. I shuddered as we traipsed past the flaming cook fire in the kitchen to a long dark room beyond. That night as I lay down upon a thin layer of straw, the flickering embers from the kitchen fire reflected off the walls and filled the room with an orange glow.

Dear God, how it ignited the terror within my soul. That night I had a dreadful dream. I saw again the hideous leaping beast with its black coat and eyes ablaze. It bolted from the belfry of the church and then took flight across the village to the *ostal* of Na Bonata. The creature entered through an open window in the loft and leapt onto the mattress where Amelha, Blanca, and Magdalena tossed in sleepless misery.

"My fire will consume you and your people," it hissed into their ears. The three of them began to scream, and I too awoke with a start. I felt as if the dreaded beast's fiery eyes had burned a hole in my own soul as well. I wondered what evil had been loosed upon Fanjeaux and trembled on the straw until daylight.

Dominic was gone for three full days. Back then I didn't think about the challenge we presented. The red-haired priest had been intent on converting us, but he had made no plans for what to do if he succeeded! And so we hid inside with Na Gracia, praying that Bonata and Guilhabert would not find us before Dominic returned.

And, God, one more time You answered our prayers. When Dominic returned, Bishop Diego was with him. It was the bishop who spoke first. "God has been pleased," he said, "to reveal to Dominic His sacred plan. The nine of you will be the vanguard for fulfilling our mission in the Languedoc."

Dominic then stepped forward, and I was sure a Heavenly glow surrounded him. He said that he had spent the past night in fervent prayer on a rock overlooking the deserted village of Prouilhe, just a half league northeast. And then he told us what he had witnessed.

"I saw a shooting star in the western sky, and then a globe of fire appeared. It circled the old village three times then it descended to the roof of the deserted Chapel of Our Lady. There it rested, and yet the holy edifice was not consumed."

With pleading eyes, Dominic turned to our host. "My dearest Na Gracia," he began, "We are dependent on your generosity and help."

Bishop Diego then stepped forward.

"You are the only Catholic noblewoman in Fanjeaux who is not tied to heresy through choice or marriage. I wish to establish a convent of refuge for good Catholic girls whose souls have been held captive by the Albigensians. Here they might be instructed in the One True Faith and given the chance to live their lives in penitence and prayer. Indeed, their prayers might help sustain a new order of preachers to eradicate the scourge of heresy from all the Languedoc."

Upon revealing this plan, both churchmen fell down on their knees.

"My excellent Lady," Diego continued. "Last night Our Lord was pleased to reveal his plan to Dominic. God wishes us to use your sister Na Cavaer's holdings at Prouilhe for this sacred endeavor. Might you be so kind as to intercede with your sister on our behalf?"

"My sister is not so kindly disposed toward the Church as I," Na Gracia responded with great care.

Dominic drew a deep breath before he spoke. His eyes squinted as he began.

"Of that we are aware, but the land of Na Cavaers is deserted and falling into ruin. It is of no use to her. If she seems reluctant, you might suggest that it could be in her best interest to reconsider. You could tell her that Bishop Folc of Toulouse has expressed concern about her friendship with the Albigensians. Should she be so generous as to offer her lands to the glory of God, then it is quite possible that in the troubles which will surely come, he might overlook her indiscretions."

I sensed a tension in the air. But, God, I was too naïve then to fully understand what had just transpired. And so I simply held my breath and waited for Na Gracia's reply.

"I understand you fully," she said quietly. "I shall speak with Na Cavaers. And I trust you will confer with Bishop Folc at Toulouse. It is he who is the patron for the Chapel de Ste. Marie."

"I'm certain he will concur," Dominic replied. "Diego and I have already discussed our hope of forming a monastic order with the bishop, and it has met with his hearty approval."

A monastic order! Dear God, as I listened to this exchange, my heart did leap with joy. *Was Dominic suggesting that we were to be founders of a monastery? Could it be that what I had dreamed of my whole life was going to come true?* It hardly seemed possible that we might have the chance to become nuns and follow Dominic to Prouilhe.

Dominic then turned to the nine of us.

"If Na Cavaers agrees, Diego and I will go to Toulouse to finalize our plans. And it will be necessary for all of your fathers to release you into our care. On the way back, we will stop at Pamiers to speak with Clarette's family. When we return we will then meet with each of your fathers and ask them to offer their daughters to the glory of God. Until then it is best that you take care not to leave the *domus* of Na Gracia."

We all nodded in solemn agreement.

The next day Na Gracia went to visit Na Cavaers, and she

returned with word that her sister had granted Bishop Diego and Dominic permission to form a monastery at Prouilhe. By evening the bishop and his canon had left for Toulouse. As we waited in our quarters, we could not help but talk about what Dominic had said.

"God has answered our prayers!" exclaimed Clarette. "We can serve our Holy Mother Church and still remain together as sisters. I am certain my father will agree to the proposal. He raised me to be a good Catholic, and my brother Guilhem is already a priest. I know it pained him to hand me over to the Albigensians."

"I'm not so sure that our father will give his consent," said Jordana. "He doesn't like the Church and always complained about its tithes."

"Of course he will," replied Riccarda "It is his purse that he is most concerned about!"

"And how could he turn down a chance to settle five daughters without paying a dowry!" added Curstlana.

We talked excitedly until the sun was set and Na Gracia bid us all to be quiet and sleep.

Within a week, Bishop Diego and Dominic had returned from Toulouse and with them was Clarette's brother Guilhem. He seemed to me still but a pimply boy, but he held himself erect as was required by his priestly station.

"You may call me Father Guilhem," he said by way of introduction. "Dominic has asked if I would be procurator for the new monastery and serve as your chaplain when he must be away."

Clarette had been right. Her father had given his full support. He was most willing to consign his daughter to the new order. And what is more, her brother had signed an oath committing himself, Clarette, and all they owned to the new venture. Clearly, our new monastery was to become a double order, with both men and women living in close proximity. I could feel my blood warm at the thought of living side by side with Dominic and the other priests.

The next step was to arrange meetings with all our families, and I knew it would not be so easy. That very night Bishop Diego, Dominic, and I walked down the hill to talk with Papa. As we went past the church and down the *Rota Des Esquirols* together, my heart began to pound. I thought Papa would likely assent to Dominic's plan—he loved the Church almost as much as I did—but I knew Mama would be dead set against it. I also knew that she held great sway over him. As we approached the familiar stone steps to my old home, I held back.

Dominic knocked on the door, and Papa opened it with a quizzical eye. We stepped inside, and it came spilling out of me before we even stepped into the *fogana*.

"Papa," I said, "these are Bishop Diego and his canon, Dominic. They have come from Osma to save our souls from the heresy of the Good Christians. They are going to start a monastery at Prouilhe! Na Cavaers has turned over the chapel and surrounding land to them. Please, Papa, won't you let me go with them to be a nun?"

"Slow down!" Papa exclaimed as he led us into the *fogana* where Mama sat in the candlelight with her embroidery. He turned to the churchmen and said, "Would you be so kind as to start from the beginning? The good bishop can tell both of us what he does propose."

Bishop Diego and Dominic took turns talking to Papa about their mission to convert the Albigensians and their dream for the monastery at Prouilhe. They spoke about the life of prayer and penitence that we would lead. They assured Papa and Mama it would be a cloistered order in which we would be kept safe from any troubles that might be coming. They suggested once again that Bishop Folc would likely find favor with any family that offered its daughters to the service of the Church.

When they had finished, Papa sat quietly, as if assessing the worth of these two strangers. Then he turned to me.

"Are you sure this is what you desire?" he asked.

"Oh yes, Papa. I want this more than anything and have since I was but a little girl."

Papa looked deep into my eyes and knew that I spoke the truth. He turned back to Bishop Diego and Dominic.

"You have my blessing to take Elmina and Amelha with you to Prouilhe."

My eyes widened. "But Amelha is not joining us," I said quietly. "She does not wish to come."

"Amelha does not know what's good for her. She will go where her father tells her," Papa replied.

At that Mama leapt up, her embroidery falling to the floor.

"Amelha will do no such thing," she interjected. "You will not force her into the Roman Church. If you should try, you will lose me. I shall leave you to care for the boys alone and join with the Good Christians myself."

She glared at Dominic. "You are the Devil in the flesh," she hissed. "I do not know what you have done to bewitch one of my daughters, but you shall not have them both."

Papa raised his hand as if to strike Mama, but then he sat back heavily upon his chair. With a resigned sigh he uttered, "My wife has spoken."

I stood, unable to look either of them in the eye. I should have been happy that my dream to become a nun was coming true, but I was not. For I knew that my love for Your Church had torn my family apart and there was nothing I could do to change it.

Once Bishop Diego and Dominic had met with all our fathers, they gathered us together and Dominic spoke.

"The huts and Chapel de Ste. Marie at Prouilhe are in a state of great disrepair," he said. "It will be some time before we can make them fit for habitation. We have procured masons from Carcassonne and several brothers from Toulouse to assist us in making some repairs. Most of you will remain here with Na Gracia until we finish our work. The signora's daughters Guillelmette and Raymundine have been given leave to return from Toulouse. They have received a Catholic education and will instruct you in the catechism. You will search your hearts in constant prayer to discern whether God truly calls you to this most noble of vocations. Before you settle at Prouilhe, I will examine each of you to ascertain your fitness for religious life. You may go now in prayer."

As we bowed our heads and turned toward our quarters, Dominic called out. "Berengaria, Clarette, and Elmina, would you remain? I need a word with you."

I cringed as the others returned to their quarters. Dominic had discerned the envy in my soul that first day we had met at the market. *What if he had reconsidered? What if he thought my heart unfit to be a nun?* I approached with trepidation.

But that was not what Dominic wanted to speak to us about. "Bishop Diego must return to Toulouse to seek alms for our endeavor. I will remain to oversee the work at Prouilhe." Dominic turned his slate eyes upon the three of us. "Elmina, you have shown much courage in leading your sisters out of the grips of heresy, and all of you have demonstrated great devotion to God and his Church. Are you certain that you wish to continue upon this path? It will not be an easy life. You will live in greater hardship than the Albigensians, eating but twice a day and eschewing all luxury and comfort. You will offer yourself in total obedience to God. You will do daily penance for the path that you have followed heretofore and mortify your flesh through constant prayer and fasting. Do you desire to commit yourselves to such a life and emulate the sufferings of our dear Lord?"

We glanced at one another and nodded our heads as one. On that July evening, standing there with Dominic, there was nothing we wanted more. "We so desire," the three of us affirmed together.

"God has confirmed your hearts," Dominic replied. "I will instruct you in the catechism at Prouilhe. It is necessary for us to go there now and begin to prepare a domicile for your sisters. You three will come with Guilhem and me. I know that you were gardeners at the *ostal* and we need you to sow an autumn garden to sustain us through the coming winter."

Dear God, I never dreamed that what I'd learned from Aude would prove to be so helpful or allow me to spend two months working side by side with Dominic. The next day, after our morning pottage, Na Cavaers gave us each a blanket and a coarse towel. We wrapped our nightshifts to make a pack and followed the two priests, walking along the northern wall until we reached a rock outcropping.

"This is where God revealed His plan to me," said Dominic. I looked out across the fields to the Black Mountains beyond and then noticed a little village nestled far below. Prouilhe! Dear God, how my heart did take flight! I could make out the walls of the Church of St. Martins. And to the east lay a small stone chapel, surrounded by thatch-roofed cottages. *Is this where God intends us to live out our days?* I wondered as we picked our way down a stony path to the valley below. As we descended, my life with Mama and Papa and Na Bonata melted into the distance. You know that I did not even look back. My eyes were fixed on Dominic, and I trusted that with each craggy step he was leading us closer to You.

Chapter 9

PROUILHE

B ut, God, I must confess that as we drew nearer to Prouilhe, a little doubt crept in. From the distance, the village had seemed picturesque, but I soon saw that much of it was falling down. The town walls were crumbling so badly that we had no need to find the gate. As we picked our way through the rubble, Berengaria, Clarette, and I exchanged worried glances. *Most surely God could not mean for us to live among such ruins*, they exclaimed.

But of course, God, that is exactly what You had planned for us. We walked north along a rutted path that grew wider as it reached the ruined Church of St. Martins and its enclave. The church's barrel-vaulted sanctuary had once been the destination of pilgrims on the way to Spain or St. Gilles, but now its west wall sagged and its roof was caving in. A circle of empty tile-roofed stone houses encircled the church. We wound our way north past them until we reached a group of small thatched-roof hovels built of wood and mud. The huts surrounded the cobbled courtyard of the little Chapel of Ste. Marie.

Dear God, as soon as I saw it, the chapel pulled at my soul. It was a simple oblong structure and its stones were the same ochre and grey as the distant hills. There was a small tower along its western wall, and from its alcove a stone carving of Our Lady bid us enter. Together Dominic, Guilhem, Berengaria, Clarette, and I walked up its four stone steps and pulled open an arched door with flecks of red paint still clinging to it. We stepped inside, and, God, I felt Your presence reach into my very bones. Clarette and Berengaria must have had the same sense of awe, for I heard their breath quicken and none of us uttered a single word.

At first all I could see were three faint streams of light from the apse windows, but as my eyes adjusted to the dark I made out a carved altar with two wooden choir benches behind it. To the right was a door that led into what must have been the sacristy. To the left, a carved wood statue of the Virgin stood as tall as life. Her wavy hair flowed down upon cerulean robes, and in her arms rested her dearest child. The gaze that bound the two together invited me into their hearts as well. I bowed my head in grateful adoration and noticed that the stone floor was dotted with chunks of limestone. *Where is this coming from?* I wondered. When I looked up, I saw that the beams of the vaulted ceiling were sagging, and there were great cracks in its plaster. I feared the chapel might be beyond repair, but when I looked around the nave, I saw that the columns looked strong. They were still covered with most of their plaster. And they were painted the same blue as the Virgin's robes and stenciled with flowers and vines.

As we turned to leave, I quickly knelt before the Blessed Mother and thanked her for answering our prayers. Then Dominic ushered us through the side door to the stone sacristy. Its arched walls and vaulted ceiling made it seem like a tiny chapel. It was painted a deep blue, with gilded stars shining from it. We all gasped and Dominic nodded his approval.

"This will be our chapter house," is all he said.

"What is a chapter house?" I quietly inquired.

"It's where you will pass many of your hours. Here you will pray the minor hours. You will meet each day to listen to your prior and conduct the business of your community."

I wasn't sure what he meant by minor hours, but I nodded anyway. When we stepped back outside, I looked to the east beyond the sacristy and saw three apple trees and a field of straw beyond. *Our garden!* I thought and my heart leapt with joy. To the north of the churchyard was a row of decrepit sheds along the crumbling village wall. They would do now for drying herbs.

Dominic then led us to a row of three hovels along the western side of the courtyard. They stood askew as if the earth had already begun to lay claim on their daub and timber. They were built of wood and mud and had thatched roofs, but they seemed too small to call houses. Our eyes widened as we took stock of them. The largest had both a door and a window.

"This house will serve as the kitchen, refectory, and warming room," Dominic declared.

"Warming room?" I asked him.

"It will be the only room that houses fire," Dominic replied. "When frosts descend you will be allowed to enter once you have finished with your prayers and labors. We looked inside and saw there was a fire pit in its earthen floor. We then walked over to the smallest hut whose walls were most intact. Dominic bid us enter its dank blackness, and we were met with the frantic screech of a family of black rats fleeing their nest. The only light filtered like Heavenly stars through holes in the thatched roof. As we stood upon the earthen floor littered with straw and dung, Dominic exclaimed, "And this, my daughters, is where you will make your beds."

Dear God, you know how my stomach did churn! I did not wish to make my bed among the rats. Suddenly I longed to be lying safely next to Amelha in our straw bed at the *ostal*. The earth smelled dank, and I had heard that rats will eat a baby if they are hungry. I wondered if they would also nibble upon grown girls.

"Will we have mattresses?" I inquired.

Dominic turned steely eyes upon mine. "You cannot mortify the flesh upon a soft mattress," he answered in reproach. "I sleep each night upon stone and give God thanks for my discomfort."

Our faces must have shown alarm, for Dominic reconsidered. "You may cut straw to cover the floor if your woman's flesh requires it."

For an instant, I wondered if we all had made a great mistake. But I took a deep breath. We'd come too far, and I was too filled with anticipation to let a few rats or a dirt floor soil my dreams. I thought of the Christian martyrs of old and knew this was little torment compared to what they had endured. After all, we had seen black rats at the *ostal* and at Papa's house too, and they had never harmed us. Once I got over my first repulsion, I told myself I didn't really mind the dirt or dung or dampness. We would take care to hang our robes and keep the floor swept clean. Most likely with all three of us in the room, the rats would find themselves a new home.

That afternoon, while Dominic withdrew to the chapel to pray, Guilhem taught us how to repair our roof. We gathered clumps of straw from the field behind the chapel and tied one end into a knot. Then we pounded our straw clusters into the holes. We swept the floor and gathered up clean straw to sleep upon. As our eyes adjusted to the dark, we noticed pegs along the walls. We hung our cloaks and nightclothes and lay our blankets upon the straw. By nightfall our dormitory was prepared.

Dominic allowed us an evening meal of bread and watered wine, and afterward we lit a candle and solemnly processed from the refectory across the cobbled courtyard into the Chapel de Ste. Marie. He led us in the vespers that would mark the close of day for the rest of my life. With his deep and resonant voice he began chanting, "*Gloria in excelsis Deo et in terra pax hominibus bonne voluntatis . . .*

Glory to God
and on earth peace and goodwill to men
We praise Thee, we bless Thee, we worship Thee,

We glorify Thee, we give thanks for Thy great glory."

Dear God, how I ached with joy and gratitude at hearing the sacred words of my girlhood church flow over me again. Then Dominic chanted psalms of thanksgiving and taught us the antiphonal responses. How I loved lifting my voice up in song! I thought I could be happy doing only that for the remainder of my days. We listened to Guilhem read earnestly from the holy scriptures, and his words seemed filled with the import of the endeavor on which we were embarked.

Then Dominic led us in prayer, "*Paternoster, qui es in caelis, santificetur nomen tuum . . .*"

My eyes filled up with tears. I now could recite the Paternoster without having to receive the *consolamentum!* O God, that night I was so happy. I longed for nothing more than to spend the rest of my days in this hovel of a convent, praying and singing Your praise with Dominic.

We passed the next three months in the daily work of turning Prouilhe into a habitable home. Right from the beginning, our days were shaped by prayer. We awoke before daybreak and gathered for lauds in the chapel. Dominic taught us the Daily Offices and urged us both to sing sweetly from the depth of our souls and to join our voices in harmony with one another. O God, I'd been so jealous that You'd given the gift of song to Amelha, but at Prouilhe I too came to learn the joy of singing! Dominic would raise his glorious voice, and my heart would soar as I joined in response. I must confess to You that there were times I almost forgot that Guilhem, Clarette, and Berengaria were by my side.

Just as Dominic had instructed, our first job was to clear land for a garden. We chose a plot behind the orchard that had a small creek running near it. Together Berengaria and I cut down the straw. We removed stones from the surface and swung a mattock to dig out the larger rocks and loosen the soil. It was too late to sow the oats and barley we would need to see us through the winter, but Diego and

Dominic provided hearty seed: beets and turnips, cabbages, cauliflower and kale. We even sowed feverfew, chamomile, and lemon balm to dry for flu and indigestion, knowing that we would need to wait until spring to plant strong herbs.

Once we had sown our garden, Clarette and I gathered reeds along the river. We wove wattle to rebuild the walls of other cottages and tied bunches of reeds together to repair the holes in their roofs. Dominic and Guilhem had invited two other Cistercian monks to work along side us, and by the time the trees had shed their leaves, we had prepared four cottages for our use: two for our dormitories, one for the kitchen and refectory, and a cottage in the enclave surrounding St. Martins where Dominic and the men stayed.

The new monks had learned carpentry, and they set to work making furniture. They built a long table and two benches for the refectory. They carved benches and a tall chair for the chapter house. Dominic had procured a painted crucifix to hang on the wall in the chapel and a brass goblet and dish for the Eucharist. He and Guilhem had fashioned a long altar of wood and laid down stones that we might kneel before it.

As I busied myself in the work of creating a monastery, I seldom thought of Na Bonata. But they, of course, knew just where we had gone. How could I have thought that it might be otherwise? I had not prepared myself for that chilly September afternoon when she and Guilhabert arrived at Prouilhe. We were at prayer in the chapter house when we heard a loud knock on the door. Guilhem continued to lead us in prayer as Dominic left to attend to the visitors. It was hard not to be distracted by the muffled words emanating from the courtyard. Finally, Dominic appeared in the doorway and beckoned us out.

"Guilhabert, Martin and Signora Bonata have arrived. They refuse to leave until they hear you say that you have willingly made the choice to be here," he exclaimed. "I bid you speak with them."

Looking down at my soiled skirt and mud-caked shoes, I wondered how it must look to these Good Christians who had so recently been our guardians and teachers. We followed Dominic to the courtyard where Father Guilhem stood with the two perfecti. I could feel a cold fury seething behind Guilhabert's eyes and dared not raise my own.

"Elmina," he said in measured words. "I believe that you have been seduced by this red-haired devil of a priest, that he has kidnapped you and holds you hostage here. The pious dog insists that he is blameless, that you have led your sisters into this land of perdition by your own free will. What have you to say?"

When I opened my mouth to speak, tears flooded my eyes and the words would not come.

"It is necessary for you to talk to Guilhabert," Dominic intervened.

"The good priest Dominic speaks the truth," I replied, and Berengaria and Clarette nodded their concurrence. "We do not wish to be consoled or to make our lives among the heretics. Berengaria, Clarette, Curtslana, Paperin, Alaide, Riccarda, Jordana, Gentiana, and I—we have all returned to our Mother Church with the blessing of our fathers. I give you thanks for the care you once extended us and ask only that you leave us here in peace."

"It is not possible for us to leave you in peace," Guilhabert replied, "for amity with the Viper Church is not an option." He took a step forward and lowered his voice. "And what of your sister? Will you declare yourself an enemy to Amelha as well?"

I blanched, and Dominic steadied my arm. "I do not want to be her foe," I replied through my tears. "But neither do I wish to declare war against the Church. I have made my choice." Sister Bonata looked around at each of us with her soft amber eyes and nodded her farewell; Guilhabert cast us a withering glance before he turned his back and left us in the hands of the churchmen.

That evening after vespers, Dominic and Guilhem joined us in the chapel. They bid us take a seat, and Dominic said gravely,

"No good can come of the enmity between the Church and the Albigensians. Diego will be returning shortly. But we cannot wait until that time to begin your protection. I will request that Bishop Folc send more brothers to keep watch over Prouilhe. Guilhem will leave today for Carcassonne to procure masons to rebuild the village walls. Let us pray that the Lord will watch over you here and keep you from harm."

After meeting with Dominic, we retired to our dormitory in silence. It had been two months since we had fled the *ostal*, and I knew it must be past the time for Amelha's *consolamentum*. Perhaps only last week she had endured her night of trials and was now living as a Good Christian perfect. And, God, tonight I need to know this, were You there by her side or did You despise Amelha for her apostasy?

Huddled in the darkness on our beds of dirt and straw, we sensed the coming storm and knew that there could be no turning back. Dear God, how I longed for the safety of the cloistered life. The world beyond Prouilhe seemed fraught with danger, but no more so than the chaos of my own heart. I thought about how Guilhabert had said Amelha and I must be enemies. The thought filled me with dread, for I knew I had been a cruel older sister. I was not certain which of us You would favor in the oncoming battle. That night I dared to hope that strong new walls might offer me protection not just from the Albigensians but from my own demons also. But that, of course, was not the way that it worked out.

By Your grace, God, the next month provided us with little time to dwell upon such thoughts. Right from the beginning, Dominic taught us the importance of working hard. He said that labor was necessary, "in order the better to avoid idleness, the cause of so many evils." You know, God, that we were never idle. We awoke before dawn to gather in the chapel and sing Your praise for the gift of a new day. Until the grain ran low, we had some wine and horsebread before beginning the day's work.

Our first task was to make mortar for building the cloister walls and to repair the ceiling of the Chapel of Ste. Marie. Guilhem had procured quicklime and had it barged down the river. We mixed it with sand and water and then used wooden buckets to carry the mortar to the masons. Slowly the walls began to take place. First the masons made repairs to the village wall that went behind the chapel and the garden. Then they started work on a new barrier that snaked behind our dormitories on the west and turned south to sep- arate our cloister from the brothers at St. Martins. They inserted but one gate in the southern wall. Each day as the stones piled higher, I felt a rising panic. Dear God, I knew the wall was being built for our protection, but I could not help but feel as if it were making us prisoners instead.

Yet we had made our choice. And Berengeria, Clarette, and I had other work to do. Each morning we kneaded yellow split peas with coarse flour to make horsebread, and set a vegetable pottage on the fire to simmer. In the afternoon, we tended to the gardens and soon we brought in turnips, beets, and onions to supplement the grain and oil that Guilhem had procured as alms from Carcassonne. In the evening we set out food for the men and prayed there would be enough left over to fill our bellies.

Of course it was hard work. The quicklime burned our hands and our skin turned to leather in the still brilliant sun. Our muscles ached. At night we often felt too tired to kneel for vigil. Even so, the labor had its full rewards. We were doing it for You, and my heart swelled to see the ancient village and chapel restored.

Still, God, You know that as we worked I sometimes thought about less holy things. On warm days when I was delivering mortar or bringing in vegetables from the field, my mind was pulled from You to the strong Castilian priest who worked beside us. I secretly watched as beads of sweat glistened in his copper hair and his wiry muscles pushed against the fabric of his robe. When I walked by him with my heavy loads, I sometimes passed so close that I could feel his heat. And then, Dear God, I'd sense the sinful pangs within me. I'd quicken my step and pray that he had not taken note of my rapid breath. If I am to tell the truth, I must say that I imagined that he too felt fire beneath his robe. And I dared hope that if I labored well enough, dear Dominic might take note of me and bless me with his favor. I cast glances in his direction and crossed my ankles in the choir stall.

Still Dominic seemed to take no notice. And as the days grew shorter, I had less time to pine after him. We had wanted to complete our repairs before the first frost of winter and that is what we did. By the middle of November the walls of Prouilhe were completed. The masons packed their tools and returned to Carcassonne. All was ready for our sisters to join us.

Chapter 10

SAINT CECILIA

O f course I know I should have welcomed my sisters with open arms. But I could no more embrace their arrival than I had Amelha's fourteen years earlier. Dear God, as we began our new life at Prouilhe, I dared to hope the demon envy might loosen its grip upon my soul. But once more that was not to be.

One week before the feast of Saint Cecilia, our sisters joined us at Prouilhe: jovial Jordana, timid Curtslana, gentle Gentiana, feisty Riccarda, lovely Alaide, and little Paperin. I greeted them and showed them the chapel and the garden we had now harvested. When I brought them to our dormitories, with nine blankets laid neatly on the straw, I noted with pride how much improved they were after just three short months. I tried to answer all my friends' questions and share in their excitement, but I felt a familiar gnawing at my heart. The truth is, I did not welcome six more sisters. I did not want to share Dominic with so many others.

Still, there was little time to nurse my envy. There was too much to do preparing for our first sacred feast together. Diego had returned from his travels and gone to Toulouse to appeal to Bishop Folc for alms. He appeared at Prouilhe with bags of oats and barley and wheat, too, and rich, sweet cream for butter. With great glee, he urged us follow him to the field behind the chapel. We found eleven speckled chickens huddled there and a red-combed rooster standing among them.

"Riccarda and Jordana," Diego instructed. "You will be in charge of caring for the chickens and bringing in the eggs. By day they will run free. They'll eat insects and fertilize the garden. Guilhem will build a henhouse, and your job will be to make sure they are locked inside each night."

"I wish that we could eat one of them for our feast," lamented little Paperin.

"We need to keep them for their eggs," Diego admonished with a wink. "But I've left the best treats for last," he added and pulled from under his robe a fine hen ready for the plucking and a packet of *poudre-douce* that smelled of cinnamon and cloves.

Dear God, what a feast we prepared! With the *poudre-douce* Riccarda made a sweetened, spiced wine. We boiled the hen and used the broth to make a sauce with parsley and sage from the garden and eggs from our new chickens! I busied myself by cutting the head and tail and whiskers off the turnips and putting them in the stew pot to boil. Clarette made a parsnip pie with figs and raisins, and Berengaria set about turning apples and eggs into a *Rique-Manger*.

We had lived on vegetables, horsebread, and watered wine for almost three months, and it seemed like a Heavenly repast. After we finished eating, Dominic bid us rise and follow him across the courtyard to the chapter room.

"It is fitting," he began, "to celebrate your first day together on the feast day of Saint Cecilia. Hers is a life that you may all seek to emulate. She was a young woman who preserved her chastity and gave herself entirely to Our Lord. Listen to her story. Cecilia was of noble Roman birth, yet she did not flaunt her station. She dressed in simple robes and wore sackcloth against her skin. She fasted and prayed daily that God might preserve her virginity. Cecilia's parents were not sympathetic to her wishes. They betrothed her to a noble suitor named Valerián, but on the eve of her wedding, she entreated her new husband, 'I will tell you a secret if you will swear not to reveal it to anyone.' And when he swore, she said, 'I will marry you, but I am to remain a virgin. There is an angel who watches me, and wards off any who would touch me.' Valerian asked to see the angel, but Cecelia told him that he must first be baptized."

"Wasn't he mad at Cecilia?" asked Alaide.

"No," Dominic replied. "He loved her very much and wanted only to please her. And so he went to Pope Urban to be instructed. He saw the glorious angel and was baptized. Then he became a devout follower of Our Lord. After he returned to Rome, he worked with others to provide a burial for martyred Christians. When the Romans arrested him, he refused to bow down to their gods and was executed by the sword."

"That's so sad," Paperin exclaimed.

"What then became of Cecilia?" I inquired.

"She began to preach and converted over four hundred souls," Dominic answered. "She, too, was arrested and sentenced to suffocation in the baths. The fires were stoked, but Cecilia did not even break a sweat that night. She was ordered beheaded, but the executioners struck three times and her head was not severed. She lived three days to sing of the glory of Our Lord, while crowds gathered to collect her holy blood."

This is the life we're asked to emulate? I thought in horror. But Dominic continued.

"Cecilia is the patron saint of music. On her wedding day and on her deathbed, she filled her head with divine music and found the strength to endure. You, too, will do the same. The sainted Augustine once wrote that to fall in love with God is the greatest romance; to seek him, the greatest adventure; and to find him, the greatest human achievement. I wish to teach you how to chant the psalms, for when you sing to God, you will become enchanted with your Savior.

"Chanting is just like speaking, but it is set to music. Do not be timid in your chanting. Let your voice emanate from the depths of your soul, but do not become enamored of its sound. Allow your voice to join in harmony with those around you so that together you make one prayer to God. Just listen and repeat after me:

Audi Filia et vide et inclina aurem tuam . . ." sang Dominic in a fine voice so deep and clear it brought tears to my eyes.

"Hear, O daughter, consider and incline your ear;
forget your people and your father's house,
and the king will desire your beauty."

We all followed.

Dear God, I knew that at that moment something had changed. No longer could I imagine that I was singing alone with Dominic. As my voice swelled it joined in harmony with all my sisters, and Dominic's voice grew dimmer. Please, God, I remember praying, don't let them steal Dominic from me. I sang louder, hoping my piety would draw his attention, but Dominic flashed me a withering glance. When we had finished, he offered his rebuke,

"The purpose of your singing must always be for the glory of God. To let your voice stand out among the others displays the sin of pride."

How my soul ached with shame. I was certain that Dominic could read my thoughts and knew why I had raised my voice, and I was certain that my sisters knew his words were meant for me. For the remainder of the feast day liturgy, I mouthed the words in silence as my sisters sang around me.

And, in the weeks following, I thought of Saint Cecelia and sought for other ways of winning Dominic's approval. Perhaps it was not possible for me to earn his love, but if I could be more like her I might regain his admiration. I kept my eyes directed downward. I practiced walking chastely, taking small steps and trying not to let my hips sway from side to side. I learned to blend my voice with my sisters so that I could not be accused of pride. I indulged myself in fantasies of martyrdom, imagining that I was burning at the stake, so deep in prayer that I could not feel the flames searing my flesh. And all the while I prayed that Dominic was noticing my meekness and devotion.

Now that the masonry had been completed, Dominic had less chance to observe me. There was no longer need for us to work alongside the men. All nine of us were charged with more womanly tasks. We took turns gathering water and sweeping the caked dirt floors. Gentiana and Alaide took control of the kitchen. They ground oats and barley, when they could get them, to make our bread; they rationed the winter vegetables and kept a pottage simmering on the fire. We had been given wool with which to make our habits and Paperin and Curtslana spun it into yarn. Riccarda took on the job of weaving, and Jordana became our seamstress.

Berengaria, Clarette, and I had laid the garden to rest for the winter. We had not yet the herbs to make a real apothecary, but we prepared what we had harvested. We dried the chamomile for tea to sooth the stomach and the nerves; we soaked the feverfew leaves in wine to make a tincture to ease headaches; and we crushed lemon balm with oil as a salve for insect bites or wounds. When we had time, we helped Jordana with the sewing.

When we were not engaged in work and prayer, we spent our days preparing to receive our vows. Dominic took charge of our religious formation. In the morning after nones and in the evening after vespers, he gathered us in the chapter house for instruction on the Bible, theology, and the ways of the Church.

"There is but one truth, handed down from the apostles and preserved in the teachings of the Holy Catholic Church. You have been poisoned by the lies of heretics," he asserted from behind the small altar, "and you must be certain of this truth before you ask God to receive you into his Church as postulates."

And so, each night, he addressed the errors that Guilhabert had taught us.

"There is only one God," he began that first evening. "It is He who created all within the heavens and the earth and then declared them good."

"But isn't God eternal spirit?" Riccarda objected. "How could he deign to create finite things?"

"God is pure love," responded Dominic, "far greater than that of which your mind can comprehend. Our Lord Jehovah made all things that he might pour out love upon them and receive it in return."

"But Bruna says Jehovah is a demon," asserted Paperin.

We all flinched in unison as Dominic's fist hit the altar. "You will not speak such heresy within these walls," he spat. "Jehovah is the One True God. I know that you have been taught that an Evil God created the material world, but it is not so. Just look around you. Every particle of creation—from the intricacy of a rose to the stars of the cosmos—they all reveal the glory of God to those who have the eyes to see."

"How can we know this to be true?" inquired Jordana.

"We know it because both the holy scriptures and God's gift of reason tell us it is so," Dominic replied. "The heretics withheld from you the book of Genesis and the sacred psalms. As you chant the Daily Office, you will come to know the glory of God's creation in your heart. Listen to the word of the Lord." Dominic raised his arms. And as if in a trance, he began to chant Psalm 19:

"The Heavens declare the glory of God,
    And the firmament shows his handiwork
Day to day pours forth speech and the night declares
    knowledge.

There is no speech; there are no words; their voice is not
      heard;
Yet their voice goes out to all the earth,
and their words to the end of the world."

I too stood entranced. Dear God, I truly was not sure whether the
longing I felt was for Your glory or the one who sang of it. I was hardly
aware of the tears that leaked onto my cheeks as Dominic continued:

"In the deep has he set a pavilion for the sun
      it comes forth like a bridegroom from his chamber;
      it rejoices like a champion to run its course.
It goes forth to the uttermost edge of the Heavens
      and runs about to the end of it again.
Nothing is hidden from its burning heat."

I barely knew that I had joined my voice with his in the final
antiphon. But he knew. For a precious moment his searing eyes
locked onto mine. Quickly, he looked away and urged the others to
join in the singing. They all did so, but it was too late. I had seen the
rise of color in his cheeks and a hint of longing flashing in his eyes.
My hope remained alive.

As the days moved into winter, I was most truly lost in reveries
of sweetest love. At morning prayer, I told myself it was Your Son,
Our Lord, who filled my heart to overflowing; but by the evening,
when Dominic returned from his labors, I was not so certain. Was it
a sin, Dear God, for me to long for him, for my head to spin when he
walked through the door and my breath to quicken when he stood
behind the altar?

Santa Deu, of course I know the answer. The pangs I felt for
Dominic are most surely signs of my original sin. If I were favored
by Your grace, I would wish to live as chastely as Cecilia and our

Blessed Lady did. But Lord, I could not help myself. My yearning for Dominic distracted me from catechism and tainted my devotions. You know, God, how I tried to keep my longing trained upon Your gracious Son. I offered fervent prayers that You might turn my heart from Dominic. I fasted, and I knelt in nightly Vigil on the jagged stones until my knees were raw. And God, you must have heard my plea for You chose to send Guillelmette to Prouilhes.

We had just completed sext psalms, offering thanks for the fullness of the day, when Father Guilhem came into the chapter house and bid Dominic come with him. We had finished with our midday meal by the time they returned, followed by two young women. I recognized them instantly as the novices I had once met in the church in Fanjeaux. The younger one was small and round with a warm glow in her brown eyes; the older was tall and graceful, with the look of one who commands authority.

"Elmina, Berengaria, and Clarette, I don't believe you have met the daughters of Na Gracia. This is Guillelmette," he said pointing to the tall, lovely one, "and her sister's name is Raymundine. They will be joining us here at Prouilhe. Both are sisters of the Cistercian Order and have received a Catholic education. Guillelmette can read and write Latin." Dominic looked at her with an admiration that made my stomach churn. "Please make them feel welcome," he declared, "for they will be of great service to our community."

I wondered whether they remembered me as the small girl they'd met praying in the church at Fanjeaux, but they gave no sign of recognition. That evening at vespers, I could hear Guillelmette singing. Dear God, her voice was like an angel's, floating high and clear above the rafters. *Why does he not rebuke her for making her voice heard?* I wondered sullenly. But Dominic said nothing.

After the service we again gathered in the chapter house, this time eleven in number.

"Might I ask a question?" ventured Berengaria.

"Please speak," responded Dominic.

"You said yesterday that God created all the world and called it good. If that is so, where do the demons come from?"

"Guillelmette, would you like to answer Berengaria?" Dominic responded.

"The Devil and the other demons were created naturally good by God, but they were jealous of God and fell into death out of envy. They listened to the voice of temptation and chose of their own free will to rebel against God," she answered, basking in Dominic's approving nod.

But that doesn't explain anything, I wanted to scream. *If they were envious of God, they were created in sin. Where did the sin of envy come from? How could a loving God allow a soul to become so consumed that she turns her back on God?* But I said nothing and prayed that Dominic did not see the sullen anger building within me.

It was only a week later that Dominic called us into the chapter house for an important meeting.

"The time has almost come for you to become cloistered as postulants to your Savior," he began. "You will prepare to take the vows of poverty, chastity, and obedience. You will look to our Blessed Lady as your example, remaining pure in all your ways, and welcoming our Holy Savior into your body, heart, and soul. Two days after Christmas, on the feast day of St. John the Evangelist, you will each receive your habit."

"What will our habit look like?" asked pretty Alaide. "Will we receive a veil?"

"You will wear white tunics of the wool your sisters have woven. They will be covered by a mantel and a veil of black," he replied. "You will adopt an order of silence and abide under the Rule of Saint Augustine, that you may live harmoniously, intent upon God in oneness of mind and heart."

"An order of silence?" queried little Paperin. "Will we not be allowed to talk?"

"Of course there will be times when you may speak," Dominic replied. "You will sing God's praises in the Daily Office. You will offer your confessions. You may request to speak at meetings in the chapter house and to hold counsel with your prior and prioress. But remember this, my Paperin—there is great joy in holding silence before the Lord, and you will come to know it. You will receive from God the gift of contemplation, and through your prayers you will support our sacred mission."

"Pray tell," inquired Clarette, "what is that mission?"

Dominic took a deep breath and his eyes began to shine. "Our sacred mission is nothing less than to spread God's truth throughout Christendom. The Languedoc has fallen into error and its people do not fully understand the sinfulness of their ways. Its priests are ignorant of both scripture and theology, and they are easily swayed from their path. God has called me to found an order of preachers to teach the truth and eradicate the scourge of heresy. We will live in simplicity as the Albigensian perfecti do. We will travel from town to town and demonstrate to all we meet the error of their ways. And you, my daughters, will support our mission through your prayers and penitence. We have appealed to Pope Innocent III for his support. Meanwhile we will work with the papal legates. Bishop Diego is going to Pamiers, and I have been assigned to preach throughout the countryside of the Narbonne. I will be making my home in Carcassonne."

I froze wide-eyed and let out a gasp of alarm. "You're leaving us?" I asked in disbelief and tried to search his eyes.

Dominic did not return my gaze. "God calls me to far greater work. It is no longer possible for me stay here at Prouilhe," he said. "But of course I will often return. This monastery and the nurture of your souls are dear to my own heart."

If that be so, why are you leaving us? I wanted to cry out, but asked instead, "How will we continue with our studies if you are absent? Who will teach us our catechism? Who will consecrate the host and lead our singing of the Daily Office?"

"You won't be left alone, Elmina," Dominic attempted to assure me. "Clarette's brother, Guilhem, will celebrate the Mass and serve as chaplain to your spiritual care. I have appointed Guillelmette to be your prioress. She will instruct you in the Bible and the teachings of the Church. She will lead you in singing the Offices. You will obey her as your *domina*, and she is charged with discipline and the enforcement of the Rule."

Dear God, I could not breathe. My head began to spin, and I barely heard as Dominic continued.

"Your days will now fall into gentle rhythm as you chant the Daily Offices," he said. "Each morning you will rise to sing the Angelus, and the Blessed Virgin will lift your souls to God."

"I fear I do not know the Angelus," Jordana admitted.

"Guillelmette will teach it to you," Dominic replied, "and many other things as well. There is a great deal you have yet to learn."

No one else raised her voice. Clarette glanced toward me and could surely read the sorrow in my eyes. When Dominic dismissed us, we both arose and left to finish hanging the last of the chamomile to dry.

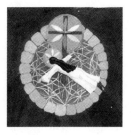

Chapter 11

OUT OF THE DEPTHS

When we had reached the drying hut I turned to her in my despair. "What will become of us when Dominic is gone?"

"Don't be afraid," Clarette responded, "for God is present, whether Dominic is here or not. You know that the Blessed Virgin watches over you and that Jesus will guide you if you turn to him. His Holy Spirit will not leave you comfortless."

"But I don't want to be alone with the Blessed Virgin or Jesus or the Holy Spirit," I wailed in protest. "It is Dominic whom I love."

"Shush," replied Clarette. "Do not speak such a foolish thing." But her words came too late.

"You are a little whore!" a voice behind me hissed. I swung around to find Guillelmette glowering at us. "You've been instructed to observe the rule of silence, and in its stead have spoken blasphemy against our Holy Mother and her Son. How dare you give devotion to your brother Dominic? I've noticed how you pass close by him in the chapter house. I've seen you fix your eyes on him in chapel. Do you not know the Rule of Augustine? It is a sin to gaze upon a man or look upon one with desire or wish him to desire you."

Dear God, I knew that she was right. I lowered my head in

shame, and Guillelmette grabbed my arm. "Clarette, you are dismissed," she uttered curtly. "Elmina, you will lay down your basket and follow me. She led me to the chapel and pointed to the wooden crucifix above the altar. Then Guillelmette bid me lie down upon the icy stone floor and stretch my arms as if I, too, were on the cross. "Heed well the Rule of Augustine," she warned and started to recite the words that would become so familiar to my soul:

"Do not say that your heart is pure if there is immodesty of the eye, because the unchaste eye carries the message of an impure heart. And when such hearts disclose their unchaste desires in a mutual gaze, even without saying a word, then it is that chastity suddenly goes out of their life.

"You will not move until morning. You will remain in penitence and contemplation of your wretched sin. And I shall pray that God have mercy on your piteous soul," she said. Then Guillelmette spun around and walked away.

Do You remember, God, how I lay prostrate there before You? I thought about the suffering You once bore upon the cross, and my shame flooded over me. I shook and cried until the tears would come no more. At vespers and at compline, the sisters processed around my miserable body and sang the Office as if I were not there.

That night, the sharp December wind that heralds winter howled through the belfry and seeped into my soul. The frigid floor sucked out my body's warmth and my heart became as ice. I feared that I might freeze to death without the benefit of final rites, and I begged that You forgive my sinful longings.

Were You listening then, God? Perhaps You were, for You did not see fit to take my life. It must have been past midnight when I heard the iron hinges of the oaken chapel door and Dominic's footsteps striding up the nave. As he came near, I closed my eyes and held my breath.

"The sins of the flesh are not so easily subdued," I heard him say
as if he fully grasped its truth. "But know these words of the Apostle
Paul: 'If you live according to the flesh you will die, but if by the
Spirit you put to death the deeds of the body you will live. Those
who belong to Christ Jesus have crucified the flesh with its passions
and desires.'"

Dominic moved slowly past my prostrate body and stood before
me. He bid me look at him as he removed his tunic and his hairshirt.
I should not have done so, for I observed his dear scarred back and
recoiled.

"'Tis not an easy thing to tame the flesh," he said, "but I can
teach you how it's done."

He then took out a wooden *flagellum* with knotted ox-hide lashes
woven round its base. He started chanting in his most resounding
voice, "*Domine ne in furore tuo arguas me . . .*

O Lord, do not rebuke me in Your anger
      or discipline me in Your wrath.
For my iniquities have gone over my head;
      they weigh like a burden too heavy for me.
My wounds grow foul and fester because of my
      foolishness.
I am utterly bowed down and prostrate;
      all day long I go around mourning.
For my loins are filled with burning,
      and there is no soundness in my flesh.
I am utterly spent and crushed;
      I groan because of the tumult of my heart."

As he sang out, Dominic began to swing the whip from side to
side so that its lashes cut into his back. He did not falter as his flesh
turned pink and then in time to deepest red.

He kept on chanting as if in a trance. "*De profundis clamavi ad te Domini:* Out of the depths, I have cried out to You, O Lord. Lord, hear my prayer."

Soon welts arose, and drops of blood dripped down his naked back. When he had completed six full Psalms, he laid the whip beside me.

"This is my gift to you," he said as he walked away.

Dear God, that night is burned into my soul. I had loved You since I was but a little girl. I had longed for You and had wished to offer up my life to be Your bride. But God, my longing was not pure and chaste. I dreamt of earthly love. And in my heart I did commit adultery and worshipped Dominic as if he were my God.

It is a shameful thing to live as woman, God. As I lay there, I begged to know why You created us with yearnings and desires. I asked, *Why would You tempt us as You tempted Eve so long ago?* I ask it still. *If You abhor our mortal state, why did You make us thus?*

I thought then, God, about the Good Christians. They too despised their corporal state and vowed to shed its deathly hold. Their perfecti also mortified their flesh and lived a life of fasting and denial. But they at least attempted an answer to my question. They simply claimed that You were not the one who made our bodies.

As I lay rigid on the stone, the cold coursed through my veins. The hours stood still and morning would not come. Finally, I raised my head to look upon Your body, hanging from the cross, and dared to pray. I asked for Your forgiveness and begged our Holy Mother to reveal her way of chastity and grace. When I lowered my head, I stared in horror at the *flagellum* beside me, and I knew what I must do. Rising to my knees I freed my arms from their sleeves and slipped my tunic to my waist. I grabbed the whip and gently stroked its knots and ox-hide lashes. Then I took a deep breath and raised my arm. As I brandished it across my shoulders, I barely felt its smart. And so I swung more forcefully. The ox-hide seared my flesh and I recoiled at its sting. Over and over again, I let its lashes cut into my flesh as I prayed the words of Augustine, "*Domine Jesu, noverim me, noverim te . . .*

LORD Jesus, let me know myself and know Thee
And desire nothing save only Thee.
Let me hate myself and love Thee.
Let me do everything for the sake of Thee.

Let me humble myself and exalt Thee.
Let me think of nothing except Thee.
Let me die to myself and live to Thee
Let me accept whatever happens as from Thee."

Dear God, I felt Your Spirit stirring through the numbness of my body, and I prayed more fervently:

"Let me banish self and follow Thee,
And ever desire to follow Thee.
Let me fly from myself and take refuge in Thee,
That I may deserve to be defended by Thee.

Let me fear for myself, let me fear Thee,
And let me be among those who are chosen by Thee.
Let me distrust myself and put my trust in Thee.
Let me be willing to obey for the sake of Thee."

Ah, God, Your Spirit moved along my spine and settled in the darkness of my hidden parts. It made them to burn with a blessed fire, and I did not know whether my stifled scream was one of pain or pleasure. I ended my prayer:

"Let me cling to nothing save only to Thee,
And let me be poor because of Thee.

Look upon me, that I may love Thee.
Call me that I may see Thee,
And forever enjoy Thee."

I put down the *flagellum* and pulled up my tunic. I lay again upon the icy floor, stretched out my arms and sank into a deep, deep slumber.

Before the break of day, Guillelmette walked into the chapel. She saw my bloodied tunic and the *flagellum* beside me and nodded her approval. She then bid me rise for matins.

That morning Dominic was gone. It was Father Guilhem who led the service and celebrated Mass. My sisters looked away when I stumbled in. After we ate our bread, Guillelmette handed me another tunic. "Go to the river and scrub your own until it is clean," she said. I did as she instructed, and of that night we did not speak again.

The next two weeks were filled with preparations. At breakfast as we ate, Guillelmette read the Rule of Saint Augustine aloud.

"Before all else, dear sisters, love God and then your neighbor, because these are the chief commandments given to us. The main purpose for you having come together is to live harmoniously in your house, intent upon God in oneness of mind and heart." She told us that it is to this end we will follow the precepts of the early Church as found in the acts of the apostles. They had all things in common and made to each one according to her need.

"You, too, will call nothing your own," Guillelmette continued. "Even your mattress and your habit are but yours on loan. You should consider it a privilege to share them should the need arise."

I couldn't help but think how much the Rule resembled that of the Good Christian *perfecti*, and once more I wondered if Amelha was now one of them. But Guillelmette fixed her eyes on me and broke into my musings with her words:

"Subdue the flesh, so far as your health permits, by fasting and abstinence from food and drink. In your walk, deportment, and in all actions, let nothing occur to give offense to anyone who sees you, but only what becomes your holy state of life. Although your eye may chance to rest upon some man or other, you must not fix your gaze upon any man. If you notice in some one of your sisters this wantonness of the eye, admonish her at once so that the beginning of evil will not grow more serious but will be promptly corrected."

I blushed and glanced around the room. Several sets of eyes met mine before I looked away.

"Please know that I hold no ill will toward any of you," Guillel-mette continued without taking her gaze from me. "It is my duty as your prioress to hold you to the highest levels of propriety."

She then read on:

"Just as you have your food from the one pantry, so, too, you are to receive your clothing from a single wardrobe. Your clothing should be cleaned as the superior shall determine, so that too great a desire for clean clothing may not be the source of interior stains on the soul."

We had begun to sew the tunics and the mantels we would wear at our enclosure, and a wave of anticipation flowed over me. Dear God, I dared to hope that when I donned the habit, it would cover my shame.

Next Guillelmette read of "the superior." She was, of course, speaking about herself:

"'The superior should be obeyed as a mother with the respect due her, so as not to offend God in her person, and, even more so, the priest who bears responsibility for you all.'"

I must take care to obey Guillelmette, I thought, *for I do not wish to offend Dominic in any way.* Then the sinking realization came. Dominic was no longer with us. It was Father Guilhem who now served as our priest. I sighed and listened vacantly as Guillelmette concluded:

"The Lord grant that you may observe all these precepts in a spirit of charity as lovers of spiritual beauty, giving forth the good odor of Christ in the holiness of your lives: not as slaves living under the law but as women living in freedom under grace."

Dear God, I must confess that living under the Rule as enforced by Guillelmette did not feel like freedom. For a moment I wondered if I should have chosen a different path. But then I realized that there is no freedom for a woman anywhere. She is always under the rule of a father or husband, a perfect or a mother superior. I prayed that one day I might come to experience life at Prouilhe not as a slave but as a woman living in freedom under Your grace.

By Christmas Day, all was prepared for our enclosure. Nine white tunics and nine black mantles lay folded in the chapter house. Nine veils lay waiting in the chapel. We had swept the floors and polished the brass until it shone with a light befitting our reception into our Savior's arms. And best of all, Dominic had returned from his travels. He would officiate at all three Christmas Masses and be present for our enclosure.

Dear Lord, it was a sacred Christmas day. We arose at the first hour. The Angelus bell struck three times and Dominic again led us in chanted prayer, "*Angelus domini nuntiavit Mariae,*" he sang. "*Ave Maria, gratia plena . . .*

The angel of the Lord declared unto Mary . . .
Hail Mary, full of grace, the Lord is with thee.
Blessed art thou amongst women,
    and blessed is the fruit of Your womb, Jesus."

At dawn we sang the Shepherd's Mass and at the twelfth hour we gathered again for the Mass of the Divine Word. Our Christmas meal was modest, for we were saving our stores for the grand feast to come two days hence. But Curtslana and Alaide had added chicken to our pottage and made a Buche de Noel decorated with meringue mushrooms. On that day, God, I set aside my jealous longings and joined in the festivities.

The next day, Bishop Folc arrived from Toulouse with his full entourage. Guillelmette told us that he would call each one of us into the chapter house to confirm our devotion and desire to enter the religious life. We went about our daily tasks anxiously awaiting our turn. I had just laid down my pails from gathering water when I heard the bishop's servant call my name, "Guilhemina de Beaupuys."

Dear God, I froze in place. I thought upon my shame and wondered what of it the bishop had been told. With sinking heart, I followed the servant into the chapter room. "Good morrow, Guilhemina" he said to me. "Our Holy Father has blessed us this day with your desire to serve him."

With my eyes lowered, I knelt before the bishop and responded, "I give thanks that you have come to sanctify our convent and vocation. And if it please you, I am called Elmina."

"And so, Elmina, why come you to this house of God?" he asked.

I took a deep breath trying to remember the words that we'd been taught. "Since I was but a girl, I've loved the Holy Church and wished to do the bidding of Our Lord and Savior. I did blaspheme and live among the heretics, but I have ever longed to serve the One True God. I know that Jesus Christ did live as flesh to free us from our wretchedness, and in his shelter I, too, wish to live my life. I pray that I might make my home among my sisters and dwell in purity and chastity as did the Blessed Mother," I answered him.

"That is all well and good," the Bishop answered. "But you have gazed upon your prior Dominic and disavowed your loyalty to God."

My heart did sink at the realization that he knew everything. I hung my head and tears welled in my eyes. "It is so," I replied. "My heart has lusted after Dominic and I have greatly sinned. I have lain in prostrate penance for my transgression and mortified my flesh before our Savior. I will continue in such vigil the remainder of my days, if I might have the chance. O my most reverend Father, I beg you to absolve me; please do not hold this sin against me forever."

The bishop breathed a deep sigh and then placed his hand upon my shoulder. "Elmina," he said, "your flesh is weak. You will continue with your nightly penances and wear the cilise to remind you of the curse of your flesh."

What is the cilise? I wanted to ask but held my tongue.

The bishop continued, "But I can see you love Our Lord and long to serve him. I shall allow you to assume the habit and pray that God has mercy upon your wayward soul."

Dear God, You know the joy that welled within my heart was tempered by my shame. I kissed the ring upon the prelate's pudgy finger and rose to join my sisters in their final preparations.

The night before we were to take the veil, Guillelmette put a bowl upon our head. She took the scissors Bishop Folc had brought and, one by one, she cut our hair above our ear. When she had cropped my russet locks, she offered me two crowns: a crown of flowers and a crown of thorns. "Which one do you prefer?" she asked.

"The crown of thorns," I answered dutifully. She nodded at my choice and bid Gentiana to come forward next.

When she had finished cutting all our hair, the floor was covered with intermingled locks of golden curls and flaxen, black and russet tresses. I stared in quiet shock as Alaide cried and Guillelmette swept away the glory of our maidenhood.

I passed the night in silent vigil with my sisters and shared my anxious thoughts with You alone. Tomorrow I would be enclosed and never step into the world again. I wondered if the walls of Prouilhe would be my sanctuary or my prison. Dear God, You know I had a passing wish to leave behind my shame and penitence and flee. But where might I find haven? And how would I survive?

As I knelt in the darkness I came to feel Your presence swirling in the air around me.

"Abide with me," You seemed to say. I took a deep breath and then glanced around the room at my sisters, also deep in prayer. And I knew this was meant to be my home and they my family. I was naïve enough to entrust my young life to Your Holy Church.

When daylight came we sang the Angelus at lauds before we gathered in the chamber house. It was the feast of St. John the Evangelist, but there was no Holy Mass that morning. Instead Dominic entered to speak with us.

"My dearest daughters," he began. I stared intently at the floor. "We must give thanks to God for saving you from sacrilege and bringing you to safety in this place. Your souls were in great jeopardy, and now through God's great mercy, they may come to find salvation. As to your former heresy, may you be ever penitent and pray unceasingly for other heretics to follow your example. There still is much for you to do before the twelfth hour of the Mass. I shall retire and let Guillelmette instruct you."

Dear God, I took great care that my eyes not betray my heart, but the hair upon my arms took note as Dominic walked past me to the door. Reluctantly, I turned my mind to Guillelmette.

"You each will need to bathe before you bow to take the veil," she said.

"A bath?" objected Paperin in horror.

"A bride must always bathe before her wedding," Guillelmette replied. "Elmina, you will go first." She'd hung a linen sheet around a barrel in the corner, and she bid me stand behind it. She first picked lice from my cropped hair; she ordered me to shed my tunic and my shift and step into the barrel. Then she handed me a cloth and soap made from olive oil and salt. I noticed there a bucket filled with water. "First wet the cloth, and wash the dirt from off your body," instructed Guillelmette. "And do not let your washcloth linger upon any place," she warned. I did as I was told. "Now bend over the bucket and wet your hair," she said. I did so and she handed me a mixture of egg whites and ashes. "Use this to clean your hair," she said. "Then pour the water over you to rinse yourself."

The icy water made me shriek. I feared that I might catch my death of cold, but I did not. She handed me a towel and gave me a clean shift. Dear God, I did feel ripe and cleansed before You, ready to commit my life into Your care.

When we had bathed, we went into the chapel to decorate the altar. Berengaria, Clarette, and I had saved dried flowers and herbs for the occasion, and Alaide had made a full livre candle that would burn through all the ceremony. Beside our veils there lay a stoup of holy water and the aspergillum the bishop would use to sprinkle each of us. Before the altar lay the *prie-dieu* where we'd kneel to take our vows. All was prepared.

We gathered in the chapter house to don our habits, but Guillelmette beckoned me to step outside. She handed me a heavy belt with iron rings and inward-pointing tines. "This is your cilise," she said. "Tie it around your waist to mortify your flesh and keep you mindful of your need for penitence."

I took the heavy object from her hand and stared at it with horror.

"It will not do you harm," said Guillelmette. "You will soon become accustomed to its prongs. Go quickly now and put it on. No one need know that you are wearing the cilise."

I did as I was told. I raised my shift and placed the icy rings around my waist. I pulled the hemp cords so the tines pressed at my flesh and tied them tight. I hung my head and stepped back in the chapter room. When I lifted my arms to don my habit, the tines of the cilise poked at my tender belly. *Is this how I am to live the remainder of my life?* I asked of You, but I knew well the answer.

At the noon hour the tower bells began to toll. We formed a line behind Guillelmette, and Dominic appeared to lead the way. Slowly we processed across the frozen ground toward the Chapel de

Ste. Marie. With every step the tines of the cilise reminded me of my unworthiness.

As we entered the chapel, I was surprised to find it filled with people. I quickly scanned the room for Mama, Papa, and Amelha, but of course they were not there. There were monks with robes of the Cistercian Order and fancy ladies dressed in silk, but I recognized no soul but Na Gracia. Our cloistering would be complete, and there could be no heretics within its sacred walls.

Dear God, You know the pang of loneliness that welled within my heart. But then Dominic began to chant the Angelus. My eyes darted in his direction. Quickly, I lowered them to the floor, and he alone took note of my transgression. As we processed, the tines against my skin awoke me from my maudlin reverie. My heart then turned to You, God. I thought of Your Dear Son as he walked the road to Calvary. I saw that in my trifling pain I would be joined to the enormity of his, and grateful tears began to form. My heart rejoiced as the last chorus ended and we took our places kneeling at the altar.

Dominic opened the service with a prayer.

"Graciously enlighten thy Church, O Lord," he intoned, "that she may be illumined by the doctrines of Saint John, thy apostle and evangelist, and thus obtain the gifts of eternity."

Father Guilhem read from the Gospel of St. John the Evangelist the verses that remind us, God, that You are our creator:

In the beginning was the Word, intoned Guilhem.
And the Word was with God and the Word was God.
He was in the beginning with God.
All things came into being through him,
and without out him not one thing came into being.

For a moment I thought about the Good Christians. They too recited John at the *consolamentum*, although they saw it differently.

I remembered Sister Bruna teaching us that in Jesus, not one material thing came into being. My mind again fled to Amelha, and I ached to have her here. Most certainly by now she was a perfect, and I wondered if she ever thought of me. For one short moment I dared hope that You might bless both my cloistering and her *consolamentum*. I bent in earnest prayer until a sharp prick from the cilise brought me from my musings.

I remember full well the beauty of that day, the words and chants that brought us to the moment of our vows. Berengaria went first and Guillelmette came forward to pin her veil to her wimple. One at a time we each lay prostrate on the floor as Bishop Folc reminded us of what we were to do. When my turn came, I lay again upon the icy stone. The cilise pressed against me, lest I forget the stain upon my soul.

"*Profisciere anima Christiana de hoc mundo,*" intoned the bishop. "Go Christian soul, escape the prison of your body, because Heaven offers you freedom. You have now shed the garments of your former life; you have donned the habit that you may be dead unto the world, your family, and all that is without."

I lay there, God, and saw again the Blessed Mother by my side. My heart opened in prayer:

My Queen, My Mother, I offer myself entirely to thee.
And to show my devotion to thee,
I offer thee this day, my eyes, my ears,
my mouth, my heart, my whole being without reserve . . .

I heard the bishop's words as if in distant echo, "Rise now into the sacred arms of Christ." As I stood up, he bid me kneel upon the *prie-dieu* and repeat my solemn vows.

"I, Guilhemina de Beaupuys, do take the vows of poverty, chastity, and obedience to God and to the Blessed Virgin, according to the Rule of Blessed Augustine."

I swallowed hard and continued.

"I also vow obedience to my prior Dominic, my prioress Guillel-mette, my priest Father Guilhem, and their successors."

Then Guillelmette, as *domina* of our little order, set a wimple upon my head. She let a long black veil unfold and pinned it there.

Dear God, I was then wed unto Your precious Son, in body, mind, and spirit. I felt His presence in the air I breathed, and His dear love came coursing through my veins. I vowed to You and to my very soul that I would ne'er forsake my vows. And I promised that to Your Holy Church I would be ever true.

Chapter 12

IN NEED OF MERCY

A nd so, God, we began our cloistered life. The day after we
took our vows, Dominic left for Carcassonne and after
breakfast Guillelmette called us into the chapter house. The
pricks of my cilise were already becoming familiar.

"This is your daily schedule," she said holding a paper lettered
in her careful hand.

    Midnight: Matins
Morning sleep
    Dawn: Lauds
Prayer and devotions
    Sunrise: Prime
Wash
Morning meal and readings
    Midmorning: Terce and Mass
Chapter
Opus Manuum
    Midday: Sext
Dinner
Opus Manuum

Afternoon: None
Instruction
    Eventide: Vespers
Study or prayer
    Before Retiring: Compline
Evening Sleep or Vigil

"You will commit it to your memory and follow it with diligence. I will ring the chapel bell to signal it is time for Daily Offices. It matters not what you are doing—you will cease your work or prayer immediately. For matins, lauds, prime, and vespers you will gather in the chapel choir. For terce, sext, and none we will meet here in the chapter room."

"But, Guillelmette, what if we don't wake up for matins?" Paperin inquired.

"You will address me as *domina*," the prioress corrected. "And you may not break the rule of silence, Paperin, unless you have received consent to do so," she added in rebuke. "If you desire to speak, you will place your hands together thus," she said and brought her fingers to her lips.

Paperin nodded.

"I will make sure that you awaken after I ring the bell," the *domina* continued, "but you will soon adjust to the rhythms of your day and awaken on your own."

Alaide bowed her head and touched beseeching fingers to her lips. Guillelmette nodded her consent.

"Are we to remain awake once we have sung our matins?" she inquired.

"After you've offered prayers to God you may return to bed until lauds," Guillelmette replied.

Then Gentiana gave the sign she wished to speak.

"I'm very sorry for my ignorance, but I do not read Latin," she began. "Pray tell what is the *opus manuum?*"

"It is the sacred work that you will give to God," Guillelmette explained. "For now, most of you shall continue with the labor you have already been given. In time, you will learn to do all the work and rotate jobs. Berengaria, Clarette, and Elmina, during the growing season you will continue to oversee our gardens and the apothecary, but in the winter months I will assign you other tasks to do. Berengaria, you will be our cellarer. You will take charge of our provisions. You'll make a list of what we have and inform Father Guilhem of our needs."

Berengaria nodded her assent.

"Clarette, I will teach you how to make candles. It will be your job to make sure we are never without light."

Clarette opened her mouth as if to reply. Then she remembered the silence and gave a nod as well.

"And, Elmina, you will be the keeper of the kitchen fire. You will bring in wood and gather kindling. Throughout the winter months you will light the fire each morning before matins and keep it from dying throughout the day."

Keeper of the fire? I almost gasped. My childhood terror reared its ugly head. I could not do that job. Did not Guillelmette know that fire sets off a terror in my soul? Had she not noticed that I avoided the fire pit and always sat in the refectory with my back turned to the flames of the kitchen fire? I felt the color draining from my face and raised my fingers to my ashen lips.

"Please, *Domina*," I whispered. "I don't mind carrying the wood or gathering kindling, but I am afraid of flames. I beg of you not to make me keeper of the fire."

Guillelmette looked at me as if I were a begging cur. "Just yesterday you vowed obedience to your superior. Have you so easily forgotten? Come. I will show you what you have to do."

I'm sorry, God, I was not able to obey her. My heart was pounding, and my breath came fast and shallow. *Please no,* I begged her with a silent pleading. Just as at Dominic's disputation, I felt the blood drain from my head. The room began to spin, and I tumbled into a heap upon the floor. I heard my sisters rushing to my aid, but the prioress pushed them all away.

"*Perfect faith casts out fear,*" she intoned. "Elmina must stand up and face her fears. She will do her assigned task." Kneeling down she took me by the shoulders and shook me gently. "You will get up and learn to tend the fire," she ordered not unkindly. "And you may wait until tonight to do penance for your disobedience."

I stood up slowly, as if in a trance, and followed Guillelmette across the room. Dear God, I still do not know how I obeyed her. I looked upon the smoldering coals and shrank away. But the prioress pulled me forward. Handing me an iron rod she said, "Use this to push the coals into the center of the fire. Then lay more wood atop them." I did as I was told. The flames leapt up as if they were the very fires of Hell, and I released a scream. But every hour throughout the day I added yet another log and kept the fire alight.

That night after compline, I remained alone in the chapel. I recalled my disobedience and Guillelmette did not need to show me what to do.

Santa Deu, that first winter at Prouilhe, how You tested us. By February, the stores that Dominic had brought from Carcassonne were almost gone, and our late garden had not yielded vegetables enough to feed us. We no longer baked bread. Our only food was a thin pottage that Alaide and Curtslana kept upon the fire. They added barley, beans, and rye to the water in their pot and put in bits of beet and onion. On days the hens produced, they would put in an egg as well.

Dear God, from times of fasting I had known the pangs of hunger, but that winter was different. Our skin grew pale, and we cast our gaze upon the cross through sunken eyes. My cilise hung loosely round my waist and rattled as I walked. Slowly the pain of hunger just died away, and thoughts of bread turned into distant memories.

In their place I began to feel a deadness and fatigue that would not ease. O God, I called to You in my distress, but I could hear no answer. I must confess that a fury flared within me. *Why did Dominic bring us to this hovel of a monastery only to abandon us here? Why do You turn Your back on us when we have promised our whole lives to You?* I tried to do penance for my anger, but not even the *flagellum* brought relief to my soul.

Berengaria spoke with Father Guilhem and begged him to procure more food to see us through the spring. I am certain he did his best. Each week he would go out to ask for alms. Sometimes he would return with moldy oats or a sack of beans; but often he would come back with his head hung low and pockets empty. Neither the Church nor the Good Christians of Fanjeaux seemed to care much of our survival.

But God, despite my anger I did not sicken, for You graced me with the gift of a strong body. Others among us fared far worse than I. Jordana and Curtslana were the first to suffer with asthenia. Each day their strength drained from them, and soon their feebleness confined them to their beds. We did not yet have an infirmary, and so we nursed them in their hut and listened to them moan at night from costiveness. We had neither violet nor flax seeds to relieve their bowels; all we could do was urge them to drink chamomile tea and offer them an extra egg in their pottage when one was to be had.

Perhaps we all began to wonder if we had made a mistake following Dominic to Prouilhe, but beautiful Alaide was the most vocal about it. She'd look with horror when she caught the reflection of her gaunt face in the brass chalice or a bowl of water. One night she broke the silence as she slipped into her nightshift.

"This is not how I thought it would be," Alaide lamented. "I didn't follow Dominic to starve to death in some mud hovel. I thought we would become a proper monastery and live in more comfort than we had at the *ostal*. I pictured how lovely we would all look in our white habits as we knelt to sing the hours. But there is no beauty here. It is just ugliness and hardship. I do not wish to stay."

"But what would you do?" whispered little Paperin.

"I would agree to marry Jacques!" she answered without hesitation. "He wanted me and always told me that I was the most beautiful girl in Fanjeaux. Look at me now! I am so thin he would never even rest his eyes on me. And my lovely nose—it was my best feature, and now my face is so sunken it looks huge. Oh, what am I going to do? I do not want my beauty to waste away!"

Dear God, I knew Alaide's vanity was repugnant to You, but I would be lying if I said I did not have some of the same feelings. I too had not expected life at Prouilhe to be so hard. But I had no suitor who would take me back. I had made my vows, and I could not give up the hope that Dominic would soon return to us. And so I had no choice but to trust that You would see us through.

Then little Paperin took ill. She had become so thin it seemed that she might float away, and her bloated belly pushed against her ribs. She weakened so very quickly. It was as if her body did consume itself. She no longer wished to eat and wouldn't even drink the chamomile tea we prepared for her. Poor little Paperin. She moaned so softly in her sleep that we could barely hear her. As the February snows built up around us, Jordana and Curtslana grew slowly stronger. But not so dearest Paperin. Each night we took turns holding her and keeping vigil in the chapel. You know, O God, how hard we prayed for You to save her.

I begged to know why You would cause such a dear soul to suffer so. In my distress I went to Father Guilhem, forgetting he was a young man but five years older than me. I bowed my head and touched my fingers to my lips as Guillelmette had taught me, and I placed my right hand on my heart. He nodded and bid me to speak. And, God, You know how my foul doubts poured forth.

"Pray tell me why God makes Paperin to suffer so," I cried. "Why did He bring her to this place only to let her starve?"

Father Guilhem took a deep breath and spoke as if from a great distance. "God's ways are not our ways," he replied. "You must pray that her soul will find release."

"I cannot pray to any God who would allow such cruelty," I countered as tears began to stream upon my cheeks.

"Elmina, you utter blasphemy. Do you presume to know better than God? You will not speak such words again. Go to the chapel now. Prostrate yourself, and pray the Hail Mary one hundred times. And you will beg God to have mercy on your soul."

I bowed my head and fled into the chapel. Lying down before our Blessed Mother, I did begin to pray, "Hail Mary, full of grace, the Lord is with thee . . ." My tears turned into sobs, and the words rang hollow in my head. But I continued, "Blessed art thou among women and blessed is the fruit of thy womb, Jesus." Slowly the familiar cadences began to calm me, and when I had completed them a warm glow spread about my prostrate form. Lord Jesus, I looked around to see Your broken body on the cross, and I did feel Your arms around me, holding me and rocking me in Your eternal grace. I could almost hear You saying to me, *Dearest Elmina, all is well.*

I do not know how long I rested there in Your sacred holding. Time had stood still. I wished with all my heart that Your embrace might last forever, but of course it did not. My attention returned to the chapel and to the icy floor on which I lay. I was cold and sore. And yet, I knew that I was changed. I sensed with wordless certainty that my soul rested in the holy glow of Your eternal love. And I offered up to You my fervent prayer. *Indigent Misercordia Domine:*

"O God, we are in need of Your compassion,
especially our sister little Paperin.
Please make her well.
O my Jesus, forgive our sins, save us from the fires
of Hell; lead all souls to Heaven, especially those in most

need of they mercy.
Amen."

When I returned to the dormitory, Berengaria and Riccarda
were bathing dear Paperin. My heart sunk as I saw them gently dry
her flaccid limbs. But then, I heard her stir!
"Paperin's fever has broken," said Berengaria. "God has intervened on her behalf. Go quickly and bring some warm pottage." For
a moment I stood frozen, as if in a trance of wonder. *Was it possible,
God, that You heard my prayers and answered them?*
"What are you waiting for?" Berengaria repeated urgently. I
snapped to my senses and scurried across the courtyard.

It was during the early thaws of spring, two days before the feast
of the Annunciation, that Dominic returned, accompanied by two
new brothers.
"Please greet Brother Bernard and Brother Noel," he instructed.
Brother Bernard surveyed our withered frames and offered a
stiff bow. Brother Noel let his eyes settle on each one of us and
nodded his greeting as he did so. The two were laden with alms of
grain and oil. They carried medicines and new seeds for our garden.
That afternoon Jordana and Curtslana baked flax seed bread, and its
aroma filled our hearts with wild anticipation.
At eventide, we savored all its doughy goodness, and Dominic
again stood at the lectern. Instead of reading from the Rule or the
Lives of the Saints, he spoke to us of glorious news. Pope Innocent
had given his support to the mission of Diego and Dominic and
had set forth a new strategy for converting the Albigensians. No
longer would the legates and the missionary priests be asked to tra-
verse all the Languedoc. Instead, each one would focus on a single
region. Twelve new Cistercian abbots had been appointed to the
mission. Arnaud Amaury of Citeaux had arrived to join the legates at Montréal; Bishop Diego would stay in Pamiers; and Dominic

would maintain a base for the preachers right here at Prouilhe! They would live at the Church of St. Martins. Our part would be to provide food to nurture their bodies and prayers to support their sacred work. The archbishop, Berenger of Narbonne, had blessed this new approach. He'd given funds to help defray the costs of the endeavor and given a charter to what was now the *Sancta Praedicatio,* the Holy Preachers.

"My precious daughters of Prouilhe," Dominic asserted in his resounding voice, "we are together the body of Christ and we have been blessed with a most holy mission. Just as our bodies have many parts, so does the body of Christ. Diego, the brothers, and I will serve as its legs and voice, spreading the word of truth to the lost souls of the Languedoc. And you shall be the body's heart and hands. Through your sweet prayers and contemplation, you shall bless all our endeavors. Your steadfastness will give your brothers courage in the task that God has set before them. And through the work of your hands, you will provide the food and clothing and medicine that the Holy Preachers will need to fulfill their mission."

O God, as I listened to Dominic, I scarce could contain my excitement! I did not raise my eyes once as he spoke, but my soul did rejoice at having the red-haired preacher back at Prouilhe. The gleam in his eyes and the passion of his voice made my heart quiver, and I too was filled with a most holy zeal. I thought of my experience in the chapel, surrounded by the great love of Your Dearest Son. And I wanted to be a part of the *Santo Praedicatio*. At that moment, Dear God, I did forget that the Good Christians already knew the fullness of Jesus's love. I didn't think about their kindness or the sacred power I'd experienced at Aude's *consolamentum*. Instead, I too began to think of them as heretics in need of Christ's salvation. I even came to believe that Bonata, Aude, and Amelha would be damned to Hell if they were not brought into the Catholic Church. And I would be part of a mission to save them.

※

That spring of 1207, as the sun warmed the earth and shed its glow upon us, we were content—all of us, that is, but Alaide. We sang the Daily Offices with renewed joy as our voices blended with those of Dominic, Guilhem, and the new brothers. But Alaide grew quiet and morose. A melancholy air settled upon her face, and lines of worry marred her lovely brow. In prayer, she was distracted. She'd pull at her cropped russet locks and run her finger down her perfect nose. One afternoon in chapter, she touched her lips to ask if she might speak. Guillelmette nodded her consent.

"I cannot stay here," cried Alaide. "My heart is plagued with melancholy, and I can no longer pray. I do not belong in a monastery. There was a man in Fanjeaux who admired my beauty. I beg you to release me so that I might go and find him."

"Dear, Alaide," Guillelmette replied. "Do not be tempted by the demon of vainglory. You're young and you are foolish. It's true that you are beautiful, but your beauty will fade, and the man who admires it will look elsewhere if beauty is what he desires. The only true beauty is to be found within your soul. I will not give you leave to forsake your vows or sacrifice communion with Our Lord for such temporal pleasure."

"Please let me go," Alaide begged again. "My presence is no longer a blessing to the monastery."

"I've spoken," Guillelmette replied. "You will be silent now and ask God to keep you from temptation. You are dismissed."

Alaide bowed her head and slowly shuffled back to the kitchen.

The next day the sun shone brightly, and Berengaria and I went out together to begin work on the garden. We swung our mattocks to loosen the earth after the long winter and raked away the weeds. We dug a pond for water. And then we placed our precious seeds into the ground: onions, garlic, and chives; kale and white-headed cabbage; fennel, turnips, and red beets and beans. With every seed we planted, God, we offered prayer that You might give us food to survive the next year.

Once we had planted our kitchen garden, we tilled the soil to grow our herbs and medicines. Brother Bernard had come from a Cistercian monastery and had brought seeds for many herbs and healing plants. We thought of how we'd longed for medicine just two short months ago and took great care in planting them. We had most all we needed. We'd saved seeds from the fall, and to them we added those that the brothers brought. But I noted with a tinge of disappointment that he had not given us mandrake root.

I made bold to sign my desire to speak and asked if he might find it for us.

"The mandrake root," he hissed in disgust. "Do you not know that it is of Satan? Its form is like that of an obscene woman and its fruit will turn a soul from God. Is that what you desire?"

I shook my head and turned back to my labors. Aude had not told us that some plants were created by God and others by the Devil.

As Berengaria, Clarette, and I worked side by side, it was almost as it had been in Na Bonata's garden. We plowed the fertile earth and set our seeds to grow. We carried water from the river. But there was one big difference. No longer was it words that bound our hearts in friendship. We worked together silently. Dear God, it was Your very presence that wove itself among us and joined our hearts in amity and peace.

That April morning was like all the others. Clarette was sowing violets, Berengaria had been digging a row to plant our poppies, and I was raking out the grass and stones for a field of flax. It was a balmy morn, and I half-wished that I might work all day out in the sunlight. But then we heard the noontime bell ring out for sext. In haste, I threw my rake upon the ground. We rinsed the dirt from off our hands and raced back to the chapel.

Once more we knelt in prayer upon the choir bench. Once more we joined in harmony to sing our psalms of praise. Dominic's rich bass anchored us while Guillelmette's sweet tones floated up above. Once more Father Guilhem read the short *captuluum* and offered words of prayer. But this time Alaide was not with us. Just as we started to pray the Paternoster, we heard a loud scream coming from the garden. Guillelmette jumped up, but Dominic signaled for her to remain seated. He ran outside while we completed our prayers.

And then we all rushed out to join him. There was Alaide upon the ground, her lovely face covered with blood. Already it was swelling and her perfect nose was smashed and bent off to the side. I saw the rake beneath her foot and knew what had occurred. We took Alaide to the kitchen and used moss to stop the flow of blood. I made a tea from yarrow leaves the brothers had brought from Carcassonne and bid her drink from it.

Alaide could see the horror on our faces, and her cries of pain turned into sobs of anguish.

"I am no longer beautiful," she wailed, and none of us denied it. "I can no longer go into the world nor make my lover desire me. What am I now to do?"

"My dear, Alaide," Guillelmette responded. "I know you do not see this accident as good fortune, but you will come to know it as God's will. God can forgive your foolishness and so can we. You will do penance for your vainglory and disobedience, and you will come to know well your real beauty. Dearest Alaide, you once believed yourself to be called to the religious life. Turn again to your God and your vocation."

Alaide hung her head and nodded her resigned consent. She stayed with us and over time she gave her heart to You. We all did as that halcyon year of 1207 unfolded.

Chapter 13

THE SUMMER
OF OUR CONTENT

D ear God, You know how deep was my contentment that summer of 1207, as the garden grew and we settled into the sublime rhythm of the hours. At first it seemed a hardship to get up at the early morning hour, but just as Guillelmette had predicted, my body adjusted. I found myself awake before the bell was rung, my soul ready to raise its voice in sacred song. When our *domina* rang the bell, all ten of us would wipe the sleep out of our eyes. We'd don our habits and process to the chapel to sing the psalms and offer prayers for the departed.

And after matins, I would fall again into a dream-filled sleep. It was as if the angels met me then and filled my head with holy visions for the day to come. Sometimes Papa or Mama and Amelha would visit in my dreams. They seemed to be content and so alive that when I woke, I'd look to see if they were by my side. I'd wonder then if they ever missed me or even thought about me any longer. At other times, I could hardly recall Amelha's face, for my life with her and the Good Christians had disappeared into a distant fog.

As the dawn rose at the first hour, I would join my sisters in the chapter house for lauds. The venerable Saint Basil once wrote, "No other care should engage us before we have been moved with the thought of God." Morning prayer consecrated to God the first movements of our minds and hearts.

And so we started each morning with supplication. "O God," we would enjoin, "Come to our aid. O Lord, make haste to help us." And as we sang our hymns and chanted psalms of praise, I did rejoice, for the Lord Jesus rose just like the sun to shine upon us all.

Each day after lauds, we would file into the common room to wash our hands and faces. Sometimes Jordana would heat water so that we might cleanse our bodies in the private places we could never name. And then we'd gather in the chapel for the Eucharist.

Most often it was Father Guilhem who said the Mass, but sometimes it was Dominic who led us. Dear God, You know how on those days I longed for the sweet concord of the communion. When he spoke the words of institution and raised the perfect circle of the host, I could not take my eyes away.

"Qui cum Passioni, voluntarie traderetur, acceptit panem," he would intone, "before He was given up to death, a death He freely accepted, He took bread . . ."

Each time he broke the bread, I felt myself the pain of our Savior's broken body, and when he took it to his lips it was as if I too had eaten of the glorious meal.

After the Mass, we would retire to chapter so that we might get instructions for the coming day. That summer we had bread to eat while Guillelmette read to us from the Church Fathers or the Lives of the Saints. If we had need to speak, Guillelmette would bid us do so. If we were to be disciplined, she would rebuke us and direct us to do penance. After the morning meal, Raymondine or Berengaria would read from scripture for our *lectio divina*. We meditated upon the sacred words and let them be our silent prayer. With God's word resting in our hearts, we then walked the courtyard that served as our cloister or retired to the chapel for private devotion.

Dear God, I found that Guillelmette had been right about the silence. It filled me and surrounded me as if it were a warm wool mantel. I could feel Your presence shimmering in the air around us while we ate and worked and sang our prayers. You alone know how much the hours fed me. The cadence of the psalms drew water from a wellspring deep within my soul. And I drank deeply. I found the resonance of my own voice and learned to make it swell and fall with all my sisters. It seemed at times as if the angels had become a part of our small choir and lifted up our music to the highest Heavens.

And, *Santa Deu*, how our gardens did flourish! After we sang terce in the chapter house, we each commenced our *opus manuum*. It was high summer, and Berengaria and I could barely keep up with the weeding and the harvesting. We picked our fill of carrots and green beans and laid the fava beans upon a cloth to dry. We brought in radishes and bitter lettuces for Alaide to make into a salad. Our eggplants and cucumbers were swelling in the summer sun and soon we'd have beets, onions, and parsnips too. With every crop we gathered, we planted seeds again for a fall harvest. We dug out a deep hole on the north side of the chapel and lined it with grasses to make a cool root cellar. We vowed that, with Your help, we would not let another sister starve.

O God, that summer all of us felt the bounty of Your most gracious gifts. We even had ripe fruit to eat. Some days Guillelmette gave us leave to walk down to the river where we foraged for wild strawberries and melons. Bishop Folc had granted us five olive trees beyond the walls of Prouilhe and apples from an orchard on the west side of the chapel. The brothers brought home olives for Alaide to put in brine, and Clarette and I picked apples to dry.

And, if that weren't blessing enough, our herb garden also prospered. We cut the leaves and flowers and dried them in the sun so that we might have the herbs and tonics we would need to see us through the winter.

Dear God, in the joy of working in Your gardens, I wanted to forget the cilise tied around my waist. But I had grown less thin, and when I bent to dig the root cellar or pull out onions, its tines served to remind me of my carnal sin. Sometimes the demons of doubt whispered to my soul, and I began to ponder things I should not have. *Why it is that You grace us with the bounty of Your harvest and then wish for us to fast and mortify our flesh? Why have You given us so many healing herbs, when You alone have destined if we are to live or die?*

You know that I did not understand Your ways. I wished that there were someone I might talk with, but I knew that Guillelmette and Father Guilhem would demand that I do penance for such blasphemy. And I feared that Dominic would judge me as a heretic if I presented him with queries such as these.

And so I kept my doubts and questions to myself. It was enough that I could see Your presence in the Sacred Host and feel it in the rich loam of the earth. Back then, I trusted that it would be always so and that my heart would stay content to rest within Your gentle grace.

For us it was a blessed summer, but Dominic was sorely distracted. Just after the feast of the Annunciation, he had left for Pamiers to see Bishop Diego and attend another debate there against the Good Christians. The day after he returned to Prouilhe, he spoke to us at chapter about what had happened.

"The heretics have no shame," he said disdainfully. "We met for disputation at the home of Raymond Roger, and his sister Esclarmonde attempted to join in. She did presume to argue like a man on issues of theology. The legate Stephen quickly put her in her place, saying 'Go Madam, and attend to your spinning; it does not become you to take part in this debate.' Do the Albigensians not know that women's virtue rests within her meekness and her silence?"

I remembered Esclarmonde from Aude's *consolamentum* and admired her courage in speaking before such learned men. I kept my eyes lowered as Dominic spoke, and I hoped that he could not read my mind. I longed to learn if any others from Fanjeaux had been there, but I knew better than to ask. I bowed my head more fully as he continued.

"There is yet more news," Dominic asserted. "Our dear Bishop Diego is making plans to travel to Spain to raise alms for our mission. His hope is to be back with us next year, but he has asked that I might continue to serve as prior to Prouilhe while he is gone. In six weeks time I will accompany him as far as Couiza and then return to you."

As Dominic spoke of the departure of his mentor, I could feel the sorrow that flowed from his dear heart. The two had been together almost fourteen years, and the bishop had been his best friend and confidante. I glanced up just in time to see a single tear form in the corner of his eye. Now he, too, would have no spiritual companion, and he would need to face his demons on his own. Dominic saw my glance and knew that I had noted his sadness. He flinched and then returned my gaze with one of rebuke. I quickly looked away, and he went on.

"Bishop Diego is not the only one who leaves the Languedoc this fall," he said. "Abbot Arnaud de Citeax is also departing. As general of the Cistercian Order he must attend the Chapter General in Marseilles. He and his entire entourage have given up their preaching, and there are rumors that his twelve Cistercian abbots soon will follow. Only the legates Raoul and Pierre de Castelnau are left working with me to carry out God's work among the Albigensians. Our apostolic mission is in danger, and it rests now in the hands of God. I ask that each of you would pray for its endurance."

We all filed out of chapter on that morning with the weight of Dominic's news on our shoulders. The sun shone bright and warm, but we could tell the chill of fall was lurking in the air. All day I thought of Dominic, and Lord, You know my heart was heavy. That night after compline I stayed in the chapel to pray. It had become a comfort to be prostrate upon the floor before Your Son. As I lay there in fervent prayer, I did not hear when Dominic came in. He must have crept quietly along the northern wall of the chapel and knelt before our Blessed Mother.

"*Ave Maria*," he implored and startled me from my prayers. "Have mercy upon me, O Holy Mother, for I am weak. Please intercede on my behalf. My Father did call me to the *Santa Preditacio*, to speak His word among the heretics. But I fear I cannot stay this course without Diego by my side. At every town the Albigensians oppose me, and they find no virtue in my preaching. Like Our Lord, I am debased and humiliated. The crowds shout insults and throw rotten fruit. My cross is heavy. I beg that You would ask Your Son to help me to carry it."

I did not turn to look at Dominic, but soon I heard his chanting and his groans above the rhythmic strokes of his *flagellum*.

By the time that Dominic returned from Couiza without Diego, we were preparing once more for the feast of Saint Cecilia. Who would believe that we had been here at Prouilhe for a full year? So many things had changed! The *ostal* and the Good Christians were but a memory. No longer did we face the choice of marriage or becoming heretics. No longer did we fear for our survival. We would not starve this winter, for we had brought in a second harvest and our root cellar was well stocked. Bishop Folc had replenished our stores of grain and even brought us wine to drink. But most importantly, we had entered richly into our cloistered life with You. No longer did we wonder what each day might hold or forget when it was time to come to prayer. The rotes and rhythms of our lives were as familiar as our own soft breath. We knew when we would eat and work and pray and sleep. Most of us had even come to learn our prayers by heart and some of the psalms as well.

Of course, we sometimes grumbled at the little hardships of living at Prouilhe. It was getting cold again, and Alaide begged Father Guilhem to procure more straw and linen that we might make mattresses. Curtslana was always hungry and asked once why we couldn't have vegetables with the morning meal before starting our labors. After all, she pointed out, our larders and our cellars were no longer empty. But Guillelmette rebuked her and replied that hunger is a way to mortify the flesh.

"Whenever you feel the desire for food," she instructed, "you must kneel before Our Lord to seek the grace of gratitude for what you have and ask the Blessed Virgin to plead on the behalf of those poor souls who have not even one meal every day."

We all knew she was right. On Fridays, and during Lent and Advent, we ate only bread and watered wine but once a day, and we moaned inwardly with our desire for food. But, God, I learned to follow Guillelmette's advice. And when I began to feel the pangs of hunger, I knelt in prayer and turned my heart to You.

That first year at Prouilhe, Dear God, I did confront my demons face to face. I'd learned to still my terror of the kitchen fire and only flinched a little when I had to lay a faggot on its smoldering coals. When my jealousy flared at Guillelmette's lovely voice and beauty, I saw that it was the same ill spirit who had haunted me since Amelha was born. When I resented her authority and raged at her corrections, I recognized that I was in the grip of my childhood anger and made penance upon the chapel floor. And in the longing I still sometimes felt for Dominic, I knew the evil power of the demon lust. I begged You, God, to grant forgiveness and to help me subdue these evil spirits.

And so I came to welcome mortification as my chance to do battle with the Devil. Each time I suffered pain or even small discomfort, I knew that I was joined to the suffering of Your most precious Son. When I was thirsty after working in the garden and I took no drink, when my knees were scabbed and sore from kneeling on the stone steps of the altar, when I was cold from lying prostrate on the stones, when the tines of my cilise or the thongs of the *flagellum* cut into my flesh—all my afflictions were but skirmishes in my war to shed the body's mortal coil. And I gave thanks to You.

Through all the challenges of that first year, I came to trust that I had made the right choice in following Dominic to Prouilhe. But God, sometimes I thought about the Good Christian life I'd left. It seemed to me that it was not so very different from this one at Prouilhe. It, too, was a group of women who desired to give their lives to You. They spent their time in study, work, and prayer and came to be as family to each other. They too did see the flesh and its desires as evil, and they mortified themselves through chastity and fasting. Like us, they knew the power of Satan to divert us from God's path. They, too, supported brother preachers with their prayers and sought to free the souls of men and women from the Devil's evil grip.

Dear God, in Your omniscience, You must know how to answer this: *why did two paths that sought Your Truth so earnestly have to declare each other to be mortal foes?* I could not help but wonder about Amelha. Did she, too, have thoughts like my own? Did she ever question why it was that we must live apart? Did Amelha ever guess how much I missed her clever songs and easy joy, how much I longed to see her smiling face just one more time? Did she, too, find it difficult to think upon me as her enemy?

Before long, frost descended on the fields around us. We celebrated Christmastide that year awaiting the return of Diego from Spain, and two days later, the feast of the Evangelist. It was the first anniversary of our enclosure, and how we honored it with psalms of gratitude and a great feast! Dominic led morning Mass, and we all shared the Holy Eucharist. When he did break the bread and raise the body of Our Lord to Heaven, my tears were those of deepest gratitude. *How could my life in one short year have brought me to such a sacred moment?* I thought then that my joy might last forever. But that, of course, was not to be.

It was only one week hence when we heard the news that Bishop Diego had died in Spain. At first, dear Lord, I did not think it possible. He was one of our founders and the guide who had led Dominic and all of us to Prouilhe. His was the apostolic vision for our mission. I wondered, *Who would Dominic be without his dear companion? What would become of us?* That night, these questions wrapped around us like a shroud as we gathered in the chapel to pray for the safe passage of Diego's soul. Dominic led our prayers through tears that flowed without restraint.

Dear God, You did receive so many prayers that winter as we brought our sorrow to Your Blessed Mother. As I knelt in the chapel, she received our dolor and blessed it with her own before she lifted it to her precious Son. We were so much absorbed in our own grief that we barely registered the import of another tragic death. One morning in the cold of February, Dominic spoke to us in chapter. That day his booming voice was hushed as he recounted an event that had occurred three weeks before in the south of France.

"My dear daughters, there has been a calamity. Our friend the papal legate Pierre de Castelnau has been murdered. Pilgrims from Toulouse discovered his body along the banks of the Rhone."

"Who would do such a thing?" Alaide blurted out without thinking to ask for permission.

Dominic did not seem to notice. "There were many who desired the death of Pierre de Castelnau," he said. "The legate had been most outspoken in his hatred of the Albigensians, and he was advocating a crusade. He'd once lamented that 'religion would never raise its head within the Languedoc until it had been watered with the blood of a martyr.'

"But there are those who say that Raymond of Toulouse is behind the murder. The count also had reason to hate de Castelnau. The legate had excommunicated him for harboring heretics, and the count had threatened de Castelnau with death if he would not reverse the sentence. Our brother was returning from a meeting with Count Raymond the morning of his murder. He had said Mass beside the River Rhone and then released his civil escorts when two young men approached him. They say it was a squire of the count himself who dealt the mortal blow."

I raised my fingers to my lips, and Dominic bid me speak.

"What will this killing mean for us and for the people of the Languedoc?" I asked.

"I fear it means there will be dreadful times ahead," he replied. "The pope has confirmed Raymond's excommunication and warned him that 'The hand of the Lord will descend upon thee most severely.' There are none who can flee the wrath of God this murder has provoked.

"We cannot know just how our pope will carry out God's hand. But this is certain—he will demand revenge. If ever there were days the Church requires your prayers, those days have come. Tonight you will hold vigil for our Holy Mother Church," Dominic instructed solemnly. And then he added, "You might pray, too, for all the souls who will stand before its wrath."

Dear God, I did not then know why, but when he spoke my head grew light, and an icy shiver passed along my spine.

Your wrath, O God, it was so short in coming. That spring, the pope called for a great crusade against the Albigensians. He sent letters not only to all the barons and bishops of the Narbonne and its adjacent provinces, but he also called upon the kings of France and England to join in his holy cause.

"Attack the followers of heresy," he cried. "Forward then soldiers of Christ! Forward, brave recruits to the Christian army! Let the universal cry of grief of the Holy Church arouse you. Let pious zeal inspire you to avenge this monstrous crime against your God." Such was his rallying call.

But God, if You do truly know the hearts of men, You know that this is not all our good pope declared. He pledged that whosoever fought for forty days would be granted indulgences (thus assuring their souls would fly directly to Heaven). He attracted nobles from the north by offering those who took the land of heretics and their protectors the spoils of their conquest. And, O Dear God, he gave his army leave to deal with the vanquished as they pleased.

I did not know this yet, for I was but a young and cloistered woman. I trusted then that the crusade would be the army of Your righteous justice. I thought that it would bring Count Raymond to repent for his assault upon our legate and restore his lands into the service of Your Church. And so I knelt in prayer with all my sisters that the pope might find success in raising an army. And that did come to pass. But Lord forgive me, for I cannot accept that all that happened next was part of Your great plan.

Chapter 14

THE COMING STORM

D o You remember, God, that year of 1208? We passed it
in sweet prayer and in service to You, as if there were no
gathering storm around us. Each dawn, we awoke to lauds
and prayed the *Angelus*. Each day, we took our morning bread and
listened to Your Word. We celebrated Mass and did our labors in the
kitchen or the laundry or the fields. We sang the psalms at terce and
at none. At dinner, we all shared the bounty of our garden and the
alms that were provided us. And then as the sun set each evening,
we sang the vespers and gave thanks again for one more day spent
in Your loving arms.

O God, I loved You so. I was devoted to the Blessed Mother and
gave my heart each day to Your Dear Son. Your Holy Spirit flowed
within me and around me so that whether I did work, or pray, or
even sleep, I felt Your presence wrapped about my soul. I could not
then imagine that the love I knew would ever fade. But, *Santa Deu*,
You know that demons have their ways.

That year Dominic was frequently gone. He traveled all throughout the Languedoc to preach the Word of God. Now that he'd lost
his dear Diego, he often went alone. On calloused feet he walked

barefoot along the packed dirt roads that led to Nimes, Toulouse, or Carcassonne. I liked to imagine that he passed the lonely hours humming Aves or singing psalms of praise. He preached in churches and spoke on street corners, just as he had when I first heard him at Fanjeaux. Each time he left, he asked for us to pray for the poor heretics he would encounter, that they might find their way back to the One True God. I do not know if Dominic ever slept. Whenever it was my night to do vigil, he was there in the chapel praying and lamenting. I do not know the sins that caused him so to mortify his flesh. Hot tears streamed down his anguished face as he prayed for the Albigensians' souls. I wonder now which he lamented more, their eternal damnation or the terror his Holy Church would soon inflict upon them.

Each time that he returned, Dominic would speak to us during chapter and tell us tales of his journeys. Often he was ridiculed and spat upon by cruel heretics who chased him out of town. He told of one time he was ambushed by two angry peasants in the fields outside of Montréal.

"They threatened to kill me if I would not stop preaching," Dominic told us. "And I said to them, 'I welcome the chance to be a Christian martyr. If you would kill me, I would beg for you to do it slowly, cutting off my limbs one at a time. Then I might know the torture of our dearest Lord upon the cross.'"

He said the peasants were touched then by the light of the Spirit. Not only did they lay their weapons down but vowed obeisance to You.

At chapter, Dominic did more than just recount stories. He talked to us about the great importance of religious women in carrying out God's work among the heretics.

"Your task is more necessary to our work than ever. It remains the same as when you first arrived here at Prouilhe," he said with impassioned words. "Still you are to lend the power of prayer unto our sacred mission of advancing the Word of God. For two years, we have tried to reach the hearts and minds of heretics through preaching and debate. And there are souls who have come to accept the One True God.

"But the pestilence of heresy is spreading, and it will take much more to stem its growth. The Church within the Languedoc is in distress, for the Albigensians will never stop with just one brutal murder. All Catholics face grave danger until we put an end to the heretics' insidious power. You know the pope has called for a crusade against the Albigensians. The kings of France and England say they will not lend their armies to the pope, but they have given leave for their vassals to enlist in the crusade.

"And so my daughters of Prouilhe, the Church does need the sacred balm of your sweet prayer." Dominic raised his arms in supplication as he implored us. "Your entreaties to God must be constant that they may reach the lords and barons of all Christendom. You will pray night and day that they be moved by the plight of the Languedoc and send their armies to our aid."

And God, I was sorely moved by Dominic's request. I thought upon his bravery and his willingness to be a martyr to his Lord. I wanted nothing more than to support him and the Holy Mother Church in their struggle against the Albigensians. I wanted to defend the One True Faith against their wretched heresy. I prayed with fervor that the noblemen of France would heed our prior's call. I knelt for hours in vigil asking that you might raise up a mighty force to carry out the vision of dear Dominic. But, God, I beg that you forgive me for my prayers. I must confess that I did not consider even once the evil that might be set loose by such a force.

Instead I continued to live a simple life of work and prayer. I praised You that we didn't starve that winter, but with the coming of spring rains our supplies began to dwindle. And so Dominic ordered that Father Guilhem travel with him in the hope of procuring alms of both oil and grain. He appointed Brother Noel as our chaplain, to teach us and to celebrate the Mass and hear us in confession.

Dear Brother Noel, with his round belly and jovial ways. You sent him to us, God, because You knew we'd need to have a guide and comforter in the distress to come. He well upheld the teachings of the Holy Church, and he helped us to understand Your Holy Trinity. He told us it was futile to attempt to wrap our heads around its sacred truth. Our minds, he taught, think in duality. That is why when we turn only to reason in our search for God, we stumble on the Devil. We think in opposites. And we find ourselves within a world created by the demons in our head.

He tried to explain what he meant in chapter. "That is the problem with the heretics," he said to us. "In their attempt to discredit the Catholic Church, they've made a God-forsaken world and would have us believe the Lord can't reach us here. The only answer to their dualism is the truth of God's great love. And that can be known but through the Trinity. The venerable Anselm explained it well when he wrote, 'When I love anything, there are three things concerned—myself, that which I love, and love itself.' He who does love is God the Father; His beloved is Christ Jesus, who gave his life that we might know we too are God's beloved; and the Holy Spirit is the reality of love itself, binding you to Our Lord and to one another. If any be removed, there is no Trinity, and love cannot prevail.

"But the Lord does reach out to us here on this earth," Brother Noel continued, "to each of you, His precious daughters. You know God's presence in the beauty all around you, and in the harmonies you lift each day in prayer, and in the deepest recesses of your own hearts. There will be times ahead when you are tempted to forget that God is with you, but this I beg you. Hold tight onto your faith in the one God in three, and turn a deaf ear to the demons of doubt and despair."

Dear God, when I listened to Brother Noel, I wanted to learn more about him. *Where had he come from? How did he understand so well the Albigensians' heresy?* He spoke as one who had once known his demons and had overcome their power.

For the first time I started to look forward to confession on the first Friday every month. We would gather together in the chapter house with Brother Noel to admit our sins and talk about the demons that attacked our soul. I still remember the first time I dared to speak about my doubts. He asked us how we tame the demons that do tempt the flesh, and I told him of my fasts and vigils on the stone, and of the cilise and the flagellum. There was compassion in his eyes that gave me leave to ask my question.

"Why is it that God gave us flesh if he wants us to destroy it with mortification?" I asked.

Brother Noel did not answer immediately. Instead he responded with a question of his own, "What have you learned from your mortifications?"

I knew the answer I should give. "I've felt the pain our dear Lord suffered on the cross," I said, "and joined my heart with his." But then I added tentatively, "I feel cleansed of my sin and do take pleasure in the stripes of my mortification."

"Do you think that our dear Lord took pleasure in his suffering?" Brother Noel queried.

"I do not think so," I replied, "for he had no need to cleanse himself of sin." I paused. "But I am not like the Son of Mary," I went on. "There are so many demons in my heart I would that I could vanquish."

"And do your mortifications vanquish them?" Noel returned.

I hesitated as I thought of lying bruised and bloodied on the chapel floor. "I am not sure," I said quietly. "It seems the demons do release their hold on me for a short while, but then they return with yet greater power."

"You've made an important discovery," Noel observed. "When you combat your demons they grow stronger. That is the way with mortification. If you deny your flesh out of love for your Savior, it will increase your faith a hundredfold. If you do mortification in penance, it will increase your sorrow for your sins and you will come to know the breadth of God's forgiveness. But if you seek to mortify your flesh in anger or in hatred of your demons, you only feed them. You think they're in retreat, but they are just feasting upon your sins. They will most surely return stronger on another day.

"Do you wish to speak of your demons in confession?" Brother Noel inquired.

I nodded slowly as I knelt before him and began to pray:

"I confess to almighty God,
and to you, my sisters,
that I have sinned through my own fault
in my thoughts and in my words,
in what I have done,
and in what I have failed to do;
and I ask Blessed Mary, ever virgin,
all the angels and saints,
and you, my sisters,
to pray for me to the Lord our God.

"I have dared question God and almost gave my heart to the Albigensians. I have blamed him for the illness of our dear sister Paperin. My pride has made me think that I know more than God, and I have railed against our precious Lord in anger."

"Is that all that you need to confess?" asked Brother Noel.

"No, there is more," I did reply. "I live with a great evil smoldering in my heart and sometimes it flares up like the fires of Hell. It is the demon envy. I have hated my dear sister Amelha because of her great virtue and her joyful heart," I declared aloud for the first time in my young life. "When I was young, I wished her dead. I have felt great jealousy toward our *domina*, Guillelmette." And then I paused, and spoke again more quietly. "And I have lusted after Dominic."

"My daughter Elmina," Brother Noel replied. "Your sins are not as great as you imagine them to be and God offers you absolution.

This shall be your penance: you will pray the Ave Maria one hundred and fifty times, and you will prostrate yourself before your Savior and listen to all your demons have to say."

I nodded, but I could not help exclaiming, "Listen to my demons? I'd prefer to drive them out with my *flagellum*."

"Dear Elmina," replied Brother Noel. "Did you not hear what I have said? The ancient desert father, Evagrius Ponticus, taught us that you cannot beat your demons to submission. You must allow them to give voice and listen to their words. Only in that way can you release their hold on you and offer them unto your blessed Savior."

I wasn't sure what Brother Noel meant when he said listen to my demons, but even so I knew within my heart he spoke truth. I vowed that I would try to do as Noel instructed. But You know that I could not keep my vow.

It was but one week later that Dominic and Father Guilhem returned to Prouilhe and brought much news. *Santa Deu,* it seems that all winter You'd been listening to our prayers. For by that spring of 1209, Pope Innocent had raised a mighty army. Barons and knights had journeyed from as far as Paris and Cologne. There now were tens of thousands of them gathered on the coast at Montpellier, and the papal legate, Arnaud Aumery, had become their commander. They had been joined by *routiers* returned from the Holy Land in search of opportunity for greater spoils. Dominic said that any day now they would start their move against the Albigensians along the coast of France.

One more time our prior implored us. "The soldiers of Christ Jesus are now gathered. They are prepared to shed their blood to put an end to those who would destroy the Church. Tonight you will offer yourselves in prostrate vigil and pray daily for their quick success."

And, God, You know that their success did come. That summer

as we reaped the harvest of our gardens and began to put away our winter stores, the very air seemed charged with lightning tension. We offered daily prayers for the crusaders, and we took turns holding vigil for their cause. Within the week Dominic and Guilhem were on the road again, and we had no word from them. We prayed each night for their safe return, not knowing whether warfare had begun.

But it was not Dominic who brought our first news of the awful crusade. How can I 'ere forget that scorching morning after lauds, not long before the feast day of Bartholomew? We'd just completed Mass when a great pounding on the cloister gate cut short our adoration. Brother Noel told us quickly to retire to the chapter house, and then he went to investigate. We sat upon our benches, and I reached to take Clarette's hand. She squeezed mine in return. In a short time Brother Noel returned, accompanied by three disheveled women whose eyes were aflame with terror.

"These are Maria, Catalana, and Valencia," Noel announced offering a nod to each. "They come to us from Carcassonne. They say they are good Catholics and would like to join us here."

We searched the newcomers for some hint of what had brought them, but they would not return our curious gazes.

"It will be necessary for Dominic to meet them and discern their call to the religious life," Noel went on. "Until then, I will have them stay with *Domina* Guillelmette for their protection."

He motioned for the three to follow him, but then he turned to us again to say, "I will remind you that we live under a rule of silence. It is important that it be well observed."

We saw the three new women every day. They sat at the rear of the chapel as we sang the hours. Each afternoon one of them stepped into the kitchen to fetch food. And in the evening we would hear them pacing as if caged by some great secret horror.

One night I too could not find sleep, and so I crept out to keep vigil in the chapel. And there I saw Valencia, her shoulders shaking as she bent in deepest prayer. At first I prostrated myself upon the floor and listened to her quiet sobs. But then, O God, You know I disobeyed Your rule of silence. I went and sat beside her as she cried. And then I gently asked if she wished to tell her story.

Dear God, You know what happened next, the horrid tale that poured from her sweet lips. It's true she'd come to us from Carcassonne, but she had fled there from the coastal city of Béziers.

Santa Deu, how can it be that what she said to me was so? How could Your Holy Church have committed atrocities so pitiless and cruel? I still can barely speak to You about the words I heard that night.

In voice so soft I had to strain to hear, the young woman spoke. "I am called Valencia," she said, "and I come from Béziers. You will not want to hear my tale, for it is more than any human heart can bear."

I shuddered, but I bid that she continue.

"It was the day before the Feast of Mary Magdalene," she said. "An army of crusading men arrived outside our city gates. They had bright flags and bore the shields from many different lands. Their leaders carried the pope's white and yellow banner. We stared in awe, wondering what they wanted.

"Our bishop, Renaud de Montpeyroux, bravely went out to talk with their commander. He returned with word that the crusaders would spare Béziers if he would hand over the heretics who live within our city. The good bishop gave him a list of names, but he refused to hand over his neighbors and friends. He then gathered all the Catholics within the church and asked us if we wished to flee. Most said no, they would not leave their city. My father too said he would stay, but he begged the bishop to take my sisters and me. Only a handful of us left that night. We walked among the army and the hired *routiers* until we found the tent where the priests were praying.

"By the next day more crusaders had arrived and were setting up their tents. We all believed there would be a long siege and time for more negotiations. But our beliefs were unfounded. It all started so quickly that I know not just what happened. A soldier from Béziers was shouting insults at some drunken *routiers*, and a brawl ensued. The soldiers made a quick retreat and the mercenaries followed them. When the crusaders saw the gate was breached, they all charged in. We could not see what happened, but, my God, we heard such screams as the armies did plunder our fair city. Soon we smelled smoke, and all Béziers became engulfed in flames. The screaming and the stench of burning flesh still haunt my days and nights. It wasn't until all was over that I learned what had occurred.

"Our people had fled into the churches and the great cathedral, both Catholics and heretics alike. It's rumored that the knights went to Arnaud Amaury to ask what to do. And he replied, 'Just kill them all, for God will know his own.' I know not if that's true. But the knights and the *routiers* broke open the doors of all three churches and then set them on fire. Nobody got away."

Valencia began to sob more loudly. "I cannot bear it," she moaned through her tears. "My papa is gone and all my friends. Everyone I know was burned alive."

Chapter 15

IGNIS CONSUMENS

D ear God, I sat with poor Valencia throughout the early hours of the night. And then, before we rose for matins, she departed to her quarters. One by one my sisters filed in as we began to sing:

O God, You are my God, I seek You,
my soul thirsts for You;
my flesh faints for You,
as in a dry and weary land where there is no water.

My words echoed the *Te Deus Laudamus* in praise of the new day, but I could not find the praise within my heart. Valencia's story pounded in my head and could find no exit.

The fires of Béziers ignited the flames that had smoldered in my soul since I was born. I had been mistaken to think that they had been vanquished. It was as if Valencia's story ignited an ancient memory. The flames leapt up as an *ignis consumens*, Your all-consuming fire. And, God, how it did burn! My sisters' gentle voices floated all around me, but I was deaf to them; instead I heard only the frantic screams that echoed from Béziers.

I passed that day in dizzy mindlessness. I sang the hours; I ate my meals and sat through Clarette's reading of the Lives of Saints; I carried water and weeded the garden; but I barely knew that I had done these things. After compline I fell into my bed, but no sleep came to me. Instead the fires swirled up to my head. They caused my breath to quicken and my heart to race. I prayed to Mother Mary for my soul's relief, but 'twas to no avail. It must have been past midnight that I dragged myself again to the chapel and found with gratitude that there was no one there. I took my *flagellum* from its appointed place and laid upon the floor in desperation.

"Please, dearest Savior," I did beg of You, and thought about the way You healed the Gerasene demoniac. "My demons too are legion, and they will not give me rest. You are the only one who has the power to subdue them. You did it once for Jesus in far off Gerasa; will You not do the same for me?"

I carefully removed my night shift. I folded it with care and lay it neatly on the floor. Then I took up the *flagellum* and knelt down before Your cross. I let the lashes thrash into my back, but I felt nothing. I swung it harder. I could tell the leather thongs were cutting at my flesh, and yet there was no pain—and no relief. And so I raised the whip more furiously, in frantic hope of driving out the demons burning in my heart. I do not know how long I did go on 'til I fell deathlike to the floor. That morning before lauds, Guillelmette discovered me lying in a pool of blood.

She quickly called for Berengaria. Together they helped me arise and took me to my bed. Dear Berengaria removed my cilise. She warmed a kettle of water and bathed me. Then she took a balm of aloe and balsam from the apothecary and gently rubbed it on my wounds. She soaked bandages in wine and wrapped them around me. Meanwhile, Guillelmette summoned Brother Noel. She returned with a clean shift and my habit. "You will put on your clothes," she said, "and meet with Brother Noel in the chapter house." I very slowly did as I was bid.

I dared not look up as I stepped inside the small stone room. "You have been very stupid," Brother Noel began, more sternly than I had ever heard him speak. "It is a sin to do such violence to your body."

He waited for me to give some response, but no words came to me.

"Do you remember what we talked about during your last confession?" he went on.

My mind went blank. I could remember that I had believed his words, but not what he had said. I slowly shook my hanging head.

"We talked about mortification," he reminded me. "I said that it could help you when it's done for love of Jesus or in sorrow for your sins."

I nodded as his words came back to me. So he went on, "But when you mortify yourself out of anger or hatred for your demons, you blaspheme God."

I shook my head. "That isn't so," I whispered. "I did not blaspheme God."

"Ah, dear Elmina," Brother Noel replied, "but you did. You took upon yourself to do what only God can do. You tried by your own hand to exorcise your demons. And you don't believe that it just makes them stronger. Try to remember. What did I say that you must do instead?"

I did recall then what Noel had told me. "You said that I must listen to my demons," I replied. "But I do not know how to do that, and I am not sure I want to."

"Perhaps I can help you," said Brother Noel. "But first you must tell me what happened last night."

"I sinned," I quietly responded.

"That much is clear," replied Noel. And, God, I think I almost saw him smile. "You'll have to tell me more," he said.

"I broke the rule of silence," I continued. "I could not sleep and so I went into the chapel to pray. Valencia was crying there, and I asked her if she wished to tell me what was wrong."

Brother Noel released a long, sad sigh. "Did she tell you her story?" he inquired.

I nodded as the tears began to fall upon my cheeks. "Please tell me if what she said of Béziers is true."

"I can't know what she told you," Brother Noel replied, "but, yes, horrendous things happened at Béziers."

"How can that be?" I asked in desperation. "That was the army of our Mother Church, sent to the Languedoc to do the will of God. We've prayed all spring for their success." And suddenly my questions spewed forth. "What is it that we've done? Have we been praying that whole cities might be razed and Catholics and heretics alike be burned alive? How can the Church claim to be the body of Christ and yet commit such evil?"

When I had asked my questions, I held my breath and dared to look into Brother Noel's eyes. I there beheld both fear and great compassion.

"Elmina, you must listen," he said quietly. "There are no easy answers to the questions that you pose. And it is not your place to ask them. Our Holy Mother Church, she is indeed the body of Christ acting in our world. Both you and I have pledged our lives in service to her. But that does not mean that the Church is immune from the sins of men. We may not understand the will of God in all she does, but we are called to offer full obedience and pray that God forgives her shortcomings. Tonight you will do penance for your doubt," he said and added, "but not with flagellation. You will spend one hour in prostration and then say your Aves to the Blessed Virgin."

I nodded my assent.

"Meanwhile, I wish to speak with you about your demons," Brother Noel said. "What can you tell me of them?"

I was afraid to trust him with the truth, but a small voice within urged me to continue. I still believe, God, that the voice was Yours. "The demons have been with me for as long as I remember," I replied. I told Noel of the smoldering cinder in my heart, and how it flared with envy and with anger. I shared with him about the terror that I felt as a young girl each time I caught a glimpse of fire and I told him the fears had returned to haunt me. I even talked about the faintness and the spinning in my head when I am sorely confused about the truth.

When I had finished, Brother Noel sat quietly before he spoke. "There are two things that I want you to do," he said. "The first is sleep."

"But I cannot," I answered truthfully.

He asked, "Is there a remedy for sleep in your apothecary?"

"There is none," I replied. "When we were at the *ostal* we did make a potion of poppy, henbane, and the mandrake root, but Brother Bernard will not bring us mandrake root."

"Ah, the remedy known as the Great Sleep," Brother Noel responded. "I will see what I can do. Meanwhile you need to make friends with your demons. Tonight while you do penance do not ask them to depart. Instead note in your heart the things they say or do. Then, tomorrow after Mass and chapter you will talk with me again. There is something that I would like to give you."

And so that night I lay prostrate upon the chapel floor and closed my eyes. My head was spinning from my lack of sleep, and it did not take long for the demons to show their faces. They started as an inky black that spread before my eyelids. I thought to open my eyes and make the vision go away, but then I recalled Brother Noel's words. I let the black grow larger and I could feel it seep into my very soul. It was the height of summer, and yet a chill surrounded me. My teeth began to chatter and my hands and feet grew numb.

"Dear God," I called aloud to You, "what is it that I see?"

And then the black took shape into a vicious cat. Its eyes were red as fire; it had long claws and teeth as sharp as swords. It was the same beast I had seen at the church in Fanjeaux, that first night we had talked with Dominic. I shrieked, and then I felt the lesions on my back as if the beast were scratching them anew. Yet still I did not move. I stared into its fiery eyes and they began to glow into the *ignis consumens*, the all-consuming fire. Again I wished to look away, but I did not. The fire filled the chapel with a blaze as hot as any ironsmith's. And then I heard the screams. Before my eyes I saw the fire engulfing women's hair as they held tightly to their children.

"Please, no" I howled, in the hope that You could hear me. And I sobbed and sobbed the way Valencia had last night.

Slowly the vision dissipated. I knelt before our Blessed Mother and did pray to her the way I had been taught:

Holy Mary, full of grace, the Lord is with you.

Blessed art thou among women and blessed is the fruit of thy womb, Jesus.

And then my soul added a plea:

Holy Mary, Mother of God, pray for us sinners now and in the hour of our death.

When I had repeated my prayer one hundred and fifty times, I went back to bed. I fell asleep and did not wake again until I heard the matins bells.

That morning after Mass and chapter, Brother Noel bid me remain with him. "How was your night?" he asked me quite directly.

I told him of the vision I had seen in my penance, and he nodded his approval.

"The cat is a sign of great evil," he replied. "Your demons are surely speaking to you." Then Brother Noel reached into a sack by his side. "I have something I'd like to give you," he repeated. He took out five small vials stopped with lamb's wool and laid them upon the table.

I stared curiously. "What are those?" I inquired.

"They are paints," replied Noel. He pulled the stoppers from them, and I could see that each contained a different color. "They're made with ground pigment and gum Arabic. These two are red and yellow ochre," he said pointing to the golden and red paint around the rims. "And here we have a black from charcoal and a white from lime. This blue one is called azurite; they say it comes to us from ancient Egypt."

I could not take my eyes from them. "They're beautiful," I said. "Where did you get them?"

Noel hesitated for just a moment. "A dear woman gave them to me not long ago," he replied. "I think perhaps that they were meant for you."

"But I do not know how to paint," I objected.

"I will show you," replied Brother Noel. He took a small miniver brush and dipped it in a bowl of water. "These are called watercolors. They are rare, so you will need to use them sparingly. You dip your brush in water and then swirl the tip into the paint. The more water you use, the more pale and transparent it will be. And you can mix colors on this." He took out a small piece of broken glass and showed me how the two ochres combined could make a deep rich orange, and how to mix yellow ochre and azurite to create green.

"When you see fire, you will paint it. When your demons come to you in visions, you can paint them too," Noel suggested.

"How have you come to know so much about demons and visions?" I inquired of him.

"It is not important how I know the things I know," Noel responded. "Just heed what I tell you. At times your visions may seem too frightening to draw, but I would like to show you something." With one smooth stroke, he formed a perfect circle on a piece of linen paper. "This circle is the sacred host," he said. "It is the fullness of Our Lord's perfection. If you draw it before you start to paint, then whatever vision falls upon the paper will be held in His embrace. And it will seem less terrifying."   ˙

I gasped. "Aude made paintings such as these. She was one of the perfecti at the *ostal*."

Brother Noel ignored my shock and continued. "When you

have made one painting, you must ask God what it has to teach you. Be sure of this. Our Lord will speak to you. And He will lead you to the next vision you have need to paint. I have but eight sheets of paper; please use them wisely."

I longed to take them and begin painting right away, but then I thought of a problem. "The sisters will be jealous if I have paints and they do not," I said.

"I will talk with them at chapter," Noel replied. "The Rule of Augustine requires that each receive according to her need. Today you are in need. Your sisters know that and will understand. We'll keep the paints and paper here in this cupboard," he said. "And I have a candle you can use. If you have a vision and wish to paint it, you may do so after matins in the chapter house."

Chapter 16

ELLA

I.

Dear God, I still remain thankful for Brother Noel. I did not know how he had learned to paint within the circle of the host. Nor did I know why he had such compassion for my nighttime terrors. But I surely loved him for it, not with a girl's infatuation or a woman's passion, but with a gratitude that flowed beyond all words. Without him, I fear that I would have succumbed to my demons before I reached my nineteenth birthday.

That night after compline I did again do prostrate vigil as Noel had urged. Again I lay upon the floor beneath the crucifix of Your Dear Son and closed my eyes. I prayed that He protect me from the demons in my mind and then invited them to speak. It was a while before the fire blazed full within my head. I stared at its reflection on my eyelids and began to feel the terror well within me. My breath grew shallow as I saw the shadow of a girl emerge within the flames. She wore a muslin tunic and must have been ten or twelve years old. The first thing that I felt was a burning pain rippling through the recesses of my most private parts. Then came the spasms, so strong that I feared I could not lie still upon the floor. And then the shame. Dear God, I was embarrassed to be lying like that before You. Once more I heard Brother Noel's voice urging, "Let them speak." And so again I did. I listened to this young girl's screams and then saw that she held a small boy in her arms. She rocked him back and forth as tears flowed from her eyes. I heard a distant cry that seemed to echo from another time and place, "Please, please, God, No. Please not my little brother." I looked more closely still, and I could see the blood that flowed from his entrails and knew that he was dead.

Once more my body trembled with a sobbing grief, and I know not how long I lay upon the floor. Once more I knelt and prayed before the Virgin and then fell into my bed for a deep sleep. That morning after matins, I went to the chapter room. I lit the candle in the coals, took out the paint and paper from the cupboard, and filled a cup with water from the cistern. Then I sat down upon a bench. I drew a circle on the linen paper and began to paint.

When I was finished I looked down at my drawing and did as Brother Noel had instructed. I asked it questions and I trusted, God,

that You'd reveal the things that I should know. I asked the girl, "What is your name?" and she replied, "Ella."

"Where do you live?" I asked, and she answered, "I do not know. It is a land beside the sea. There is a rocky shore with villages and a grand monastery."

I looked upon the girl in my painting and gently asked, "What happened in the fires?"

She spoke with silent words that pounded in my head. *I lived in the village with my mamai and my daidi and my dearest brother Bradán. I'd taken him with me to do the wash along the shore, when I heard the warning* calls within the village. I looked around and saw fierce ships along the coast. They were like dragons with red and white sails, and men were rowing in small boats onto the shore. I grabbed Bradán's tiny hand and pulled him to a cave among the rocks. There we heard screams and awful cries, and then we smelled the thatched roofs of the village as they burst into a ball of fire. I knew at once that my mamai and daidi were burning among the flames. There were people running in all directions. Some were on fire and coming toward the shore, with the invaders pursuing behind. I held tight to Bradán and prayed that we would not be found. But God turned a deaf ear unto my plea.

What happened next is terrible. As the invaders came onto the shore, I saw that they had horns upon their heads and thick rough beards of red and brown and black. They found us in the cave and dragged us out. One pulled dear Bradán from my arms and thrust his spear right through him. The others shoved me to the ground, and one by one they did the things of which I cannot speak. When they were done, one took me by the neck to strangle me, and when he thought that I was dead, he flung me down upon the rocks.

I do not know how long I remained there, but when I awoke the village was but smoldering ashes, and Bradán lay there stiff and cold beside me. I took his little body in my arms and sang to him a gentle lullaby. And then I laid him in the cave. I crawled back toward the ashes that were once my home and crumpled to the ground.

'Twas there that old Donagh found me. He, too, had survived the attack and saw that I was yet alive. He gently lifted me into his arms and carried me across the hills. When we arrived at the monastery, he told the nuns of what he knew, and they did take me in.

I looked again at what I had painted, a young girl with her little brother's lifeless body amid red, swirling flames. This was the image that had haunted me for my whole life. *How is it that I have such a vision locked within my soul?* I wondered. *Where do these words I've heard come from?* Dear God, I did not know.

That day after Mass, Brother Noel asked how I was doing with my painting. When I told him the story of Ella and showed him what

I'd drawn, I saw a look of fear flash in his eyes. He quietly sat down and bid me do the same.

"It is important for your soul that you continue to paint your visions, Elmina. There is someone from the past who does haunt you, and you must come to know her. But it is not safe. The Church would not approve of what we're doing. Should anyone see your painting, he might think that you are bewitched or perhaps a heretic."

"A heretic?" I quavered. "Why would they think that?"

"The Albigensians believe that we live many lives. And we carry the anguish of each one until we release our soul from the confines of flesh."

"But I don't want to be a heretic," I wailed. "I only want to serve God and find rest in Heaven."

"I want that for you, too," replied Brother Noel. "And so does God. It's why he sent his Son, Jesus, that we might be freed from the cycle of birth and death. Do you understand?"

"I do not think so," I admitted.

"There is but one thing that can free us from our earthly toil, and that is embracing the fullness of God's love. Because Our Father wanted us to know this love, he sent Jesus to live and die among us. He showed us how to find the love of God within our hearts. From him we learn how to share it with others. When each of us has learned what Jesus came to teach us, we have no further need for earthly life. Then we will abide fully with our Lord in Heaven."

"I do not yet know how to love as Jesus loved," I answered.

"Few of us do," Brother Noel replied. "And such love is not possible when you are tormented by demons. Painting within the circle may help you, but we need to keep your work secret. This is what you must do. Each night when you finish your painting, you must bid it farewell, then lay it on the fire and let it burn. Take care that there is nothing left before you leave. You need not fear; you will not lose the things that you have drawn, for they will yet abide within the confines of your soul."

Still, God, I was afraid. I did not want to be a heretic or go against Your Church. I did not want to be plagued by the demons of a girl from long ago. I did not want to burn my paintings. And yet I understood just what Noel was saying. I slowly stood and laid my drawing on the fire. I did not even turn my eyes away as it burst into flames.

II.

My God, all day I prayed for little Ella. I felt as close to her as to a dearest sister or even to my very soul. You know she rested in my heart as I weeded the garden, and she flowed out through my tears as I did chant the hours. I wondered if there was more to her story, and if I should come to know it.

That night after compline, I stayed once more in prostrate vigil in the chapel. This time the fire was dim and far away. I lay in darkness and wondered if perhaps I'd have no more visions of Ella. But then it was as if my inner eye adjusted to the night, and I began to see a wall of stone surrounding me. I wondered first if I were looking at the stones of the chapel, but, God, You know my eyes were closed. The wall before me seemed to curve, as if it were a chamber in the turret of a cloister.

And there was Ella kneeling on the floor, crying as if her heart had been forever broken. In the wall above her were two long slits that shed a holy light upon her form. She was held safely there within the sacred circle while a red fire burned about her. Black slashes cut through it as if formed from the charcoal of burned bones.

Dear God, how my heart did cry out to hers. I lay in silent prayer that Our Dear Savior was there with her. I hoped that he was holding her within his arms. And yet, I could not help but ask: *how can it be that You love us and still let so much grief abide upon the earth?*

Again, I waited until after matins, and I painted what I'd seen. I asked again, Dear God, what I must know, but Ella could not speak. I stared at what I'd drawn and thought of what Noel had said about *Evagrius*. The early fathers of the Church had gone into the desert so that they might meet their demons face to face. And then I wondered if the anger and the darkness of those slashes might one day find their way into Ella's soul.

III.

For several weeks I did not stay for vigil after compline. I was too tired, and I was not sure that I could hold any more of Ella's suffering within my heart. Also it was harvest time, and there was work to do. Guillelmette asked Noel if Valencia might aid us in the garden, and he agreed. And so together we all worked in silence, picking turnips, beets, and ripe white beans to store for winter. We gathered herbs to dry on strips of linen in the summer sun. And then we turned the soil to plant a second crop of carrots, fennel, kale, and leeks.

For a short while, I slept well in the night, and Ella slipped out of my daily thoughts and prayers. But slowly I became more agitated. I woke up long before matins and often could not get to sleep again. I found myself distracted when I sang the hours and oft forgot the psalms. The first Friday of September we gathered with Brother Noel for our monthly confession, and I shared that I had been remiss in prayer. When Brother Noel assigned my penances, he said he thought it time for me to do vigil again. And I fully understood.

That night I lay once more in penance on the stone floor of the chapel and thought of Ella in her cold stone chamber. And again I had a vision. The fires that had surrounded her were now receded to an emptiness flecked only with a few leftover ashes. She sat within a wall of stone that had become a prison. She was surrounded by a grey and violet grief, and the only thing that penetrated through those walls was a dripping of black despair. Dear God, I wasn't sure my heart could stand to paint so deep a pain, and yet I did, knowing that You held Ella in Your arms.

Before I placed the painting on the coal, I asked of it what You needed for me to know. *It's the beginning of acedia,* I heard Your voice as if it were my own. *The fires of her passion that once burned so bright have given way to numbness; the demons of doubt and despair now feast upon her soul. She thinks the only path out is through death. Keep listening, Elmina. She still has much to teach you.*

IV.

And, God, I did keep listening. The next night, I lay down upon the stones and prayed that You might help dear Ella find another way. As I lay there all I could see was a grey fog and specks of darkness all about it. I tried to make out Ella, but at first I couldn't see her. I became afraid of what she might have done and begged You that it be not so.

And then I saw a hint of light and her dim frame seated upon a lilac sea of grief so pale it made me gasp.

"Don't let her disappear!" I begged, but just the way it had appeared, her image vanished. All I could see were charcoal flecks where Ella had once been.

That morning as I painted my vision, I asked, "What can I do to bring her back?" It was a still, small voice that answered me, *You can but love her. She alone must find her way to God.*

V.

You can but love her.

Dear God, how those words echoed through my soul. I thought of Ella locked within the sea of her own grief. She'd spent her tears, and yet mine flowed like rain. I know You'd said that she alone could find her path to You, but I dared to hope that I might lend my prayers. At the next vigil I lay down and prayed that she might come to see Your light.

And then another vision pierced my soul.

I saw the windows first.

The largest one was round and stood within the arch of a stone chapel. The window looked like that which shines above the altar at Fanjeaux, but there was not just one triquetra but six, all dancing within a stone circle. Above the windows was a little hole that looked just like a clover. Below it were two openings, with small circles above, and iron bars that formed a checkered grid. Behind the arch there was a circle of the deepest black, but it, too, was surrounded by an ochre light.

And there beneath the windows stood Ella. She was dressed in the poor clothing of a servant girl, but her arms were raised as she beheld the wonder of it all.

That morning I looked at what I had painted, and I saw the hope I'd prayed for in the night. Ella had seen her own vision of You. A seed of light had entered into her numb heart. And, God, You know how hard I prayed that it might take root and begin to grow.

VI.

The next night I could not wait for compline to end. When all were gone but those who were absorbed in their own vigils, I eagerly lay down. I asked You if Ella had found her path to You. But I received no answer. For a full hour I prayed to You, but no vision would come. I offered prayers unto the Blessed Mother and then went to bed and tossed about until matins.

I came back the next night, and still one more before I saw another vision of Ella. As I lay prostrate, I began to see a pool of blood flowing around me on the stones. I shuddered in terror but let the demons speak to me. Slowly the blood congealed into a red pillar, and then it started to take the form of a tall priest. He stood between Ella and the church windows and glared down upon her.

My heart did shiver at the sight, and my head began to spin. I did not want to comprehend what I had seen and fled out from the chapel. I tried to go to bed, but I could not lay still. My heart was pounding like a hundred masons cracking stone, and my only thought was how I might take flight. But there was nowhere I might go. I dared not return to the chapel, so I paced the cloister fence until the bell rang for matins.

Dear God, I begged, *please tell me what to do.* And You responded as I knew You would, *Sing morning psalms and paint your demons.* And so after matins I went into the chapter room, and once again I painted. When I was done I said, "Dear Ella, speak to me," but she said nothing.

"Why do you kneel like that before the priest?" I asked and waited in the silence until her answer came.

He made me do things you don't wish to know about, she said. *But if you want to hear the things he said to me, you must be strong enough to listen to the demons.*

VII.

I had to know more. So the next night, despite my lack of sleep, I passed another vigil in the chapel. Again I saw the pool of bloody red. Again it did congeal into a priest. And once more he stood there between the dancing light and Ella. I did not hear his words so much as see them.

"You are a whore, and you're not fit to set foot in the church," he said through sneering lips and voice of deepest scorn. "There is no light for you. There is no God, no joy, no voice, no love. There is no color and no music. You have no life, no purpose on this earth but to do penance for your vile sin. You'll have no sleep. And you will offer service as I do demand it. For you there's no way out and there is no one to help you here. Perhaps God will take mercy on your filthy soul."

With that he turned his back and walked away.

I let the demons' voices resonate within my soul. A silent scream rang out from deep within me, *THE PRIEST DOES NOT SPEAK THE TRUTH!*

Dear Ella did do nothing to deserve such foul contempt. She could not help what those men did to her. Her soul is pure and only longs for God. I begged that Jesus purge her of her demons, and I heard his gentle voice respond, *Her demons are your own.*

And then I knew the meaning of what Brother Noel had said to me. I had to hear my demons and know full well that they did not speak the truth. I had to leave them at the cross and trust that Our Dear Savior would dispose of them. That night I did just that. I returned to the chapel and imagined them resting at the feet of Your

Son. Then I went to bed and slept in a realm far removed from any demons. Would that I could have done the same throughout the dark times that were yet to come.

VIII.

I thought on Ella every day as I went through my daily work and prayer. I wondered how it was that she could live so closely in my mind and heart. Of course the Albigensians would say she came through transmigration; that Ella was my own soul living in a different time and place. They'd say the sacred circle had enabled her to speak. But, God, I was a Catholic sister of Prouilhe and not a heretic. I had no way to make sense of dear Ella in my life.

I had but one more piece of paper and was almost out of paints. For days I did not hold vigil with Ella, for I was afraid to hear how her story would end. But once again, my sleep became restless and I could tell that there was one more thing I had to see.

And so, the next Sunday night I lay another time in vigil on the chapel floor. I closed my eyes and entered into prayer, asking our Savior for one more vision of sweet Ella's life. And when the vision came to me I gasped out loud. I saw a bent old woman kneeling on the floor and scrubbing with a brush as red as blood. Behind her was the wall of windows and of light, so faded I could barely make it out. Around it was a ring of angry fire and deep slashes of both red and black across the sacred circle.

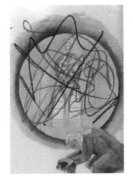

The vision did arouse alarm and pity in my soul. I moaned aloud, "Please God, it can't be Ella."

But I knew that of course it was. She had believed the red priest's evil words, and year-by-year the demons had destroyed her soul. "Dearest Ella," I gently wept, and painted the last circle of her life. I slashed red and black lines over the light that once had given her such hope. I knew for her there truly was no joy, no peace, no life, no love, no God.

With greater sorrow than I'd ever known, I placed this last painting upon the coals. And then I knelt and begged of You, *Dear God, please hold me tight and keep me from such desolation.*

Chapter 17

CRUSADE

*S*anta Deu, You know how hard I tried to shake the end of Ella's life out of my mind. But it was etched within me. Her misery became a bitter gall that tainted all my days. In dark moments I wondered, *Would I, too, come to hate Your priests and be cut off from You? Would I, too, end my life in deep despair?* I wished that I might share my fears with my dear friends, but I knew Brother Noel had been right. If I were to speak of my visions, I would be thought a heretic or else possessed by demons.

And they would have been right. I knew I was infected by the heresy, for I began to hope that Ella's soul really did live within me. I prayed that I might teach her to sing the hours. No longer would a priest deny her tortured soul access to the solace of the sacrament. She had a place in the choir, sitting right next to my own. Sometimes I even sensed that she was singing with me, and my voice took on a fuller, richer timbre. On those days my heart did rejoice.

But there were other times I felt Ella's presence as an iron weight upon my shoulders. Her grief was always with me. I took it to the chapel, and I offered daily prayers that You might find it in Your heart to lift it from me. I felt dear Ella's sorrow in the dark hours of the morning after matins and in the evening after compline when I longed for sleep. The heaviness grew worse with every passing week, as we heard news about the armies in the south.

It was the height of summer, on the Feast Day of Saint Bartholomew, when Dominic and Guilhem returned to Prouilhe with a full entourage of men, both priests and soldiers. They stayed at the Church of St. Martins, and we could hear their raucous voices late into the night. The day after his arrival, Dominic spoke with us during chapter. I raised my eyes to look at his and saw that they had changed. It's true that there had been a passion in his eyes when he was with Diego, and I cannot deny that it had pulled hard at my young girl's heart. But now his eyes flashed with a different kind of fire. They darted back and forth and gave off an unholy gleam, as if he had witnessed an unspoken horror and his soul had been taken hostage.

I did not know this Dominic. His fiery eyes scared me and ignited the demons I had once thought put to rest. I could feel Ella cringe within me, and I quickly looked away. I feared that Dominic had recognized my distress, but I had no need to worry. He took no notice of me or anyone else in the room. His mind was fixed on more important things.

"I bring good tidings of the Lord's work in the Languedoc," he said to us. "Carcassonne has surrendered to the armies of the Holy Mother Church!"

Carcassonne has fallen? My heart objected silently. *But that is only one day's journey from Fanjeaux!* Were the pope's armies really headed this way? Had they wreaked the same havoc in Carcassonne as in Béziers? I wondered how I could have been blind to God's plan for the Languedoc. Had I really dared to hope that the crusaders might stay far from my own dear home?

Dominic continued, for still he could not read what was on my mind. "Carcassonne surrendered to the army of Arnaud Amaury after a siege of just two weeks." He then gave a little chuckle. "Our good abbot tricked Viscount Raymond Roger of Carcassonne into leaving his castle and coming out for a negotiation. And now that heretic sits chained in his own dungeon."

My heart released a protest yet again. *Wait, wait! It cried. You can't make light of such deceit. That's not the way the pope's army should battle. Our Lord demands his knights abide within the code of honor.*

Dear God, I know now how naïve I was. But I had given myself to Your Church and still believed that it was fighting for Your sacred truth. Dominic went on to tell us more. "Pope Innocent was sorely upset because Arnaud released the populace of Carcassonne and did not kill a single heretic. The legate sought to be relieved of his duties and asked many lords to take over as commander general, but none would acquiesce. Finally the mantel fell upon the Earl of Leicester, Simon de Montfort. He was offered the castle in Carcassonne and all the Trencavel holdings, as well as whatever else he conquered, and Simon did agree."

Then Dominic began to praise the virtues of the Earl of Leicester. "Simon de Montfort is a true and valiant servant of Christ Jesus," he began. "He fought in the crusade against the Turks and did great honor to the Church and to Our Lord. When his men wished to plunder Zara and strip Christians of their land in Constantinople, he protested and went on to the Holy Land alone. He is a clever and courageous warrior and will lead the Pope's army to glorious victory."

Dominic explained that Simon and he had met each other while consulting with Bishop Folc in Toulouse. Now the two had become friends and comrades. "We've reached a new understanding of our mission," Dominic went on to say. "Simon will be the arms of the crusade, and the Order of Holy Preachers will serve as its voice. Simon will drive the heretics from their lairs, and, with God's help, I will attempt to convince them of the truth. If they turn a deaf ear, we will destroy them. Either way the scourge of their heresy will be no more."

Destroy the Albigensians? I screamed mutely. Dominic had never told us that our mission was to destroy the Good Christians. He'd said it was to save their souls. I thought of Na Bonata and dear Amelha. What would they do if confronted with the choice of giving up their faith or facing the sword?

Dear God, as Dominic was speaking my head started to feel light. How could it be that my dear Dominic was joining forces with the leader of an army that had burned twenty thousand people at Béziers? I could not reconcile the man who'd preached the sweetness of the love of God with this crusader. Right then, as Dominic told of his passion for the cause, the room began to spin around me. I sensed a flash of light, and then the awful darkness squeezed upon my sight. Once more I slipped into a faint upon the floor.

Sister Guillelmette must have come to my assistance. For when I began to stir, I felt her gently shaking me. And then she offered me a drink of wine and water. When I'd come to my senses, I returned to the bench and tried to stay upright as Dominic told us more about his plans.

"Simon has set up residency in the Trencavel castle at Carcassonne. Most of the knights who fought under Arnaud Amaury have served out their contracted forty days and returned to their homes up north. There is no telling how long it might be before more forces can be raised. But Simon has offered me a room where I might stay and preach to the poor sinners who are infected with the heresy. You will pray fervently for our work in Carcassonne among these poor lost souls, for they do not yet know the glorious truth of our Jehovah. And you will offer supplication that God move the lords and prelates of all Christendom to enlist their vassals in this holy war."

Dear Lord, as I listened to Dominic my head did start to spin again. I grabbed fast to the table so I would not faint another time. The word "Jehovah" pounded in my ears, and a terrible thought flashed through my mind. *What if the heretics were right? What if the God of Dominic were really the evil Jehovah of the Old Testament?* If that were so, then the crusades were fighting not for You but for the Devil.

I shook my head to banish such blasphemy. *No, no,* my soul protested. *It cannot be, God, that You are the vile Jehovah. For You have created the earth and sky and all that is within and have declared them good. You were born from the chaste womb of our most blessed Mother Mary and died to free us from our sins. When I was but a little girl, You soothed my burning soul in the deep recesses of Your Holy Church. You are the One who rocked me in Your arms when I was in most sore distress. And Your compassion does surround me every hour I pray. It holds me tight each time I do my penances. Such sweetness simply cannot come from the fruit of an evil demon.*

Santa Deu, You know how freely my tears then began to fall. When Dominic had finished speaking I left quickly, hoping that no one did take note of my distress. I was grateful that there was much work to be done in the garden.

We heard no word of the crusading armies for several months. There were now four of us working to bring in the second harvest. When Dominic was here, he'd questioned Maria, Catalana, and Valencia and had confirmed their calling to religious life. Now Valencia worked alongside Berengaria, Clarette, and me, and quickly learned the art of growing. Together, we plucked the remaining apples in the orchard and laid the last of the herbs out to dry in the fast-fading sun. We plowed under our beds and covered them with straw for the coming winter. And I must admit that I took comfort in Valencia's presence, for she alone seemed to sense the depth of the troubles that now burned so brightly in my soul.

Once we had finished putting the gardens to rest, Berengaria and I set about the task of making balms and potions. One afternoon, while we were grinding comfrey root, Guillelmette approached us in the kitchen.

"Forgive me, but I must ask leave to speak with you aloud," she said.

The two of us nodded together in consent.

"Dominic has had words with me," she explained. "He told me that there will be a great need for balms and medicines when the fighting starts up again."

Dear God, You know I startled at her words. She had not said *if* the fighting starts again but *when*. I drew in a deep breath.

Our *domina* had more to say. "We have good tidings from Carcassonne. You know that Simon de Montfort was granted all the Trencavel holdings. He has made offering to God by giving from his income to Prouilhe. This is glorious news! We now have funds to fix up an infirmary and a real apothecary. Berengaria, I know that you, Elmina, and Clarette learned some things of making medicines when you were living with the Albigensians. I ask that you would make a list of all you need. Brother Noel will assist Guilhem to procure it."

I wondered briefly why Guilhem might need the help of Brother Noel, but I was too excited about the new apothecary to give it too much thought. The three of us immediately nodded our assent. Berengaria raised her finger to her lips and Guillelmette bid her speak.

"We could use the thatched-roof cabin behind the church, not far from our herb gardens. It has two rooms: a large one with a fire hole in the center and a smaller room off to the southern side. The large room could be our infirmary," said Berengaria. "And the small room with its southern light would work well for drying herbs and storing medicines. All we'd need is help rebuilding the west wall and replacing the roof, and then putting in shelves."

"I'm certain that can be arranged," Guillelmette agreed.

I signaled my desire to speak and she nodded.

"Might we three have leave to talk with one another as we make the list for Brother Noel?" I asked.

"During your *opus manuum* this afternoon you may confer," Guillelmette replied.

And so, after singing none, Berengaria, Clarette, and I remained in the chapter house. We could barely contain our anticipation.

"How shall we go about making up this list?" I asked Berengaria. "There are so many herbs to choose from."

"Let's think about the ailments we would want to cure," she replied. "Then we can take an inventory of the seeds and powders that we have and make a list of what we need."

So we began our list of ailments: wounds, dog bites and snake bites, burns, infections, pain, fever, cramps, cough, weak digestion, troubles with the heart, gout, sleeplessness, and madness.

"We have many all-heals, but we'll need self-heal for cuts and inflammation. Indeed, if the fighting begins again, we'll want to make many more medicines for wounds and pain," Clarette observed.

I caught my breath. "And also for sleep and madness," I added tentatively.

"We shall want to make the Great Sleep," said Berengaria. "We already have poppy seeds. Perhaps Father Guilhem and Brother Noel can procure henbane, cowbane, and the mandrake root."

"Brother Bernard told us it is evil to seek the mandrake root," Clarette warned.

"These are trying times," I intervened. "Perhaps Father Guilhem and Brother Noel will reconsider."

And so we did prepare our list and give it to Father Guilhem. It was too late for us to start the garden, and we knew it could take months for them to get the seeds. We would have to wait until spring's thaws to do our planting.

The war, however, did not wait for our sowing season. The fighting started up again long before the arrival of spring's thaws. Dominic had been traveling throughout the Languedoc and preaching of the Christian duty to eradicate heresy. Many fine noblemen from the north had heeded his words (although, I must admit, they may have been as moved by the pope's promise of spoils as by Dominic's preaching). Perhaps it matters not the way he did it; the result was the same. Simon de Montfort raised another army.

By the beginning of November, it had gathered outside of Carcassonne. And on the Feast Day of Saint Martin of Tours, Dominic sent word asking us to pray for a fast victory in the siege of Cabaret, a castle lying three leagues north of its citadel.

Dear God, You know I breathed a short sigh of relief. Perhaps the crusaders were headed north and would not bother with Fanjeaux. I fervently did as Dominic had bid. I asked that You bless the pope's army. I prayed that they might be victorious over the heretics at Cabaret. But I saved my most earnest prayers for nightly vigil. When I lay prostrate on the floor, I begged that You might keep the fighting far from my dear homeland and the people I loved.

Each morning at lauds, Father Guilhem led us in prayer for the brave crusaders who held siege at the walls of Cabaret. At Mass, Brother Noel offered heartfelt prayer for the souls of all those who had perished in the fight. It did not escape my notice that Brother Noel failed to specify just which souls we were praying for. I silently prayed for everyone caught in the iron grip of the crusade.

During our *opus manuum*, Berengaria, Clarette and I worked feverishly to prepare balms and medicines. We made an ointment from the yellow flowers of St. John's wort and ground boiled comfrey root into a healing paste. We used the feverfew and poppies we had grown during the summer to make pain medicines and wished that we had planted some more potent plants. Each evening we would leave what we had made outside the cloister door, and each morning it would be gone, taken away to the fields of battle.

And all the time I worried what would happen when Cabaret fell. Would the crusaders continue westward toward Levaurs, or would they turn toward Bram and then Fanjeaux? Would there be a fierce battle? Or would the pope's army simply surround each town and wait? I knew that in Fanjeaux, the *Lac de Jupiter* would provide water to outlast a lengthy siege, but how long could my people stay alive once their food had run out? Would Papa and Mama be protected because they had given their oldest daughter to the Church? Or would they be blamed because their younger daughter still lived among the heretics? And what of dear Amelha? And Blanca, Bruna, Aude, and Magdalena? Did they know of Béziers and what the crusaders had done to heretics? Were they still at the house of Na Bonata or had they fled?

All day my head would spin with such questions. I could not concentrate, and even once I forgot the words of the Paternoster. The nighttime was the worst. It was impossible for me to find sleep. Without the distractions of work or prayer, my fears tormented me. I lay awake for hours, wishing only for the consolation of blessed slumber. But when I did drowse off, it was not to the land of pleasant dreams. I would awaken in a sweat, with hot flames raging in my head. I had no way of knowing if they were a memory of the past or vision of the inferno to come. Dear God, how hard I prayed that it would spare Fanjeaux.

Each day I hoped that Dominic would bring us news. But he did not return to Prouilhe until the Feast Day of Cecilia for the celebration of our third anniversary. I wanted to beg him for news the moment he arrived, but Dominic went straight to his quarters. That morning he led Mass as if nothing were happening. We did sing sweetly for him; we chanted the psalms in full voice and perfect harmony. He spoke of the sainted Cecilia. He told us that our music did great honor to her name, but even more, our chastity. He talked again about Cecilia's martyrdom, how she was struck three times through the neck and yet did not die. She'd lived three days so that she might convert her home into a church. I couldn't help but wonder if Dominic was suggesting that we too might soon be called to die such a martyr's death.

After Mass, we finally gathered at chapter to hear Dominic tell us of the crusade. "My dear sisters of Prouilhe," he said, "You are the bloom of St. Cecilia. You live here in perfect piety, while throughout the Languedoc brave men are defending the Holy Church. Please be assured that your prayers for their success are being answered."

Dear God, my stomach churned at what he might say next.

But Dominic did not take notice. "This morning we give God great thanks," he continued, "for Fanjeaux is now cleansed of the curse of heresy."

FANJEAUX? How is it possible that the crusaders have taken Fanjeaux? I wondered. We had not smelled smoke nor heard any fighting outside the walls of Prouilhe. I barely could take a breath as the room spun about. Again I held fast to the table awaiting what Dominic would say next.

He wasted little time in telling us of what had happened.

"I had traveled with Simon from Carcassonne to Cabaret and then on to Fanjeaux, so I did see it all," he said. "When the crusaders reached the outer walls, they found the gates to be wide open. The army walked right in and met there no resistance. The town had taken flight! The castle and the palace were vacant, and there was no sign of Guilhabert de Castres. All of the heretics had fled, and even the ostals were empty. Simon did his best to find out where they all had gone, but no one seemed to know for sure. Some said that they were headed to the fortress of Montsegur; others said a group of women had set off by night toward the Black Mountains."

My head once more began to reel. What was Dominic saying? It sounded as if Fanjeaux had just been handed over to the pope's army. He'd said the heretics had left. But who did he really mean? Most all the town was connected with the heresy in one way or another. If they were not credentes themselves, they all had friends or relatives who were. Was it just the perfecti who had taken flight? Or had Fanjeaux become a ghost town to be given as spoils to the northern armies? Desperate for more news, I raised my finger to my lips. I know Dominic saw me, but he looked away.

"We can also give thanks," Dominic went on, "that Fanjeaux

has not been destroyed. Many of its nobles have become *faidits;* they have departed and the Church has seized their lands. Simon de Montfort has set up his army in the old castle upon the hill. He's granted me a room in his stable behind the church, where I will stay when I have need. And there have been donations of land to the brothers and sisters here at Prouilhe. If God continues to shine His grace upon us, we will soon have funding to repair the Church of St. Martins and build for you a real cloister and a monastery."

I softly cleared my throat and gave the sign again, but Dominic continued.

"I've asked Simon if he might give us some of the spindles and looms left by the Fanjeaux weavers, and he's assented. Father Guilhem will hire some men to repair the cottage behind the refectory and set up a weaving shop. You will now be able to spin and weave cloth not just for your own use but to make clothes and blankets for the brave soldiers who fight on your behalf."

Finally I could not hold my questions any longer. "What of my mama and papa?" I blurted out frantically. "Are they still there? Or has Papa run off and become a *faidit* too? What about Na Bonata? Did she go to her brother in Minerve? Was Amelha with them?" I asked.

My sisters gasped, and I knew instantly what I had done.

Dominic grew red around his ears.

"Your questions would suggest that you are more concerned with vile heretics than with the Christian martyrs," he exclaimed.

My face had gone white. I glanced around and saw others among my sisters looking down. They, too, had wanted to hear news of their kinfolk, but clearly we were not to seek it from Dominic.

"I beg forgiveness," I replied and bowed my head. "I did forget that I have given my life to the Church, and I have no other family." Then I offered a silent prayer that Dominic had not noted my betrayal of Amelha and Na Bonata.

Once again, God, it seems that You were not listening to my

prayer. Dominic glared at me and a quizzical smile spread across his lips.

"I did not say anything of Minerve," he said. "Is that the city where the signora's brother lives?"

Santa Deu, my heart did burst with panic. How could I have said that? Dominic had not known just where Na Bonata and the *bonnes femmes* were headed, and now I had given them into the hands of their enemies.

"I can't remember," I said in a desperate attempt to take back what I'd said. But I knew it could not be done.

That night I dreamt of Na Bonata and Amelha. They were running down a forest trail, being chased by an enormous bank of flames. *Where is Amelha, your sister?* a voice resounded in my head. I awoke with a start and looked about in panic, but I saw no one there. "I do not know," I whimpered to the darkness. "Am I my sister's keeper?"

Of course Dominic was true to his word. By the week before Christmas the new weaving room had been prepared. The roof was patched and the floor covered with clean wooden boards. One afternoon a wagon came, laden with three looms as well as benches, spindles, combs, and distaffs. It also carried piles of wool and spools of woven yarn—everything a textile shop would need. We all stopped our labors to watch it being unloaded. When the last loom was pulled off of the wagon, we looked at it and released a gasp as one. Carved on its frame, we saw the *Flor de la Vida*.

I watched as the loom was carried in and set up in the corner of the room. My breath became shallow, and I felt a choking in my throat. It was the very loom where Magdalena had taught Amelha how to weave. I could almost imagine that I saw the marks of her fingers upon the pick. Then I ran from the room, my breath coming so fast I thought that I might faint. But I did not. Instead, my abdomen contracted. I started to wretch and it seemed as if I might not ever stop. Clarette and Valencia came and knelt beside me. Berengaria took me by the arm and helped me to the new infirmary. She made me drink a tea of fennel seeds, angelica, and mint. Then I fell upon a straw mattress by the wall and pulled into the corner, wishing only that there were some potion that would make me disappear.

Chapter 18

MINERVE

Santa Deu, You know that I was so oppressed by my own torment that I paid hardly any attention to my poor sisters. Each one of them had known family and friends in Fanjeaux; each one longed desperately for news of how they fared. The silence as we ate our meals and went about our daily tasks was filled not with Your peace but with an awful tension. We sang our prayers with thin voices, as if we could not bear to tap into the deep recess of grief within our hearts.

Fanjeaux was but two leagues away. When the cloister gates were open, I could see it beckoning from its stony promontory. The green and ochre fields still wound their way right up the hill and to the city gates. All I would have to do is follow their ridges to retrace the path I had taken with Dominic a short three years ago. I would enter through the Aymeric Gate just north of the church and run down the *Carriéra des Esquirols* to see if Papa and Mama were still there. I'd hug Papa tight and beg him to tell me all that had happened. When we were done, I'd slowly walk down the *Rota de Farque*, turn past the Durfort palace, and inch my way down the trail to the *ostal* of Na Bonata. I knew full well there would be no one there, but maybe I would find something that Amelha had left behind. I'd ask the neighbors if they'd seen her go, or if they'd received any word from her.

But, God, I had made solemn vows that I would stay enclosed at Prouilhe for all my days. And, if I were to tell the truth, I must admit I was afraid of what I might find if I returned to Fanjeaux. What if everyone who I once knew had vanished? Where would I go? I thought of walking to Minerve to find Amelha. But then what? I'd made my choice. My life was not among the Good Christians, but here among my sisters and with Dominic and Brother Noel. And so I remained at Prouilhe, growing more fearful with the dawning of each day.

It was the time of Advent, the preparation for that darkest night of winter when You came to dwell among us. Three times each week we fasted, eating no meat, eggs, or cheese and drinking only water. We passed long hours kneeling in silent vigil as we awaited Your coming and gathered weekly in the chapter house to confess our sins. That winter, Dominic was living at Prouilhe. My heart still fluttered in anticipation of his serving Mass, but I missed having Brother Noel as my confessor. As I knelt with my sisters before Dominic, I dared not raise my head, for I feared what his eyes might tell me. When my turn came, I began my prayer of contrition,

"I confess to you, Almighty God, that I have sinned. It has been thirty days since my last confession. My venial sins are that I have coveted more than my share of bread at the evening meal, and I have placed my concern for my own family above my love for Yours. I do not recall having committed any mortal sins . . ." I uttered.

I did not add that I, like Cain, had betrayed my dear sister. Instead I sat among my friends with dull, blank eyes, waiting for my sisters to finish their confessions and for Dominic to dispense penances and the assurance of Your grace.

Dominic's words arrived upon my ears as if from some great distance.

"Anyone who sins has an advocate with God: Jesus Christ, the righteous one. In Jesus, we are never beyond the reach of God's grace and God's great compassion. Therefore make your souls as fitting abodes for our redeemer and prepare yourselves for His final coming."

But, God, it seemed impossible that I might make my soul into a fitting abode for You. Each time that I saw Dominic, I wondered if he had told Simon of Na Bonata's brother. I thought constantly of how I had let him know about Minerve, and my head spun in horror at what I had done. I noticed as I worked or prayed that I held my hands clenched in fists so tight my fingernails cut into my palms. At night I remained kneeling on the stone long after my sisters had gone to bed. I prayed that I had been mistaken about where Amelha had gone, but in my heart I knew that I had not. I once again began to mortify my flesh with the *flagellum*, hoping for some sweet relief from my increasing dread and guilt.

As Christmastide drew near, we all participated in Advent traditions. We embroidered signs of the Messiah and placed them on the Jesse Tree; we fasted on the Ember Days and lit candles in our awaiting; at vespers we sang the *Magnificat*, with its antiphon, but that year I could feel no joy in the festivities.

Perhaps Dominic sensed the tension in the air among us. Or maybe, God, it was You who told him what we needed. I do not know. But that Christmas he called us to chapter after Holy Mass and told us that he had a special gift. He brought out fifteen beaded strings and offered them to us. Each one had fifty carved boxwood beads hanging on a silk ribbon. They were set in five groups of ten with a knot tied between them. I picked up mine and looked more closely at the beads. The carvings were of the Blessed Virgin holding tight to her little Son. I held them with reverence and wondered what they might be for.

"These are the *rosarium*," Dominic explained to us. "They will be for you a great assistance in your prayer. Each time you offer the Ave Maria, a rose petal drops from your lips. The Blessed Mother will receive each prayer and pick it up to form a garland for her hair."

Berengaria was entranced and raised her fingers to her lips. Dominic bid her speak.

"They almost seem alive," she said with reverence, "as if they carry the heart of the Virgin. Pray, tell us more about them."

Dominic answered, "Last year after Diego died and the Cistercian abbots left us, I began to fear that our mission had been doomed. I was in deepest prayer when the dear Virgin Mother came to me and offered her consolation. She told me that I could not reach the hearts of heretics with just preaching alone. She showed me then the *rosarium*, how to attach an Ave to each bead and meditate upon the fifteen holy mysteries."

"What are those mysteries?" Berengaria inquired, her curiosity so great that she forgot to ask to speak.

"There are the joyful mysteries," Dominic responded, "and each suggests a holy virtue. The first is the annunciation of the angel Gabriel to Mary and the virtue of humility . . ."

Dominic went on to tell us of the sorrowful and glorious mysteries and showed us how to use the beads to pray them.

"You may wish to pray the Rosary alone whenever you feel sore distress," he said. "And you will pray the mysteries together each day after none."

We bid our thanks to Dominic for his fine gift and he graciously received them. The next day he left to join Simon, and Brother Noel once again became our chaplain.

At first, God, You must know that I resented having to pray with those beads. I no longer trusted Dominic with my heart, and I wasn't sure I wanted him to tell me how to pray. In our January confession, I shared my fears with Brother Noel and my sisters.

"I do not think that I can pray the *rosarium*," I confessed. "My heart's too filled with fear and sore regret. I did not mean to tell

Dominic about Minerve," I said. My tears began to flow. "It just came out. Of course he will tell Simon; how could he not? And when winter is done the crusaders will go straight to them. Dominic asks us to pray for their victory, but my prayers turn to ashes in my mouth. I have betrayed Amelha and those whom you love as well, and now I would also betray my God. I know not what I must do." My tears turned into sobbing.

My sisters all looked down, and none but Valencia would meet my eyes, but Brother Noel listened to me with a great compassion. When he began to speak I'm sure I saw a tear form in his own brown eyes.

"You will pray the Rosary just as Dominic has shown you," Noel replied. "When you have prayed the sorrowful mysteries of our dear Lord, you will go back and pray them twice again. You do not need to pray that God give victory to anyone; just pray that God stand as witness in the struggles that are to come."

And so, God, I did pray the *rosarium*—*Sancta Maria, Mater Dei, gratia plena*—I prayed the Ave one hundred and fifty times and said the Paternoster on each silken knot. I meditated on the mysteries of Your Dear Son and came to take some comfort in his sorrows. And as I prayed, my tears flowed freely and offered me some solace.

But that was the only relief that I could find. Most of the time, I passed as in a daze; I often didn't know what hour it was or even what psalms I was singing. I worked with Berengaria in the apothecary, but she chastised me for confusing tarragon and feverfew. I lost my appetite, and my cilice hung loose around my waist just as it had during the starving winter.

The worst times were the nights. Often I stayed awake in vigil until matins, for I could not find sleep. I would pace the path from our dormitory to the chapel until I was too tired to stand. I lay in prostrate vigil hoping I might find some rest upon the floor, but nothing seemed to help. In desperation, I approached Guillelmette after chapter and asked to speak with her. I told her I feared I might go mad if I did not soon sleep. She looked into my reddened eyes and took compassion.

"I'll talk with Berengaria to see if she has something in the apothecary that might help you," she replied.

I knew, of course, what Berengaria kept there and wished that we had had more seeds to plant in the fall. She chose for me a tonic made from lemon balm and chamomile, but it was of no help. It made me feel as if my head were filled with sand but brought me no closer to sleep.

Meanwhile, I prayed that it might be a long winter so that the crusaders would remain at home. But God, You chose not to make it so. The ground was thawed before the Ides of March, and I knew that Simon's army must be on the move. You know how hard I prayed that they would be heading westward toward Toulouse. I know it was a sin, God, but I asked that You take the lives of others who were not so dear to me.

That spring we began our planting early. It was on a warm afternoon, while I was furrowing a row for peas, that Guillelmette appeared. She told us Dominic was requesting that we enlarge our medical garden. He'd told her that the armies of the pope were heading north, and we must grow more herbs and plants for salves and analgesics.

"They're heading north?" I blurted out. "Where have they gone?" My eyes darted frantically, and I felt the fear move through my entrails. Guillelmette bid that I remain silent, but she replied gently, "I do not know."

It was not long before we all found out. In March, we were instructed to pray for the crusaders at Bram. Dominic returned to tell us of their quick success.

"Bram fell after but three days," he reported. "Simon devised a plan to terrorize the land into submission to the Church. He took more than a hundred prisoners and cut off their noses and upper lips. Then he blinded ninety-nine of them and left one man to lead them to Pierre Roger de Caberet. He hoped to frighten de Caberet into submission, but the stubborn heretic refused. Still you can be assured that all is not lost. The city of Lastours has surrendered without a single casualty among God's army."

He did WHAT? I screamed silently. My head did spin and blackness came again before my eyes. Dear God, what was Your army doing? How could it be Your will that a hundred men be mutilated so? It seemed as if a great evil had been let loose upon the land in Your dear name. And, God, I knew that I was part of it. I glanced around the table and saw other blank stares among my sisters. I was not the only one who felt distress. Nobody said a word, yet we all knew that Minerve was but ten leagues from Lastours.

The next day Brother Noel arrived while we were turning over new ground for our herb garden. He had a large sack slung over his shoulder. "I've brought you some things that you might find helpful," he said. He started to walk away and then turned back to add quietly, "I trust that you will use them with discretion."

I looked inside, and what I saw made my heart leap! There was Hildegard's *Book of Simple Medicine.* I saw the Occitan translation neatly written in the margins, and I knew where Brother Noel had found it. I held the book close to my chest as I pulled out several small packets of seeds: henbane, cowbane, and poppies. And then I saw their tangled limbs at the bottom of the bag. Brother Noel had dug up mandrake roots for us.

I thought to keep them hidden in the bag so no one would see the plant of the Devil. *How then had Brother Noel known to look for them?* I wondered. I shrugged my shoulders, knowing I would need to plant the mandrakes before Guilhem or Dominic caught sight of their telltale roots. It seemed unlikely either one would recognize the plant's wide leaves or purple flowers once it was in the ground.

We quickly grabbed three mandrake roots and planted them in southern light against the walls of the apothecary. The others we did set aside to dry indoors beneath the southern window.

As June turned to July, we had no news of the crusaders. I found some small relief from my haunted condition when I was tending to the garden. That summer all our plants did thrive. The white cowbane crept along the ground while the yellow feverfew danced in the breeze. The scarlet poppies waved in the sun amid purple mandrake flowers. I carefully weeded round them and gathered the seeds as their red petals fell to the ground.

Together Berengaria and I poured over Hildegard's formulas. We made salves of hemlock and monkshood that would ease the pain of battle wounds. We set about preparing mandragora. We stripped the bark from our mandrake roots and set it aside to make tea. Hildegard had written that, "if some person has been bent in his or her nature that he is always sad or in some kind of hardship so that they suffer pain continuously, he should sleep with a cleansed mandrake root beside himself in bed." I knew that I could not bring a lustful mandrake into the dormitory, but I did slip a piece of bark into my habit. After we had removed the bark, we pressed the fleshy roots to extract their putrid oil and set aside the residue to dry. By mid-July it was ready to grind into a powder. I tried to remember what I'd been taught at the *ostal* about preparing mandragora.

Aude had showed us how to boil the dried bark into a tea to help induce a gentle slumber. She had mixed the powdered root with wine to ease the suffering of those given to fits and madness. For her strongest remedy, Aude had combined the oil extracted from the mandrake root with poppy seeds, henbane, and vinegar. She had called the potion "the Great Sleep" and claimed it was so potent that it could abate the pain of surgery, "So that a man feels nothing though he be cut."

After making this most potent of remedies, we poured it in small vials and placed them outside the gates of the cloister. How I envied those soldiers who would take our remedies and find relief from all their pain. And so I secreted a vial when I was alone, tucking it into my cilise. I did recall the words of the old *bonne femme* at the market square in Fanjeaux, "It can drive you mad or make you sleep forever." But, God, I did not care. I only wanted rest and some relief from my delirium. That night after vespers, I took a draught, and it was as if You had granted me a miracle. *Santa Deu*, You let me sleep.

I did not want to risk the madness of mandragora, and so I used the potion sparingly. I'd wait for several days until my sleeplessness became unbearable before I'd take another draught. And that sufficed as the heat of July bore down upon us; that is, until the Feast Day of Mary Magdalene. Dear God, how can I e'er forget that day? I did not sleep the night before, and by morning Mass I was dizzy from exhaustion. Perhaps it was the madness of the mandrake root, but I do not believe it. I think that my soul had received a vision of what happened at Minerve.

At Mass, Brother Noel read the gospel story of Mary's brave witness at the cross. But, God, I could not keep my mind on Mary Magdalene. An eerie red light was flashing in my eyes. My head seemed to expand until it filled the chapel and then shrank into a small pinpoint of darkness. I did not know what was happening to me. The room began to spin, and when I stood to leave I fell into a faint.

Once more my sisters helped me to my feet and urged me to take food or drink. But I could not. I spent the day in sore distress. I worked listlessly in the garden. I sang the hours, but, God, my heart was not turned toward You. I counted the minutes until bedtime in hopes that I might elude my demons through kind slumber. I lay under the blanket and gratefully took a long draught of mandragora. I did fall into a deep sleep, but I awoke in the night with a fire burning before my eyes. A hundred voices screamed inside my head. I jolted wide-awake, but the screaming remained, and I heard my voice join in with their frantic cries. *Was I dreaming once more of Ella's fire?* I wondered briefly, but in my bowels I knew that this nightmare was not about some distant past.

Soon all the sisters were also awake, and Berengaria was at my side with gentle words. Still I would not be soothed, and I could not stop my screaming. Clarette ran to fetch Guillelmette. When she arrived she shook me hard to bring me to my senses, but I was flailing and I struck her in the face.

"You must stop this," she yelled at me above my screams. Then Guillelmette bid Jordana and Alaida help her drag me to my feet. They carried me across the courtyard to the chapel, and I collapsed onto the floor. Guillelmette ordered me to lie prostrate, and I did so. As the night wore on, my body quieted and the screaming slowly faded into a distant din. In its place I felt a deadness creep along my spine into my soul. I could not move. I heard Guillelmette say, "You will remain here and pray to Our Lord that you regain your senses."

I heard her words, but I could make no sense of what she said.

I know, God, that I must have lain there through the night, but I cannot remember whether it was so. The next morning Guillelmette bid me to rise, but I could not. It was as if I were not in that place, and a paralysis had settled in my limbs. Guillelmette bid me to speak, but I was mute. She had my sisters pick me up and carry me to the infirmary and told Berengaria to watch over me. My dear friend stroked my hair and offered me a tonic of cowslip and coriander. She softly sang the Angelus and prayed the *rosarium*. I sipped the tonic and then curled into a ball under the blanket. I spent the day there and did not even rise to sing the hours. That night I dozed and dreamt only of ashes in the mud.

The next day, I awoke to find Brother Noel sitting by my bedside. His shoulders were bent as if he carried a great weight upon them, and he looked as if he too wanted for sleep. Brother Noel sat quietly in prayer, and I began to match my breath to the steady rhythm of his.

"You have passed a most troubled night," he offered.

I could but nod as a tear fell upon my cheek.

"Were you again having visions of Ella's inferno?" he asked.

I shook my head. "It was a closer fire," I managed to whisper.

Brother Noel remained silent until I gained the courage to say more.

"I fear the fire came from Minerve," I dared to speak out loud.

The color drained from Brother Noel's face. "What do you know of Minerve?" he asked me.

For a moment I hesitated to divulge all that I suspected, but I trusted Brother Noel. "I think Amelha might be at Minerve," I said. "Na Bonata has a brother there."

"Yes," replied Noel, "I know."

"You know?" I queried and wanted to add, *How do you know?* But then I recognized that Dominic must have told him what I had said.

As if he had heard my unasked question, Noel replied, "I, too, have a sister in Minerve . . ." His voice trailed off.

I looked at Noel, and finally I understood.

"She, too, is a Good Christian," I asserted quietly. "Does she live at Minerve or did she flee there?"

"She fled there," is all that he replied.

"From where?" I started to ask, but before words escaped his lips I realized that I knew the answer. Someone had taught Noel about the Good Christian way. She had shown him the secret of drawing within the sacred circle. He had known where to go to get us mandrake roots.

"You are Aude's brother!" I proclaimed. "It is you who gave her the recipes from Hildegard's *Physica*. Have you heard from her?"

"I have not," Brother Noel replied without denying what I said. "I, too, live in daily fear for her safety."

"How can you sit here with me when I have betrayed your dear sister as well as my own?" I asked.

"Dear Elmina, God has a great compassion and he forgives all of your mistakes. That is the reason He sent us His Son, that we might trust the truth of His forgiveness. You must open your heart and let it in. You say you were a jealous and mean big sister, but every eldest child feels envy toward the next that comes along. You think your soul has been cursed by demons, but I have seen you face your fears with strong courage. I see your struggles, and I beg you to remember that you are the beloved daughter of our dearest Lord."

We sat in the sweet silence of our newfound bond until I asked, "How is it that you and Aude went separate ways?"

"My story is not unlike yours," Noel replied. "My mother was a *credente* who studied with the *bonnes femmes* when she was a girl. But her family was wealthier than yours, and her papa insisted that she leave to marry a nobleman. She raised us with a great respect for the Good Christian way and taught me many things. She sent Aude to the *ostal*, but my father insisted that I be trained in the teachings of the Church.

"Did you want to become a perfect?" I asked.

"No, Elmina," he replied, "I was not born to follow the Good Christian way. I admire their devotion and the purity of their lives. But I cannot accept the notion of two Gods nor, despite all I've seen, believe that a Bad God created the beauty of life on earth.

"Of course there is evil within our world," Noel continued. "And I, too, fear that the Church has fallen prey to the power of Satan. Like the Good Christians, it now looks upon the world in dualistic terms of good and evil. But the Church is not God. Dear Elmina, please try to remember that. We who have chosen to live our lives within her walls must do what is in our power to bring her back into the loving fold that is the Triune God.

"Do you remember I told you of how the sainted Anselm talked about the Trinity? He spoke of the Tripartite God as the relationship between lover, beloved, and love itself. If one piece is removed, God is distorted, and true love becomes impossible. The problem with the Albigensians and the Church is that they have both turned their backs on the Trinity. The heretics deny the Father as creator and in doing so remove God from our world. The Church clings to the Father and the Son but has become fearful of the Holy Spirit. It has severed itself from the power of love itself. Surely, Elmina, we live in an age that is a trial to the soul."

"I fear that my soul is not strong enough to weather this trial," I admitted.

"No soul is strong enough to weather it alone. That is why we are called to constant prayer."

"But I no longer know what God I'm praying to," I whimpered.

Noel replied, "Then listen to your heart, Elmina. Your heart knows."

As dear Noel spoke, I dared to hope that I might once again share his faith in the One True God. How I longed to listen to my heart and discover the Spirit abiding there. But God, You know that I could not. My guilt was far too great and the fire within my soul burned too intensely.

"My heart no longer speaks," I said, and then turned my back to dear Brother Noel. "I bid you leave so I may rest." When I was sure that he was gone, I dragged my dead limbs out of bed, put on my habit and returned to my sisters.

Chapter 19

MANDRAGORA

Dear Clarette welcomed me back with heartfelt relief. Berengaria offered me soothing teas until I had the strength to return to my work and prayer. Once again I sang the hours and prayed the *rosarium*. I harvested the first planting of the garden and put in the late summer crops. I dried the herbs and prepared balms and tonics in the apothecary. I crushed up poppy seeds to make more mandragora. To anyone watching me it might seem as if I were recovered from my madness. But I was not.

Dear God, I felt nothing and feared my soul had disappeared. As I went through my day, it was as if some other person were eating my meals and doing my work for me. The chapel no longer held its mysterious lure, and even when I prayed the *rosarium*, I sensed no sweet compassion. Seven times each day I sang the hours, but I no longer felt my voice resonating within me. I know that words and harmonies came from my mouth, but I could hardly hear them. I passed each day in longing for the night when I might drink of mandragora and sink into the darkness of deep sleep. I knew that if I took too much I might never awaken, but, *Santa Deu*, I did no longer care.

In such a way I passed my time, dreading Dominic's return when

I might learn the truth of what had happened at Minerve. But, God, You did not want for me to wait so long. It was the end of summer, when the first crop had been dried and stored for winter and the second crop had almost ripened. I was working in the garden when I heard a loud pounding on the cloister gate. I remember wondering who could be so desperate to get in. Perhaps it was the army of the Albigensians coming to exact revenge; perhaps the mercenaries of the pope's army had come to take our bodies and our stores. My heart beat loudly as I waited for Guillelmette to attend to the gate. I feigned attention to my work and watched as a young woman staggered in. I could not hear their words, but I saw Guillelmette usher her into the chapter house.

It was not long before they appeared in the garden.

"Elmina," the *domina* spoke aloud. "Berengaria is holding vigil in the chapel. "Would you please help our visitor to the infirmary and make her comfortable?"

I nodded my assent. I stepped to greet the new arrival and let out a gasp as my eyes adjusted to what I was seeing. The woman was dressed in rags and wore a yellow cross stitched on her bodice. Her feet were bare and torn as if she'd traveled many leagues over inhospitable ground. Her skin looked parched and dry, and she was so thin that her eyes had sunken deep within her face. We stared at one another for a long moment, and then exclaimed together,

"Elmina!"

"Blanca!"

I scarcely recognized the girl who had fled back to the *ostal* that night so long ago. I led Blanca to the infirmary and quickly helped her to remove her ragged dress. I gently washed her weary body and rubbed balm onto her blistered feet and her parched lips. I gave her a clean shift to wear and helped to brush the mattes and tangles from her hair. I wanted to ask everything at once. *What has happened to you? Why are you here? Where have you come from? Have you seen Amelha? Do you know what has become of her?*

But Blanca was sobbing softly, and I knew I must wait to hear her story. Slowly her weeping eased, and she fell into a deep sleep. I waited with Blanca until vespers and left to sing the hours. After dinner I took her a bowl of pottage, and she ate it hungrily. I was grateful we were in the infirmary where the rule of silence could be broken.

"Pray tell, what has occurred," I said to Blanca. "What has brought you to us this day?"

Blanca was crying again, and she could barely speak. "I cannot bear to talk of it," she moaned and shook her head. She wept silently for a while before she added, "But I cannot bear to keep all I have seen inside myself."

I remained silent and waited to see if she might continue.

"It was unspeakable, as if the Devil himself had released the fires of Hell upon Minerve. They died so piteously. I watched in horror knowing I should have been among them." Blanca's shoulders were again wracked with sobs.

Minerve! She has come from Minerve! I thought, and I bit my tongue to keep from asking all of my questions at once. I sat upon the bed, put my arms around her, and heard my own quavering voice respond, "Tell me, dear Blanca, what have you seen?"

And Blanca began her story. "When we fled to Minerve I thought we might be safe."

"When did you go?" I could not help but ask.

"It was after the fall of Carcassonne when the pope's armies started to move north. We heard that Montréal had surrendered without a fight, and Guilhabert warned us it was not safe for us to remain in Fanjeaux. He said that he was going to the mountains south of Foix, to the stronghold of Montsegur. Bruna and Esclarmonde went with him. Na Bonata had a brother in Minerve and said that he would most certainly take us in."

"Who was with you?" I held my breath and asked.

"It was just the five of us: Bonata, Aude, Magdalena, Amelha, and me. We'd all received the *consolamentum* and become perfecti. On the bones of God, I swear I do not know why I did it. That night when we heard Dominic and saw the evil cat inside the church, I was afraid. I ran back to the *ostal*, and I swear, when Na Bonata asked me where you all were, I told her that I did not know.

"Dear Lord, I do not know why I joined the Good Christians. I did not want to live the life of an ascetic perfect, but I felt so confused. Amelha and Magdalena were preparing for the *consolamentum*, and I would have been the only one at the house who had not received it." She hung her head. "I guess I did not want to be alone," she said.

"Please tell me of Minerve," I urged Blanca through the lump in my throat.

"It will not be easy for you to hear," Blanca replied.

I closed my eyes but bid that she continue.

"We left for Minerve perhaps ten months ago, as winter winds were blowing in the Black Mountains. We walked by night and hid ourselves in wayside huts and barns. Amelha had not changed. As we walked up the mountain roads, she and Magdalena hummed their tunes until Na Bonata hushed them and said we must travel quietly. We reached Minerve on Twelfth Night amid fair celebration. The lord of misrule had been named and chosen a fair queen from among the peasants. I cannot help but wonder if they knew the day when the world turns upside down might soon return again.

"Na Bonata quickly found her brother, and he willingly took all of us in. We helped his wife with her cooking and in the spring we planted gardens and replenished stores of wood for the coming winter. Life was almost as normal, and we made friends with the perfecti at the *ostals* in Minerve. We dared to hope that our *castrum* would be a sanctuary and that the armies of the pope might head west to Toulouse. But that was not to be.

"We heard of the atrocities at Bram and that the crusaders were headed into the Black Mountains. By the first of June we had sighted the dust of the army along the road from Lastours. Mother of God, how we were filled with fear! When the crusaders realized they could not cross the rivers of our moat or penetrate our walls, they did lay siege. They built wood shanties on the hill across the river. Then they set up their engines and a huge trebuchet, and they began to bombard our walls and city. We never knew who might be hit by flying stones or crushed beneath a crumbling wall. We stayed within the house all of the day except when one of us had to fetch water. It got so bad that four brave men sneaked out with oily rags and coals to set the trebuchet on fire. For a short while we thought that we were saved, but the flames were extinguished.

"Finally the trebuchet turned its aim upon our well. It filled the path with boulders 'til we could no longer get to water. By then it was July, and our cisterns were dry. There was nothing in all Minerve for us to drink.

"It was so very bad," Blanca recalled and halted her story. I stroked her forehead and handed her a cup of water.

"You are safe here," I said to her. "Please try to tell what happened next."

"Our neighbors soon began to die of thirst. By day we hid within our houses, and by night we searched the town for rotting corpses and threw them over the *castrum* walls. We were so dry that our tongues swelled within our mouths and we could not swallow food. Finally William, lord of Minerve, went out to make a truce with the crusaders. He offered all his lands and castles to Simon de Montfort if he would spare the town's inhabitants.

"But then that wretched legate Arnaud Amaury spoke up. 'We can't allow those who would profane the Church to continue in their heresy. We must interview all the residents of Minerve and ask them to swear allegiance to the Church and renounce any other beliefs. Those who do so swear will be allowed to remain in their homes without reprisal; but those who don't will die by the almighty hand of God.'

"William could see no choice but to accept the legate's terms. And so the city gates were opened to Arnaud Amaury and his priests."

His priests, I thought, my eyes almost exploding from my temples. I swallowed hard and asked, "Was Dominic among them?"

"I do not know," Blanca responded. "I did not see him at our *ostal* or later at the fires."

"What fires?" I couldn't help but ask as my stomach and entrails tightened.

"My dear Elmina, are you sure you want to know?" Blanca inquired again.

This time I could but nod.

"The priests interviewed everyone and asked them to make an oath of loyalty to the Roman Church. The Catholics and *credentes* affirmed the oath but not so the perfecti. The priests went to the perfect men, and not a one renounced his faith. Then they came to our *ostal.* The priests first asked Na Bonata and then Bruna, Magdalena, and Amelha to take their oath. One by one, each responded, 'Neither death nor life can tear us from the faith to which we are joined.'

"And then," Blanca paused and began to sob. "I cannot bear my cowardice. They came to me. I thought of how I'd come to join the Albigensians and how I had once loved the Church. I did not want to die at the hands of the crusaders. I and two other women swore their cursed oath. The priests pulled us aside and sewed this yellow cross onto our robes. Then they took the others into the dungeon.

"All night we could hear them there, as Amelha and Magdalena led them in singing hymns of praise to the Good God. When morning came, the whole town was ordered to gather up the wood we'd stored for winter. We carried it over boulders and down the steep path to a flat above the river.

"'Here 'tis we'll build the fire,' said one of the priests, 'so that we can consign the remains to the river and leave none that might be gathered up as relics.'" Again poor Blanca stopped, "Dear God in Heaven, I cannot speak of what was next."

"But you must," I quickly countered. "You cannot keep it locked within, and I have to hear it."

Blanca took a deep breath and went on with her story. "All night the army had been carving posts and setting them into the dirt. We piled the wood around them. The priests then ordered us to bring our cooking oil as well. When the pyre was laid we returned to an overlook in the *castrum* where we were told to observe all that occurred.

"The perfecti were led out in groups of four. They were stripped naked and their hands tied behind their backs." Blanca squeezed her eyes tight as if to block out the memory of what would come. "They descended the path so bravely, singing hymns as they went."

"Did you see Amelha?" I had to ask. "Did you hear her singing?"

"I saw them all," Blanca said quietly. "Amelha and Magdalena climbed down together, singing of the Magdalene."

I knew it was the song that we had learned from Beatriz:

Dear Mary, do not weep
For all that lives within the Heavens
Knows your sorrow
And the depth of your
Sweet compassion.
Seek not your Lord
Amidst these mortal ruins
But know that He abides
Within your heart
This day
And evermore.

"What of the fire?" I asked. "Did they sing then?"

Blanca hung her head and the tears flowed freely. "I wish that I could tell you that was what happened," she said. "But I cannot. When the soldiers lifted them onto the stakes, poured oil over them and lit the fires, I heard nothing but desperate screaming. I hear it still."

With that Blanca collapsed onto her bed.

Would that I could say I held her tight and that we both sobbed together. But I cannot. It was as if all sensation had vanished from my body. My arms and legs were numb. At first my head began to spin, but then all movement ceased. I knew Blanca was with me there in the room, but I could not see her. And then I felt a retching in my gut and staggered out the door. I heaved and heaved until I sensed the darkness closing about me. It was Berengaria who found me lying on the ground in a pool of vomit and took me back to the infirmary.

Most precious God, after that time I knew no peace. By day I walked about as if I were not there. I would recite my prayers and sing the hours, but I heard neither my own words nor the voices around me. My limbs felt like foreign appendages that moved at someone else's bidding. All day my head would shake from side to side as if to prevent any thoughts from entering it. At confession I could not speak, and neither Clarette nor Berengaria could penetrate my shell.

Brother Noel tried to help me. He told me to recite the *rosarium* three times a day and asked my sisters to take turns praying with me. But I could draw no comfort from Our Lady. I asked her to pray for me, "*Nunc, et in hora mortis nostrae*," and I wanted so for that hour of death to come.

All day I longed for the night when I might take my mandragora and find a blessed rest. But, God, You no longer would give that gift to me. A single draught gave me no sleep, and so I would take two or three in hope of finding some relief. Then I would collapse into my bed for a short while before my head would fill with fire. Again I would awake in a delirium of writhing and screaming. And again, I would receive no comfort.

It was not long until Guillelmette moved my bed to the infirmary so that my sisters could get some rest. Blanca had been moved out, perhaps to stay with Guillelmette. I do not know. I only know that I had the room to myself.

Dear God, You know I tried to pray to You. I so wanted to discern who You really are. When he first met us, Dominic had said You were the God of love, the One True God who rules over all that is. You were the One to whom I sang the hours. Your spirit filled my heart with such great joy when I did pray the *rosarium*. I loved Your Church and longed to rest within the peace of its embrace. And, *Santa Deu*, I did love You and trust in Your goodness and mercy.

And so I cannot understand. *If You are the God of love, how is it You could hate the Good Christians so much? How could You find their deep-held faith and simple lives anathema? How could You wish to burn a soul as pure and full of life as was Amelha's?*

I cannot help but think that the Good Christians were right. If that be so, then dearest Ella was my very own soul. She was born again into this wretched time and place in the hope that I might bring her healing. And I have failed her. I begged that I might not fall prey to the same demons of despair that tormented her life. But, God, I have.

I see now that the God of Dominic is the Jehovah who leads armies into battle. He is an Evil God. He cares only about His own might, and wishes to destroy all who would not bow down to Him. He burns the fields of the glorious land He has created. He asks that we who worship Him pray for His armies' victories, and for the death of those we love.

I cannot undo all that I have done. It's not just that I have betrayed Amelha; I've given my life not to You, the God of light, but to the warrior Jehovah. I am sorry, so very sorry, and by the bones of Your Dear Son, I swear I will not do it any longer.

Tonight I have taken enough mandragora to stop my heart from its incessant beating. *You know, of course, that I have reached the end, and I no longer even know to whom I pray. Dear God, if You are the God* of the Holy Catholic Church, the One whom I have loved and tried to serve here at Prouilhe, I will soon be damned to the fires of Hell—not for what I've done to Amelha and to my people, but for the sin I will commit this night. For the priests say that the razing of the Languedoc and burning of the heretics were done for Your great glory, but that to take my own life is a mortal sin that cannot be forgiven.

But, Santa Deu, what if the priests are wrong? What if the heretics knew the truth all along? If so, the life I thought was serving You has been offered instead to Satan. But death will bring about release from all its torments and the promise of a new life in a different time and place. If the Good Christians had it right, I may yet have another chance to love and to serve You better.

Whoever You be, God, thank You for listening to my story. Perhaps in the next life I'll find a way to quench the fire that has burned within this one and rest in Your peace.

EPILOGUE

I t's finally the end to a long winter. I hear a steady drip from the icy eaves and a gentle trickle, as rivulets of melting snow make their way around the white pine trees into the Casco Bay.

I am so ready for this thaw. For the past five years, my frozen heart has found protection in this little red log cabin on an island off the coast of Maine. Peter and I are here together, healing from burnout after a decade of ministry in refugee resettlement. My soul had sensed kindred spirits in those who had lost everything and had the courage to start over in a strange new land. But sadly, I could not carry the weight of so much sadness any longer. Now I have retired, and I take comfort in little things—my painting, piano lessons, and the beauty surrounding me.

On this Saturday morning, our neighbor has arrived for meditation. I insert a CD into the Bose Wave, sit cross-legged in the leather chair that is my perch, and let the chanted mantra flow through me:

Om Mani Padme Hum

Breath by breath, the meditation deepens and I can feel each of my chakras begin to vibrate. Soon, points of light sparkle before me and start to spin like galaxies within my head. Slowly, they congeal into a now-familiar flower of life. Its warm glow fills me with a sense of great benevolence. I breathe in the energy that binds my soul to all things and release my mind's perpetual resistance to the divine. In. Out. Pause. The flower takes on color and fades into gray and black as the background begins to shine around and through it. I am not just connected to all things but am infused with divine light. The glowing background slowly recedes and again the flower grows brighter . . . and yet still brighter. The edges are outlined with a golden thread so brilliant, that I think to shut my eyes. But they are already closed.

And then, as if a new world were being created, the flower of life explodes into three dimensions, extending in all directions into infinity. The energy and love of the Creator shoot through me, enlivening each chakra to shout out an orgasmic "Yes!" to God.

And with that "Yes!" I receive clarity. The time has come for me to step foot off this island and reclaim my call to ministry. I've been telling myself that I'm content with life just as it is, but I know that isn't true. My soul is longing for Church—not the politically correct United Church of Christ in which I am ordained, not the island's earnest little United Methodist Church where I play the organ Sunday mornings, but a Church that lives in my imagination. It has gothic arches and stained glass windows and a choir chanting glorious music. Its doors are opened in welcome and service to people from many walks of life. Its members seek to understand the sacred presence that we call God, at the same time its liturgy evokes God's great mystery.

Of course my mind takes over. *Why Church?* I ask myself for the umpteenth time. I've found spiritual connection in Hindu *kirtan*, Zen chanting, and New Age meditation. I study with a wise and wonderful Taoist teacher. And didn't a psychic say to me a few years back, "Linda, you're beyond Church. It's time for you to move on." I know he could be right. I'm not your typical Christian. I don't believe that there is just one path that leads to God. I'm not convinced that Jesus of Nazareth was God's *only* incarnation. I cannot reconcile a loving God with traditional concepts of Heaven and Hell. It even seems likely to me that in our journeys back to God, we're offered many chances at life on this Earth.

And yet I do not want to turn my back upon the Church. It isn't just that I adore its sacred space and music, or that I want community with other seeking souls. It's that God in Christ lights my path and enlarges my heart. It's the fact that the God of my understanding is a Holy Trinity: the transcendent Creator, the incarnate Presence, and the quickening Spirit that gives me life. In the images of Saint Anselm, my God is "Lover, Beloved, and Love itself." I sense that any time a piece of the Trinity is removed, the truth becomes distorted and creation suffers.

Dear God, you are cajoling me away from the safety and seclusion of winter. In my mandala journaling, you gave me a clear message, *Rebuild my Church!* I've heard you say, *Make it a place where those who share the same knowledge and doubts as you can feel at home.*

But how am I to do that? When I burned out from refugee resettlement, I also burned all the bridges to a world beyond my island. My soul began to wither, and I ceased to believe that I have anything to offer.

Om Mani Padme Hum

The chanting brings me back to the present and my meditation shifts to prayer:

Please help me, God.

I hear as a response the words to a Gospel hymn ringing in my ears:

He who began a good work in you,
He who began a good work in you,
Will be faithful to complete it,
He'll be faithful to complete it in you.

Through my tears, I ask God please to show me the way.

And, of course, God does. I see a notice on the Internet looking for volunteers to teach ESOL to refugees. I take the ferry into Portland, and each day I work with them my heart heals and becomes stronger. I'm led to a spiritual director who is also an artist and a former priest. I enter formation to become a spiritual director myself. I step off the island and find in an Episcopal cathedral the combination of mystical presence and spiritual searching that my soul has longed for. I worship and sing, attend classes, assist refugees, and teach the art of making mandalas. Each week I hold my breath, waiting for that sacred moment in the Eucharist when the broken host is held aloft, brought together, and made whole.

Like me. I'm mending, but I'm still nervous about committing my life to the Church again. I read the Bible and respond with fury at the passages portraying a judgmental, vengeful God. I can't help feeling as if I must atone for being called into the Christian faith.

I still need help, I pray to God one night. The next day, I have tea with a friend and as we talk, she says, "I sense there is something important standing in the way of your progress. I know a wise counselor who might be able to help you. I've done energy work with her, but she also does past life regressions."

"I don't really believe in past lives," I answer.

"It doesn't matter," she replies matter-of-factly and hands me a book, *Other Lives, Other Selves* by Roger Woolger. "Read this."

I read with fascination the story of a Jungian psychologist who explained that there are many possible explanations for the phenomena we may experience as past life memory. One is that we selectively recall images from things we've read, seen, or experienced in this life; another is that we draw upon pieces of the collective unconscious that hold unusual power for us; and the third, of course, is that our soul actually does live many times on its journey home to God. Woolger claimed that it doesn't matter how you interpret it, the work of doing past life regression is the same.

By the next morning I am hooked. I go to visit the wise counselor, who calls her practice "The Way of the Soul." Naturally it
feels right. Each step along my life's journey has been exactly what
my soul required. My wise counselor works from a winterized shed
overlooking a waving salt marsh. As the seasons change, we talk of
my struggles as a daughter and a mother, of my spiritual longings,
and my conflicted feelings about the Church.

We do a past life regression and discover a young Celtic girl
named Ella. For almost a year, Ella abides with me. I dream of her
at night, I paint mandalas of her story, and she sits next to me in
church. We stare together at its big rose window and I tell her over
and over,

"The big red priest was wrong. There is yet joy and happiness
for you."

Slowly the weight of her sadness floats out of my life. And so my
wise counselor and I decide our work is finished.

But it turns out that we are wrong. We have arranged one last
meeting to review our work and say good-bye. At the end of the
hour, I stand to leave. My wise counselor reaches to take my hand
and then takes a deep breath, the kind she takes when she has intu-
ited an important truth.

"I think there's one more thing," she adds. "You might want to
explore a life among the Cathars in which you betrayed your sister.
There is a girl who needs to know she got another chance and that
she is loved and forgiven."

ACKNOWLEDGMENTS

I am most grateful for those who have supported me on this journey with Elmina and made it possible to tell her tale.

In their gentle presence and faithful singing of the hours, the sisters of the international community at the Notre Dame de Prouille Monastery allowed me to find Elmina's heart and experience the times she found joy and peace in her vocation.

Cathar historian and tour guide James Macdonald of St. Ferriole not only introduced me to Cathar Country but also helped me to explore the ways Elmina's story might have evolved. His website, www.catharcountry.info, provides a wealth of information in English on every aspect of the Cathars' story, including bibliographical references and primary sources. And I thank him for his review of my manuscript and helpful suggestions.

I thank Christopher Janosik, EdD at Villanova University for permission to use their English translation of the Rule of Augustine, available at http://www1.villanova.edu/villanova/mission/campusministry/spiritualaity/resources/spirituality/about/rule/chapters.html, by Robert Russell, O.S.A. based on the critical text of Luc Verheijen, O.S.A. (La regle de saint Augustin, Etudes Augustiniennes, Paris, 1967). Used with permission.

The incident of the demonic beast that appeared in the church at Fanjeaux was first reported by Berengaria at the Board of Inquiry for the canonization of Dominic de Guzman on July 13, 1233. It has been cited in many biographies including *The History of St. Dominic*,

Founder of the Friars Preachers by Augusta Theodosia Drane, Dominic printed by James Stanley in 1891. I've used her words from that translation in Chapter 8.

Le Jeu d'Adam is a 12th-century morality play written in a combination of French dialect and Latin. It has been translated into English many times. I found my excerpts in *Medieval Drama*, David Bevington, editor. Boston, MA: Houghton Mifflin Co., 1975.

I am grateful to Joan Hunter of Fifth House Lodge, Bridgton, Maine and all those who read early drafts of *Elmina's Fire* and offered me invaluable suggestions.

I especially wish to thank those spiritual guides who have been the Brother Noels in my life: Rusty Hicks, Peg Stearn, Martha and Frank West, Sophia Morreale, Sukie Curtis, Larry Landau, Pam Curran, Bev Perkins, and Kathleen Luke who first introduced me to Ella and Elmina.

And finally I offer my most profound gratitude to my husband Peter for his unwavering support for this project and conviction that Elmina's story had to be told.

Questions for Discussion

1. Elmina is drawn to the Church from an early age. What was it about the Church that appeals to her? How does the Church give her relief from her inner demons? How does her family dynamic contribute to her feelings about the Church?

2. Elmina often begs forgiveness for being "a mean big sister." Why is she so jealous of her sister Amelha? Have you experienced such jealousy in your life? What was it like for you?

3. The morality play *Le Jeu d'Adam* introduces issues that plague Elmina throughout the book. How does it define the conflict between the Good Christians and Church? How does it echo Elmina's own family dynamic?

4. Elmina finds the Good Christian *Ostal* to be warm and welcoming. What does she learn at the *Ostal*? Why is she happy during her first year there?

5. Through the debates at Carcassonne and the teachings of Bishop Guillabert, Elmina learns about the growing conflict between the Roman Church and the Good Christians. What are the differences in what they believe about the nature of

God? About creation and its value? About the importance of priests and sacraments? About life after death? What are your thoughts on these differences?

6. Na Bonata teaches Elmina how to draw the *Flor de la Vida* and shows her Aude's spirit drawings. What does the *Flor* symbolize? Why do you think drawing within a circle can be a sacred experience?

7. As Elmina and Amelha come of age, what choices do they have to make? What does this say about the options available to medieval women? How would you respond if you were in Elmina's shoes?

8. Elmina begins to hope that "if Mary Magdalene could love both man and God as one, perhaps one day someone might come along who'd let me do the same." Is Dominic de Guzman the answer to her prayer? Why is she so drawn to him? What is the danger inherent in looking to a human being for salvation?

9. What happens at the Trial by Fire? Why does Elmina feel that she must flee the *Ostal*? What are some of the reasons her friends give for following her?

10. Elmina begs Amelha to leave the *Ostal* with her. How has their relationship changed? Why does Amelha refuse to follow Elmina?

11. Describe the village of Prouilhes. What are the physical challenges of Elmina's first months there?

12. How would you describe Elmina's relationship with Dominic? Is it reciprocated? Why is it cause for such great shame?

13. The medieval Church insisted upon mortification of the flesh. What are some of the ways Elmina is asked to torment her body and its yearnings? What are the reasons for this?

Do women today still face conflicting messages about their bodies?

14. How does Dominic describe the mission of his Order of Preachers? How do Elmina's feelings about participating in this mission change? Have you ever found yourself complicit in a mission about which you felt conflicted?

15. What is the importance of Brother Noel in Elmina's life? How does his message differ from that of Dominic and the medieval Church? Who have been the "Brother Noels" in your own spiritual life?

16. Brother Noel invites Elmina to explore her visions by drawing them within a sacred circle. What does Elmina learn from this process? Are her discoveries helpful or harmful to her?

17. New arrivals to Prouilhes brought ever more alarming reports from the outside world. In October of 2016, the Roman Catholic Bishop of Pamiers sought forgiveness for "acts contrary to the Gospel, in which the Lord Jesus gave us the commandment to love our neighbour." Is it possible to reconcile the atrocities of the Albigensian Crusade with Jesus's teachings? Are there aspects of the Christian message that contribute to this kind of atrocity?

18. What are the causes and signs of Elmina's growing emotional distress? How does she try to cope with them?

19. Elmina sees no way out of her distress. What are your feelings about the choice she makes? If you could offer Elmina your wisdom, what would you want to share with her?

20. Elmina dies in the hope that "death will bring about release from all my torments and the promise of a new life in a different time and place." Do you believe Elmina gets her dying wish? Is it possible to reconcile her hope for reincarnation with the teachings of the Christian church?

ABOUT THE AUTHOR

photo credit: Jen Dean Photography

Linda Carleton graduated from Yale Divinity School, was ordained in the United Church of Christ, and formerly worked in refugee resettlement. She now lives in Portland, Maine, where she teaches, writes, and offers workshops on mandala journaling and spiritual growth. Linda strives to integrate her own Christian faith with the world's diverse spiritual teachings and to help the world heal from its history of religious abuse.

SELECTED TITLES FROM
SHE WRITES PRESS

She Writes Press is an independent publishing company founded to serve women writers everywhere. Visit us at www.shewritespress.com.

Light Radiance Splendor by Leah Chyten. $16.95, 978-1-63152-178-2. Set in Eastern Europe in the first half of the twentieth century and culminating in contemporary Israel and Palestine, *Light Radiance Splendor* shows how three generations of the Hebrew Goddess Shekinah's devoted mission keepers grapple with betrayal, forgiveness, and Lost in the Reflecting Pool.

All the Light There Was by Nancy Kricorian. $16.95, 978-1-63152-905-4. A lyrical, finely wrought tale of loyalty, love, and the many faces of resistance, told from the perspective of an Armenian girl living in Paris during the Nazi occupation of the 1940s.

An Address in Amsterdam by Mary Dingee Fillmore. $16.95, 978-1-63152-133-1. After facing relentless danger and escalating raids for 18 months, Rachel Klein—a well-behaved young Jewish woman who transformed herself into a courier for the underground when the Nazis invaded her country—persuades her parents to hide with her in a dank basement, where much is revealed.

The Belief in Angels by J. Dylan Yates. $16.95, 978-1-938314-64-3. From the Majdonek death camp to a volatile hippie household on the East Coast, this narrative of tragedy, survival, and hope spans more than fifty years, from the 1920s to the 1970s.

The Sweetness by Sande Boritz Berger. $16.95, 978-1-63152-907-8. A compelling and powerful story of two girls—cousins living on separate continents—whose strikingly different lives are forever changed when the Nazis invade Vilna, Lithuania.

What is Found, What is Lost by Anne Leigh Parrish. $16.95, 978-1-938314-95-7. After her husband passes away, a series of family crises forces Freddie, a woman raised on religion, to confront long-held questions about her faith.